No Reservations

It was always this way with him, had been since the first moment she'd opened her hotel-room door to find him standing there nearly a year before. He touched her like he was meant to. Her body and her heart certainly agreed. Charles Dixon was her favourite addiction, even if he was an arrogant man with an ex-wife who'd ensconced herself downstairs watching Kate's Gerry Butler and probably trying to steal him, too.

'Quit it,' she managed to say, the words thick on her tongue as desire bloomed, slow like honey, through her veins. Her nipples hardened, her pussy slickened and readied for him.

'You don't want me to stop.'

She didn't. But damn him, his ex-wife was under the same roof! '*I* don't, but Eve does.'

He snorted just before he caught a nipple between his teeth, sending bright shards of pleasure/pain skittering through her. 'I don't care about her. Plus, I hate to break it to you, darling Kate, but she knows I'm having my way with you right now.'

Praise for *Taking Care of Business* by Megan Hart and Lauren Dane

No Reservations
Megan Hart and Lauren Dane

This book is a work of fiction.
In real life, make sure you practise safe, sane and
consensual sex.

Published by Black Lace 2009

4 6 8 10 9 7 5 3

First published in Great Britain in 2009 by
Black Lace
Virgin Books
Random House, 20 Vauxhall Bridge Road
London SW1V 2SA

www.rbooks.co.uk

Addresses for companies within The Random House Group Limited can be found at:
www.randomhouse.co.uk/offices.htm

The Random House Group Limited Reg. No. 954009

A CIP catalogue record for this book is available from the British Library

ISBN 9780352345196

The Random House Group Limited supports The Forest Stewardship Council [FSC], the
leading international forest certification organisation. All our titles that are printed on
Greenpeace approved FSC certified paper carry the FSC logo.
Our paper procurement policy can be found at www.rbooks.co.uk/environment

Typeset by Palimpsest Book Production Limited, Grangemouth, Stirlingshire
Printed and bound in Great Britain by CPI Bookmarque, Croydon, Surrey

1

Standing, Kate took a deep breath and smiled tightly at the other women in the house. 'I'm going to go and read for a while. Good night, everyone.'

Adrienne, Dix's younger daughter, ignored her, continuing to chatter to her mother who'd ensconced herself on the couch, right where Kate had been sitting for the last four days. Yes, Eve, the girls' mother. *Dix's ex-wife*. Still, Kendall, the older girl, got up and hugged her. 'Night, Kate. Sure you don't want to watch this movie with us? Gerard Butler, tiny leather undies? Come on, what's to say no in that?'

Kate laughed, liking Kendall a lot. Still, even her secret celebrity boyfriend in leather undies wasn't enough to keep her in this wood-panelled room filled with memories and Eve Dixon who'd just *shown up* a few hours before.

Dix looked up from his paper, surrounded by the women in his life and met her eyes. He had *that* look in them. Oh no, he did not even think she was fucking him now!

'I'll come too.' He stood, putting the paper down.

Kate took a step away from him. 'No. No, it's fine. You don't need to. I'm going to sleep right away anyway.' She sent him a look which he conveniently ignored.

He kissed and hugged each one of his daughters and nodded at Eve before he turned back to Kate. Grabbing her, he pulled her to his body and kissed her. It was quick but he made his point. Pickles, Kate's not-so-nice nickname for the ex-wife, saw it and her eyes narrowed. Kate stifled the desire to pop her one.

'Of course I don't need to. But I'm tired and I've already seen this movie with you four times. I can give time number five a pass.' The look in his eyes told Kate he wasn't going to be swayed. He wanted what he wanted and he was certainly not above turning her into a puddle of goo if he had to.

A brittle cough interrupted their little struggle. 'Well OK then! Gosh I sure do appreciate you sharing the holidays with me, Katie. It's lonely you know, being a mom without her babies,' Pickles chirped. 'It's just you and me, girls.'

Bitch.

Resisting, only barely, her urge to slap the shit out of Pickles for calling her *Katie*, Kate dug her nails into her palms and left the room. She climbed the stairs towards their shared bedroom, the heat from his body right at her back so she couldn't escape.

Once inside, she glared at him but he'd moved to build a fire in the fireplace.

'I know you're mad. I didn't know she was coming. I'll talk to her tomorrow.' He spoke as he worked, his back to her.

'Don't talk to me with your back.' She knew it sounded petulant but so be it. His ex-wife, a woman who seemed terminally unable to do stuff like open pickle jars without his assistance, had just shown up on the porch unannounced! And she called her Katie. She was *not* a Katie. And if she was, that thundertwat downstairs would not have the privilege of calling her that anyway. Over the months she and Dix had been seeing each other, the woman had gotten worse and worse. It had gotten to the point where Dix spent most of their time together at her place since Eve wouldn't dare show up there. Unfortunately, she'd taken to showing up lots of other places and Kate found that distasteful as well as pitiable. It was beyond over between Dix and his ex. That Eve was being so pathetic now with her attempts to break him and Kate up spoke volumes about how crazy or how clueless the woman was.

Finishing up, Dix covered the grate and turned to face her, the corner of his mouth twitching. 'There, it should warm up in here soon. For now, let's preserve our body heat, shall we? I hear two people naked are good for that sort of thing.' He tossed his sweater to the side, tousling his hair and looking very tasty. *Bastard*.

'Well, I'm sure Pickles will be glad to snuggle up to you then. You may have noticed, *Charles*, I'm not in the mood. I'm going to read and then I'm going to sleep. Fully clothed.'

'Do you really want me to go downstairs to a woman I ceased loving a long time ago and have been divorced from for nine years now? When you're right here and clearly in need of a little exercise to work off your mad? I don't want her. I want you. I always want you.'

Warmth spread through her at the way his voice lowered and then more as he traced the back of his knuckles down the line of her jaw.

'I love you, Kate. I'm here with you. I am sorry she showed up, but that doesn't mean you and I are any different than we were before she came.'

She arched a brow at him. 'Stop being logical. I don't want that from you right now.'

His face softened, losing that predatory gleam he had in his eyes. He pulled her into a hug, kissing her before looking into her eyes. Christ, he made her love him so much. It didn't scare her any more, but he still needed to be fended off at times when he tended to try to take control of every situation.

'How is it you're even hotter when you're being prickly? I need therapy, but I'd rather have you. I know you're upset. I'm sorry. Do you want me to go down and make her leave?'

She sighed. 'Gah, you're abominable. I told you I didn't want to be rational right now. And you had to go and be all nice.' She rolled her eyes and kissed him. 'I don't want her here. I hate her voice. Her perfume is cloying and needy, just like she is.' Kate groaned and pulled at her bottom lip for a moment. 'No. I know why you didn't make her leave tonight. I don't want you to put the girls in the middle.' Pickles had done that already.

'You're a good woman, Katherine.' The predatory gleam was back as he made very quick work of her sweater and then her bra. She sucked in a breath as he palmed her nipples. 'A good woman who likes my hands on her nipples.'

She shrugged. 'They're just hands. Anyone's hands would do. And we are *not* having sex tonight. Not with her here.'

He pushed her back and she bounced as she hit the mattress. The sounds of the movie downstairs floated up and under the door as the fire began to pop and crackle. She was never sexier to him than when she put him and his daughters first. She didn't know of course, so it wasn't about her manipulating it like Eve had done by showing up.

It'd been hours since he'd had her last. Since they'd fucked, hard and fast, still mainly clothed in the thick forest behind the house. Her breath had misted in the air as he'd backed her against a tree. Her body received him, the shock of her heat a stark contrast to the cold air. And still, he'd wanted her, even as the sweat on the back of his neck had cooled.

Whatever it was about her, he wanted to possess it even as he couldn't help but let the strength of her fierce independence shine through. That she wanted to be with him, that she sought him out and let him hold her, thrilled him and comforted him at the same time.

Right then, as he divested her of her jeans and those tiny panties, but left on the over-the-knee socks she knew he got off on so much, he was far more thrilled than comforted.

'I love those socks. So sexy and silly. Every time I see you I want to devour you in three greedy bites,' he said as he got rid of the rest of his clothes and returned to her. She was still pissed, he saw it in the set of her mouth, but it made seducing her, making her want his touch, making her crave his cock in her cunt, even sweeter.

'I want to read.' But she hadn't moved, in fact her eyes were glued to his hands as he'd unzipped his jeans and pulled them down.

'Hmm. I want to lick your pussy.'

In the low light, he caught the sound of her indrawn breath. He reached out to open the curtains, silvery moonlight flooding into the room, illuminating her as she waited for him. His cock jumped against his belly when she caught her bottom lip between her teeth.

He chuckled, taking in the way her nipples stabbed skywards and not because of the cold. Her scent, of desire flushed skin and her pussy, rose to meet him as he got onto the bed beside her.

'So, darling Kate, open your thighs for me.' He leant in and her hand rested gently against his shoulder. He wanted to laugh triumphantly, that hand was meant to push him back but neither one of them had the energy to play that game.

In the dark, in the quiet of the room with the night settled in all around, Kate couldn't help but arch into his mouth. He left hot, wet kisses down her neck and gooseflesh in his wake. Halfheartedly, her hand rested on his shoulder where she'd been ready to shove him back. Instead, she breathed him into her lungs and let him touch her.

Any way he wanted to.

It was always this way with him, had been since the first moment she'd opened her hotel-room door to find him standing there nearly a year before. He touched her like he was meant to. Her body and her heart certainly agreed. Charles Dixon was her favourite addiction, even if he was an arrogant man with an ex-wife who'd ensconced herself downstairs watching Kate's Gerry Butler and probably trying to steal him, too.

'Quit it,' she managed to say, the words thick on her tongue as desire bloomed, slow like honey, through her veins. Her nipples hardened, her pussy slickened and readied for him.

'You don't want me to stop.'

She didn't. But damn him, his ex-wife was under the same roof! '*I* don't, but Eve does.'

He snorted just before he caught a nipple between his teeth, sending bright shards of pleasure/pain skittering through her. 'I don't care about her. Plus, I hate to break it to you, darling Kate, but she knows I'm having my way with you right now.'

'That is ... oh, holy Christ, you're not playing fair.' His knuckles brushed against her labia, stroking against the slick knot of her clit.

He laughed, that dark, wicked chuckle as he inched downwards. 'I'm playing the way you like it. Hard, hot and bad. I'm going to eat your pussy until you have to scream into the pillow. And then I'm going to fuck you until every damned spring on this bed squeaks. I will have you, Kate, and then I'll have you again and once more after that.' His tongue swirled decadently around her belly button before he caught the ridge between his teeth briefly.

What could she say to that other than, *Yay*! She really should be firm with him but when he did that thing, oh yes, *that* thing with his tongue, well she wasn't a saint. Plus she sucked at being firm with him. He was bossy and pushy and arrogant when it came to sex and their relationship. Truly it was part of his appeal. Though it did get exhausting sometimes. She'd dated a lot of men but Charles Dixon was a capital-M *man* and she loved it when he played at pushing her around. As long as he respected her, she sort of liked how he took charge.

He licked through her cunt, savouring her slowly. The palms of his hands held her thighs open wide and down. That bit of restraint flipped her switch.

Her fingers tunnelled through his hair as she urged him closer, needing more and knowing he'd give it to her. He moaned then and it vibrated through her clit, up her spine, lodging in her brain, the sound/sensation fluttering like a moth.

The flat of his tongue slid back and forth over her clit. Until he pulled back. 'Mmm, you taste so fucking good. Now hush, you don't want anyone to hear you. You don't want anyone to know my mouth is on your cunt. To know I'm just about to make you come all over my face.' His voice was a breath of sound she barely heard above the water lapping the lakeshore and the wind blowing through the trees.

Still she heard it and it did her in. Her gasp was involuntary and a shiver roiled through her. 'Get to it already. All talk, you,' she whispered back and he laughed.

He surged up her body, kissing whichever parts of her were within his reach. 'Tough talk for a woman so wet, her thighs are glistening.' He kissed her, owning her mouth, not letting her take refuge but instead making his point. She wanted him and he knew it. He knew just how to get to her, knew her buttons.

Their little game and she loved it as much as he loved him.

'God, what am I going to do with you?' she moaned and he nipped her bottom lip.

'I have many ideas. First of all, stop being so uptight. No one is going to hear us. The girls are watching a movie so loud I can hear it and I don't give a damn if Eve hears. She wasn't invited. Anyway, you're not usually turned *off* by the notion someone might hear.'

'That's strangers, dumbass. This is a house full of your women.'

'If only it were as lurid as you make it out to be. I told you, the television is on so loud I can hear it and so can you. And Eve is not my woman. *You* are my woman. And right now, you're undoing my work on your pussy.'

'Your *wife* did that.' She wanted to cross her arms across her chest and glare at him but it was impossible to pretend she didn't want him to shove his cock into her even if she was pissed. The damned man was beyond irresistible.

He slid his cock along the seam of her pussy and she widened her thighs to get more contact. A grin, quicksilver, flashed across his face.

'She's not my wife. *You* would be my wife if you stopped freaking out every time I asked and just married me already.'

Gah! Not that while they were doing this. 'We've been ... oh that's very nice ... seeing each other, going steady, whatever you want to call it for less than a year. You come with a lot of baggage including Pickles downstairs. We don't need to rush. Except you need to make me come or put your dick into me.'

He started laughing and rolled her over so that she was on top. 'That's better and I'll give you five dollars to stop calling her that.'

Taking matters into her own hands, she grabbed his cock, angled him and slid down the thick stalk of him until he was inside her fully. 'If you want the job done right, do it yourself. And anyway, she invites mockery, Charles. She just *plays* at being helpless to keep you hopping.'

He grabbed her hips and slammed into her cunt and then pulled out, slamming in again. 'Mmmm, juicy. Now can we speak of something, anything else? Like how you haven't come yet?'

'I'm always willing to talk about that.' She smirked down at him, the lines of his face lit by the moon reflected on the snow outside and the golden light of the fire in the fireplace across the room. 'You're too good looking.'

'Thank you. It's all for you. Now get to work up there. I think we should start off with a nice, hard orgasm for you and then we'll follow up with another in a few minutes.'

She arched, letting her head fall back as she rose and fell, repeatedly taking him into her cunt. His finger traced around her nipple and then down the curve of her left breast. Around her belly button and then *at last* he danced the very tip of it over her clit. They gasped in unison.

'I love the way your cunt grabs me when I do that,' he murmured. 'I love the way you look, above me, gleaming in the firelight, your pussy hugging my cock. Your tits swaying as you fuck me. You're so beautiful, Katherine. Beautiful and sexy and all mine.'

He looked up at her and meant every word he said. God damn, she was gorgeous. Mouthy, opinionated, independent and damned sexy. Her pussy was an inferno and he never wanted to leave it.

Her inner walls contracted around him as he drew slick circles around her clit. She was close, he could tell. Her nipples were dark, beaded against the cool air, her breath quick and shallow as she squirmed down on him over and over, grinding herself into his fingers as they played over her clit.

He hadn't been kidding when he'd brought up marriage. He wanted to be with Katherine Edwards forever. But he'd take living together. And he'd planned to bring it up over a few glasses of wine, some sex, a fire, all designed to get her resistance low.

Instead, his ex-wife had shown up saying she'd missed their daughters and what could he say? Toss her out of the vacation house they still shared? In the presence of their daughters? If it had been just them or the girls had been away at the time, he would have, but they'd seen her drive up and he'd been trapped. Kate had been really angry but had hid it well, behaving, as always, kindly in Eve's presence, but Eve played games and he planned to have yet another conversation with her about it.

There was a steadfastness of will Katherine possessed that Eve simply didn't have it within herself to understand. Just because Kate didn't tantrum or cry didn't mean she wasn't totally immovable. That was Eve's critical mistake. She underestimated Katherine. All the things Eve didn't get were all the reasons why Dix loved Kate so deeply. Eve hadn't stood a chance at getting him back before he met Kate, but now that she was in his life, no one would take her from it.

He had no desire for anyone else and, though she was courteous in the presence of his girls, he knew it was only a matter of time before Kate unsheathed her claws with Eve.

Kate wasn't a passing phase. She was with him. *With him.* But right then, he wanted to bring her off, so he added pressure to his touch, bringing another gasp to her lips followed by a low moan. He smiled, closer, *come on then ...*

Her head shot forwards as she leant over him, her fingers tunnelled through his hair as she rode him hard and fast.

'That's it, take it from me.' He dug his heels into the mattress and surged up as she ground down on him, her cunt wet and hot. When she came he nearly lost his mind at how good it was, rippling and squeezing around him as she continued to fuck herself down onto him over and over. Thank heavens they'd finally reached the stage in their relationship where they could stop using condoms so he could feel all that hot wetness without latex between them.

'Sweet Christ,' she panted out, slowing her pace and letting him take over again.

'I take it that was to your liking, milady?' He rolled, landing on top where he could control the pace better. That and he liked the sight of her spread out beneath him, her face flushed from her climax.

'You'll do.' Her voice had gone lazy, her muscles loose as she took him in. Her fingers slid up and down his spine as she wrapped her legs around his waist, holding him against her body.

He gave himself over to the pleasure of being with her, losing all other concerns but for what he felt for the woman beneath him. No other woman had provided such a refuge for him, had accepted him the way this one did.

'Have I told you lately how much I love you?'

'Mmm, it's not like I have a problem hearing it more than once a day or say, when your ex-wife shows up with a suitcase.'

'My darling, Kate, that horse is dead. Now unless you want me to go soft, let's speak of it no more.'

Teasing him amused her. He got the cutest little furrow in his brow when she agitated him. Delicious really. Plus, he thrust into her a bit harder, and who could find fault with that?

'Fine, fine. I love you too, by the way. You're very handy when you're naked.' And he fucked like a rock star.

He stroked into her, deep and hard, keeping his rhythm steady. The subtle stretch of her skin around her clit, along with the way the angle he kept brought his cock over all the right spots, warmed her, filled her cells with pleasure. Instead of the hot rush of climax when she'd been on top, this was languorous and decadent. Much like him.

'I like that smile.' He flashed that grin of his. 'It means something naughty in store for me.'

He pulled out and untangled himself from her legs despite her protest about it.

'I was busy here the last time. Before you started bitching.' With that, he pressed his mouth to her cunt and kissed, leaving her arching and breathless.

On and on he went, his mouth, tongue, lips and even teeth working in concert to blow her mind as he went down on her. She was ready, already close, but he kept her dancing right on the edge of climax until she pounded the mattress with her need to come. He sucked her clit in between his teeth, gently but surely, and it shoved her right into orgasm with one gasped whisper of his name.

Her muscles still jumped as he slid his cock back into her pussy with a satisfied sigh. His lips met hers, tasted of her, of them. She hugged him tight as he fucked her. Harder and harder and she knew he was close. Her nails scored into the hard muscle of his shoulders, her calves ached, holding him as close as she could get him, and he grunted in her ear as he thrust as deeply as he could and came.

He lay against her as his heartbeat slowed, their sweat and body heat fusing them together in a not altogether unpleasant way. 'Tomorrow after breakfast, when the girls go out with their friends, you and me, naked all afternoon.'

'Charles, where do you propose we put Pickles during this time? Because, while I am not opposed to sex with women, I am opposed to sex with *her*.'

Oh. Yeah. He had to deal with that issue.

'I'll talk to her in the morning. And then we can talk about the whole sex with a woman thing. You know it's one of my favourite subjects.' He grinned up at her and she sighed.

'I'll take a walk then, shall I? Or maybe I'll go into town. We're getting low on milk and bread.' She stretched and he admired the long line of her body, the dips and curves of her.

'Why don't you stay? I want you to be there, I want to underline to her that you and I are together.'

'Dix, I don't want to be an underline.' She sat, arranging the comforter around her legs but leaving her breasts bare. 'I appreciate how much you've worked to make it clear to her that you and I are a couple. And I don't blame you for this little stunt. But she knows we're together. She knows I'm not a passing phase. She. Doesn't. Care. She wants you back and she'll do anything she can to drive us apart. It's boring but true.'

'Well, what do you suggest I do? If you would just move in with me, we'd have that to stand on.'

She froze. 'What? I live two hours away from you, which means my job is two hours away. I don't think I want to commute like that every day just to tell your ex something she already knows.'

'We can move to Lancaster. We'll get a house near enough to the station so you can commute and so can I. That's an hour out for each one of us. I can work from home two days a week anyway. Don't you want to be with me every night?'

She sighed. 'Why are you bringing this up right now?'

'Because it's time and because you won't marry me. I want something more from you, Kate.'

'I won't marry you right now and you know why. Anyway, what about the girls? Adrienne already hates me, if you and I move in together and she has to commute to school, or she loses the place she's lived in for as long as she has, it'll only make matters worse. It's just two more years until they both graduate.'

He truly admired the way she thought of his kids. She didn't push them out of the way, wanted him to keep his focus on being a good father. It was one of her best qualities. Still, it wasn't insurmountable.

Sighing he pushed the hair from his eyes. 'You and I are smart people who love each other. We can work this through somehow. They already spend most weekdays with Eve because of work and school. We can work this out. And Aid doesn't hate you, she's just getting to know you. Kendall likes you.' Thank God for that. His oldest daughter had taken to Kate from the first time they'd met. Eve didn't like that much but, so far, he couldn't see that she'd interfered or criticised Kate to the girls. He had the feeling that was next on Eve's list though and it ruffled his feathers. He shouldn't have to tell Eve things like 'Don't badmouth my girlfriend to our daughters.' He shouldn't have to tell her lots of things, but Eve's behaviour had only become more and more childlike and annoying the closer he and Katherine had become.

'So what? You'd give up your weekdays with your daughters? Be a weekend dad? They adore you, Dix, and they should, you're a great father. I am really not comfortable with having you spend less time with your daughters so we can live together. Even if they spend all that time with Pickles, they will blame me if you move. It's only natural. I would too in their shoes.'

'That is just an excuse to keep yourself away from me.' He narrowed his gaze at her, moving towards her to take her again.

Until he heard Adrienne call his name from the bottom of the stairs. Kate raised that damned right eyebrow at him again and he snorted.

'Go on. I need to shower anyway.' On her way off the bed, she kissed him and he grabbed her, delivering a very thorough kiss instead of a quick peck. She got up and he admired how good she looked from the rear, her juicy, tight ass swaying as she walked.

'This discussion isn't over, darling Kate. There are solutions if you really want to find them,' he called out as he pulled a pair of boxers and sweats on, following with a sweatshirt.

'Yeah, yeah. Tell it to Pickles,' she said before she shut the door on him.

2

Leather slid through Brandon's belt loops, one at a time, with a sound that sent a spiral of desire straight to Leah's too-long-denied clit. *Thwap. Thwap. Thwap.* He gripped the belt's buckle end in one of those big hands and yanked it free, finally, to dangle from his hand.

He was grinning, the bastard.

'Look at this nice new belt.' His voice dipped, husky-low.

Leah kept her chin high, expression neutral. 'I see it.'

Brandon didn't seem swayed by her lack of reaction. Looping the leather in his fists, he tugged it with another *thwap* that weakened her knees so much she had to grab the back of the nearby desk chair to keep her balance. Her pussy pulsed, her clit a tight, hard knot against the silk of her panties, but Leah was *so* not going there.

Not in Brandon's parents' basement with them doing God knew what just above. The house was quiet, but that didn't mean they were asleep. And it was the rumpus room for fuck's sake!

'What a nice belt this is.'

God, he knew just how to tease her. *Thwap* went the leather in his hands and he tucked the end through the buckle to make a loop just large enough for both his wrists. He held it up.

'Leah, don't you want to help me use this belt?'

She'd given him that belt, supple black leather with a plain silver buckle, just over a week ago. She'd given it before Christmas because they'd be spending the actual day with his family, and how, exactly, do you gift your lover with a belt you intend to tie him up with and have him open it in front of his parents?

She should've waited, she thought as his tongue swiped across his lips and all she could do was imagine it buried between her legs. Above their heads, Leah heard the skitter of claws on linoleum. That would be Scamp, the Longs' appropriately adorable mutt. That, along with the squeak of the back door opening, was also a reminder that, although the house was dark and mostly quiet, they weren't alone.

With the belt still dangling like sin from his fist, Brandon reached over his shoulder with his free hand to grab at the neck of his white T-shirt and pull it off over his head. It snagged on the belt and he tugged it free to toss the shirt onto the faded and spring-busted recliner in front of the battered television. Most of the white-painted basement had been decorated with cheery bright furniture and posters on the walls, a billiard table and Brandon's dad's prized possession, a vintage KISS pinball machine. But this guest space contained, in addition to the lumpy pull-out sofa, the cast-offs from when the Longs had redecorated. The fact Brandon had told her he'd received his very first blow job on that chair might have offended her except the thought of it had turned her on so much she couldn't look at the chair without wanting to make him forget any other woman had ever touched him.

'Brandon,' Leah said warningly and watched his pupils dilate. Fuck. She was only going to turn him on more, at this rate. Herself, too.

This could be a problem.

Bare-chested, he stood straight. It was just an illusion that the top of his dark head brushed the ceiling beams. At least she thought it was. He was seventy-thousand feet tall, after all, and she knew every single inch of him.

'Your parents,' she managed to say with another glance upwards as the door squeaked open and shut and Scamp clattered across the floor again.

'That's my dad letting the dog in. Mom's in bed. He's going to bed, too.'

But she couldn't fuck him in his parents' house, she just couldn't. It was bad enough his mom had greeted them with a cheery grin so much like Brandon's it had been startling, had given them this basement guest space instead of, as Leah had assumed, assigning them separate rooms. Brandon had seemed to take it as a matter of course, not noticing as he slung their bags onto the couch and showed her the tiny but functional bathroom that Leah had been shocked into silence by his parents' seemingly easy acceptance of their son's relationship with an older woman.

They'd been there for four days. Arrived on Christmas Eve and planned to stay until New Year's Day. It had been four days of whirlwind activity from morning until night, with present opening, visiting relatives, taking tours of Brandon's hometown and viewing the hot spots – his elementary school, high school, the grocery store where he'd had his first job.

The chair where he'd had his first blow job.

Her eyes flicked towards it against her will, and he didn't miss the look. Brandon hooked a finger in the button of his jeans and tugged it open. Then the zipper, notch by notch. When he pushed the denim over his hips and stepped out of it, still without letting go of that damned belt, Leah's heart set up a steady thumping that sounded so loud she was sure he could hear it. He had to see the way her mouth parted and her breath hissed in over her tongue. He never missed anything like that.

Down went the jeans and he stood there in his soft cotton boxer briefs, already bulging in the front. Lord have mercy, he was a knee-trembler. Her grip tightened on the desk chair, which swivelled a little.

'Brandon.' Leah tried to sound stern. 'This is not the place.'

He grinned again, damn him. 'Why not?'

Because your mother wears sweatshirts with pictures of kittens on the front, and I can't deflower her son in her house without feeling like a fucking slut. Because your dad looks just like you will in another twenty years and is only a couple years older than my last lover. Because I'd prepared myself for them to hate me, and instead they've welcomed me into your family like a daughter, and I don't know how to handle that.

She didn't say any of those things, because Brandon had moved step-by-step closer, and she could smell him. Soap and water. A hint of cold fresh air. They'd been out visiting his grandparents and aunts and uncles, had taken a walk around the neighbourhood. His hand had kept hers warm.

He was so tall and stood so close she had to tip her head back to look at his face, but she was helpless not to. With the desk just behind her ass, Leah let herself sit on the edge so she could lean back far enough to keep her neck from cricking. That was more of a mistake than giving him that damned belt had been, because all she could think about was the first time he'd gone down on her, in that Harrisburg hotel room. She'd told him to eat her pussy and he'd gone to his knees like a pro. How long had it been since she'd had his mouth on her cunt? The five days she'd had her period before they left Pennsylvania for Iowa, and four days here, but who was counting?

Leah was not a woman who gave up control. When Brandon leant down to offer his mouth to hers she didn't turn her head, but neither did she lean to meet him. His grin curved his lips and his breath teased her. He didn't kiss her.

He was waiting for her.

Oh, they'd come so far. Six months ago she'd have said there was no way this beautiful man, sexy and self-confident, strong and secure, would ever have put himself in a place where she could get him hard with nothing more than a murmured command. She wouldn't have believed it of herself, either. And yet here they were, not mistress and slave but something far, far deeper.

'I love you,' he whispered into her ear when she didn't grant him the privilege of her kiss.

Her pulse throbbed in her wrists and throat, and between her legs. Leah drew in a soft breath, not because the words were new or even unexpected, but because her world still rocked a little every time she heard him say them. He knew it, too. He was working her, but did she care?

He'd braced his hands on the desk on either side of her hips, his upper body a mere inch from hers and his mouth teasing her ear. Now Leah reached to sink her fingers into the deep, dark depths of his hair at the base of his neck. She traced the familiar curve of his skull and arched her back as his breath gusted over her skin on his hiss of pleasure.

She pulled, hard, harder than she'd have dared six months ago when this was all still new. She knew better, now, what he could take. Brandon could take a lot.

She pulled his hair as she turned her face to his and held him with their mouths a breath apart. It wasn't that her grip kept him still. She had her fingers tightly woven into his hair, but he was big enough to get away if he wanted to. She tugged again to remind him of that, and another slow exhale drifted over her face.

Leah leant in and, eager, Brandon almost kissed her. Her hand in his hair arrested him, and his dark eyes went wide. She'd surprised him.

The white, soft hum of arousal filtered out all the other sounds. Leah looked deep into her lover's eyes and felt her smile teasing him. 'No.'

Her hand cupped the back of his neck for a moment before sliding over his shoulder and down to his chest. She pinched his nipple lightly until it pebbled under her touch and his skin humped into gooseflesh. Brandon let out another breath, this time with a shiver.

'You don't want me to kiss you?'

She loved it when he asked her what she wanted, how to give it to her. How to please her. She wanted a lover, not a mind-reader. She loved it even more when he got cocky and thought he knew. Most of the time he did, without question, but there were still times like now when she was able to remind them both of the rules of the game.

'Oh, I want you to kiss me, Brandon.'

Heat had bloomed between them, more now against her thigh where his crotch pressed. It was his name, the way she said it. Turned him on, and knowing that it was his trigger got her revved up, too.

He smiled. 'Not on the mouth?'

Leah wanted to smile, too. She always did when she saw Brandon's grin. It lit him up from inside, infectious, and made her want to kiss him breathless. She raised a brow instead and kept her expression cool.

Without saying anything, she put her hand on the top of his head and pushed down. The desk creaked when he shifted and went to his knees in front of her, when he pushed her legs apart under the long corduroy skirt she'd chosen for both warmth and fashion.

The material dipped between her knees and made a well into which he pressed his face. Looking down, she ran her fingers through his hair as his hands came to rest on her ankles. She still wore her knee-high leather boots, flat-heeled for walking. He'd bought her those boots.

His nose nudged her through the multiple layers of her skirt, tights and panties. He sat back on his heels, his dark eyes alight with desire. The belt had fallen to the floor, forgotten.

Leah leant back on the desk a little and put her foot into his lap. 'Boots.'

First, he leant forwards to rub his cheek against her calf. He drew in a breath, smelling the leather. He made a fuck-noise low in his throat, and her clit pulsed. Her hips shifted, the desk creaked, and Brandon looked up at her as though he knew exactly what he was doing to her.

Which, of course, he did.

Next, he ran those big, strong hands up the leather, then found the zipper and tugged it down. Not fast. Brandon inched the zipper open without looking away from her eyes. Each separating tooth eased the leather's constriction on her calves until finally the entire boot had opened.

Heat leaked through the vents on the ceiling and the room wasn't chilly, but Leah shivered at how cold the basement air felt on her leg without the boot's protection. Or maybe the shiver came from Brandon's fingers easing the boot from her foot and how he cradled it in his lap. Her tights-covered toes pressed the bulge in his boxers.

Gently, he put her foot on the floor and lifted the other boot into his lap to repeat the process. Leah wiggled her toes, which had been slightly pinched, and Brandon captured her ankle in his huge hand. He could circle his fingers all the way around it.

Leah hooked her fingers into the soft corduroy and inched it higher, over her thighs. Winter-weight tights weren't quite as sexy as thigh-highs and garters, but, hell, it was cold in Iowa.

Brandon didn't seem to care. He ran his hands up her legs and drifted them over her knees and thighs. 'Leah.'

'Yes, baby.' She stroked his hair back from his face.

'I want to taste you.'

He wasn't asking permission, but she gave it to him anyway because they both liked it that way. 'Put your mouth on me.'

With another grin and a duck of his head, Brandon leant forwards to press his face into her pussy. Leah's legs parted wider and she gripped the desk as he lifted one of her legs to go over his shoulder. His hot breath seeped through the fabric of her tights and panties, warming her already heated cunt. He kissed her there, then rubbed his lips over her clit. Her mouth slammed shut on a groan at the pressure, which was tantalising but not nearly enough.

'Stand up,' he whispered.

She did and stood over him so he could hook his fingers into the elastic at her waist and pull her tights down over her legs. Her skirt she held high, bunched at her waist.

Brandon had to wrestle with the stretchy tights to get them all the way off, and Leah laughed. He tipped his face up to her as he pulled, laughing too.

Love swept over her in a wave so fierce it would have sent her to join him on her knees had she not grabbed his shoulder. The white hum that always tickled her ears when he was submitting to her, no matter how subtly, for a moment became a roar. Leah gasped, and Brandon's grin faded.

His brow furrowed. 'Leah?'

She shook her head. His hands on the backs of her thighs steadied her. So did the kiss he pressed to just above each knee. Her skirt had fallen on one side when she grabbed his shoulder, and Brandon pushed it aside to reach her flesh.

She loved him. This was not some schoolgirl crush or something to do to pass the time. He wasn't a man she put up with because it was easier than breaking it off. She'd chosen Brandon six months ago, and she still chose him, every day.

Leah undid the buttons at the front of her skirt and let it fall off her hips. It caught briefly on him and then fell to the floor when he moved. She stepped out of it, still in her panties and soft turtleneck sweater.

Her nipples peaked through the lace of her bra and showed clearly through her sweater. Brandon didn't miss that, and his eyes gleamed again. He put his hands on her ass and pulled her forwards against his mouth. One hand tugged the cotton to the side and then, oh, fuck yes, he'd found her with his tongue and lips.

Her grip bore down on his shoulder, her nails digging into his skin, but Brandon didn't even flinch. He moaned into her. He licked her clit and sucked gently until Leah's hips bucked forwards.

She wouldn't be able to stand for this, literally unable to keep upright while he ate her. She needed to sit, to lean, to lie down. But for now it felt too good for her to move as he spread her pussy with his fingers and nibbled her clit with teasing strokes of his tongue and lips.

It was rare they went for more than a day or two without making love, and it had been a helluva lot longer than that. Leah's cunt contracted in the first orgasmic spasm by the time Brandon had pulled her panties off. When he bent back to blow on her, small, steady puffs, Leah couldn't hold back the groan of frustration.

She looked down at him, and then he was on his feet. Stretching up, up, up, he towered over her. His hands tangled in the hem of her sweater and pulled it off over her head. When his mouth crushed hers, Leah was already wrapping her arms around his neck and jumping into his embrace. He caught her easily, his hands under her ass, and walked her to the pulled-out couch that screamed in protest when they sank onto it.

His cock, still shielded by cotton, rubbed her belly. He rolled them both until she straddled him. Mouths locked, tongues stabbing and dancing, they both worked to get him naked. Panting, Leah pulled back to ride his thighs and reach for his delicious erection. It leapt in her hand and she drew gentle, teasing fingers down the length until she reached his balls.

And she stopped.

Brandon stopped too, his every muscle tense. He licked his lips, his gaze going first to where her hand cupped his balls and then to her face. Under her touch, his skin grew hotter. He wasn't helpless in her grip, but they could both pretend he was.

'Do you still want to taste me?'

His tongue crept out again to swipe over the mouth she'd come to crave with an addict's intensity. 'Yes.'

'Well then,' Leah murmured, 'I guess it's your lucky day.'

She crawled up his body and sat on his chest, her knees next to his ears. Brandon was already holding her hips and urging her forwards until her cunt hovered perfectly over his face, but Leah didn't lower herself close enough for him to lick her. Not yet.

So much of what they did was based on trust and anticipation, she wanted to relish this just a moment longer. From this position there was no question who was in control. She could move, writhe, even grind herself onto his face if she wanted to. But for now she only teased his lips with the fluff of her curls.

Brandon could have forced her down, or lifted his head to reach her, but he liked the game as much as she did. Sometimes, based on how easy it was to get him erect and panting in her ear, Leah wondered if he didn't love it even more. He waited, each breath catching in his throat as his fingers flexed on her hips.

Without a headboard to grasp, Leah had to be satisfied with bracing herself on the back of the couch. Her hands sank into the padded fabric a little too deeply to make this comfortable, but in the next moment she barely noticed as she shifted her hips to brush her cunt along Brandon's lips.

He was ready for her. His tongue found her seam and parted it, darting inside to taste her just as he'd said he wanted. With a shudder, Leah dropped her head forwards, eyes closed as pleasure made her blind.

Brandon found her clit and sucked gently as she rocked her body back and forth. She set the pace, but he kept up. His hands roved her ass and thighs as Leah moved on his mouth.

Her thighs trembled as Brandon's clever tongue teased her clit towards orgasm. He knew just how to circle and stroke her, just how much pressure to give and when to take it away. Pleasure had taken over and stolen her control. Her body moved on its own, and Brandon didn't falter even when her hips pumped against him.

She thought about his cock as she rode his mouth. How hard it was, how thick. How it would feel inside her, in just a minute or two, just as soon as she came . . .

The knock on the door didn't register right away. When it came again, Leah's low moan strangled her. She froze, her body tipping on the edge of pleasure's precipice, so close to coming she couldn't believe she hadn't already fallen over the edge.

'Bingo?'

Shit. Caroline, Brandon's mother, was knocking on the door while her son ... wasn't stopping ...

Leah's fingers gouged deep dents in the back of the couch, and now she pushed with her hands to move herself off Brandon's face. If she ever needed a reminder he was strong enough to never obey her if he didn't want to, she didn't want it now. His hands gripped her hips and kept her still, her cunt hovering over his mouth.

'... yeah,' he said after a moment, sounding sleepy.

Don't open the door, Leah prayed. The room was small and everything in it was in full view of the doorway. Don't open it ...

'Sorry to wake you, honey, but I wanted to remind you both to toss your laundry into the basket in the laundry room, OK? I'll throw a load in tomorrow morning.'

Leah's heart was pounding, but when Brandon spoke, damn him, he let his mouth continue working its magic on her pussy.

'OK, thanks.'

Shit. She was going to come at any second, and not even the spectre of his mother listening outside the door could stop it. If he said another word, she was going to go over, go up in flames ...

'Good night, honey!' Caroline chirped as prettily as the birds she'd BeDazzled onto her sweatshirts. 'Good night, Leah. See you in the morning!'

Leah didn't know where she found the voice to reply, but she did. As the creak of the basement stairs announced Caroline's departure, Brandon set back to work with that wicked tongue.

The mood should've been broken by them almost being caught like a pair of naughty teenagers, but Brandon didn't seem to care. Leah did, or she would when she came down from this sexual high. For the moment all she could do was ride out the waves of pleasure turning her into a mass of boneless, quivering jelly.

Blinking, her muscles still twitching, Leah rolled onto her back next to him. Despite the interruption, the orgasm had been strong enough to knock her senseless for a minute. She came back to reality when Brandon put his hand between her legs, cupping her.

She looked at his smug grin and frowned as she sat up. Leah looked down at Brandon's prick, tapping his belly without shame. Obviously, he wasn't as disturbed as she was.

'I love it when you come on my mouth,' he said as serenely as if dirty talk fell from his lips every day.

Which, she had to admit, it often did. Nobody would ever guess it to look at him with that choir-boy face, but Brandon was as much a champ at talking about what he wanted to do as he was at doing it. Usually it melted her butter in a huge way, but not at the moment. It was hard to be annoyed in the aftermath of that orgasm, though, and even more difficult with that gorgeous cock staring at her.

Brandon got up on one hand to put the other on the back of her neck and pull her in for a kiss. She let him, tasting the remnants of her pleasure on his lips. Somehow she found herself on his lap and, since Leah wasn't a woman who let go of control, she had to admit she'd put herself there.

His cock rubbed her belly as she moved, but only for a second before she'd reached between them to guide him inside her. Brandon moaned into her mouth as she sank onto his cock all the way. Her cunt convulsed around him, and she moaned too. But softer, biting it back, ever mindful of where they were.

'You feel so good,' Brandon said.

'Shh.'

He blinked and looked at her, then grinned. 'Are you worried?'

She didn't want to talk about it now. Leah put her hand over his mouth, her fingers tight together. His eyes widened for a moment and in the next his hands clamped down hard on her hips as he thrust upwards.

Leah wasn't into many of the scenes most people would think of as representing dominance and submission. She'd had her share of that with the man she'd left just before meeting Brandon. Empty games that had no meaning and never got to the heart of what really aroused her. Not the props and toys, the leather, the cuffs, the floggers, but control and trust.

She and Brandon had been together for six months, testing that control and trust. Learning from each other. Testing the limits.

She'd bound his wrists but never gagged him. Now, her hand covering his mouth, her breath caught as his cock throbbed inside her. Leah stilled, her knees gripping him to prevent him from easily thrusting deeper. He moved once more, then acquiesced to her silent command.

Under her hand, Brandon's mouth was warm and wet. She could feel his lips parted slightly, and the smooth push–pull of his breath. A tiny muffled noise vibrated her palm, but her fingers kept it trapped.

She let her gaze go to the ceiling, as though assessing it, then back at him. A small shake of her head, and he got it. She didn't need to spell it out for him.

Silence.

She moved on him, rocking her hips. She moved slowly, twisting her body on each down stroke to make sure her clit rubbed just right on his belly. In moments her cunt slickened with desire, easing each thrust until they rocked together as smoothly as if they were part of one another.

His hands slid beneath her ass to make it easier for her to move; Leah gripped him with her thighs and locked her ankles to give herself leverage to fuck onto him harder. Faster.

She could have told him to be quiet and assumed he'd do his best, but this ... this was ... she wanted to make her own noises at how this made her feel. Under her hand, his mouth opened. His cries leaked out but she held them tight and quiet. Hidden. Secret.

He closed his eyes and leant into her as she fucked him. They moved together. His throat worked as he cried out with each thrust, but her hand kept him locked up tight.

The white-noise buzz filled her ears again. Great, sparkling ripples of ecstasy flooded her, and she bit back her cry as she came.

Brandon shuddered. His teeth pressed her palm and she let go of his mouth to muffle him with her kiss. She took her name from his lips inside her mouth and swallowed it, then came again as he shuddered into climax.

Sweat glued them together, and muscles she hadn't known she was using ached as Leah relaxed into Brandon's arms. He buried his face into her neck, kissing her before just resting. Quiet. She smelt his soap-and-water scent but also the unmistakable aroma of their fucking.

'Guess we'll have to wash the sheets,' he murmured, and she jerked away to look at him, appalled. 'I'm kidding!'

She moved off him to hop/skip/jump into the bathroom before she could leave a stain. 'Not funny!'

He followed her and leant in the doorway while she turned the water on in the shower. 'You really are worried, aren't you?'

Leah stepped in before the water was even hot. 'I don't want your parents to think I'm fucking you raw on their pull-out sofa, OK?'

'Not raw.'

She glared, even though with that rumpled hair and just-fucked grin she really wanted to kiss him. 'I'm serious.'

He nodded and stepped into the shower with her. There wasn't nearly enough room for them both, hell, he had to duck just to get under the spray when he was in there alone. But when he tucked her up against him so she could breathe in the familiar, beloved scent of him and the water finally got hot, how could she complain?

'I love you,' Brandon said with the confidence of a man who has no doubt his love mattered. 'And relax, my parents do, too.'

Which was, Leah thought as the steam hid her face from him, a big part of the problem.

3

Pale morning light came through the window Dix had left open the night before. Kate stretched and snuggled back against him. He'd put a shirt and his boxers on, which she knew annoyed him when she was in his bed. But his kids were in the house and, with Pickles around, one never knew when he'd have to do something any normal simian could handle.

He stirred against her and she smiled as one of his hands tiptoed up her thigh. She'd put on a pair of his boxers too, with her T-shirt, but it wasn't a barrier he had any trouble getting past. Her cunt bloomed for him as he pressed his wakening cock against her ass.

He pressed closer, kissing the back of her neck, groaning when she reached around and into his boxers to grasp him. Her thumb spread the bead of pre-come around the head of his cock.

The bedroom door swung open. 'Charles, what do want for breakfast? Oh! Oops!' Pickles stood in the doorway and Kate nearly lost her mind.

'Damn it, Eve! Don't you knock?' Dix roared as he sat up.

Kate narrowed her eyes at the other woman and asked quietly, 'Where are the girls?'

Eve, not as dumb as she led people to believe, looked caught, like a deer in the headlights. This cheered Kate immensely. The part of her that relished the courtroom, relished devouring an opponent until they were nothing but a stain on the carpet, clicked into place.

'They're already gone. Out with friends.'

Good.

Kate sat up, not bothering to cover herself. She'd rarely been as angry as she was right then. This little foray into their bedroom was a direct assault and this passive-aggressive bitch needed to be taken down.

A giggle escaped Eve. *A fucking giggle.* 'I'm sorry! I just forgot. I'm so used to coming and going in my house.' Her perfectly manicured fingers flailed around as she attempted to look frail and upset, which only pissed Kate off more.

Dix started to speak but Kate held her hand out. 'You're a piece of work, you know that? I've been nice. I've been understanding. But I'm not a doormat and you're not going to keep doing this. You knew we were in here. You slept alone, clue number one. A closed door, clue number two. You've been *divorced* for nine years, clue number three. You're not as stupid as you pretend to be so don't try to play me. He might feel guilty but I don't.'

'I'm sorry if you feel that way.' The smirk ruined that little gambit.

Kate shook her head. Amateur. 'Oh the non-apology apology. The domain of the passive-aggressive gigglers like you. Let's get this straight, you're not sorry. You *meant* to barge in here this way because you still aren't done trying to mark territory that hasn't been yours in a very, very long time. Truthfully, though, I don't care one way or the other. You don't matter enough to me.'

Dix rustled around behind her and she knew he was pulling clothes on. To his credit, he'd let her say her piece without interrupting. Moments later he stood behind her, wrapping a flannel shirt around her shoulders, pulling her back against his body. Probably to keep her from knocking Eve out as much as to comfort her.

Pickles flattened her mouth into a thin line before responding. 'I had no idea you disliked me so intensely. I assure you, there's nothing going on between myself and Charles. We share our memories and our daughters. You've made it clear you're sleeping with him.'

Kate couldn't help herself, she actually guffawed. Wiping her eyes, she cleared her throat. 'Oh, Eve, I know there's nothing between you and Dix. I just want you to knock when you come into a room where I'm sleeping. Now, I'm going into town for groceries which means I need to change clothes so you need to get out.' Satisfied, she turned her back, extricating herself from Dix and began to grab clothes to change into.

'We need to talk. Don't go anywhere. I'll be down in a few minutes.' Dix gently pushed Pickles back and closed the door in her face.

'I'm sorry,' he said, coming back to where she stood, dressing.

'Yep. Heard it. Been there, done that. The T-shirt is worn very thin.' Her anger made her brittle, her movements sharp. Her inner shrew was just about to make an appearance and she resented the situation. This was supposed to be her holiday with him. Supposed to be time when she got to know his daughters better. And now, because of Eve, it had turned into something uncomfortable and annoying. If she wanted that, she could have gone to her parents' house.

He wrapped his arms around her, squeezing. 'Darling Kate, your anger makes you magnificently hot. I'm dealing with it right now. Clearly this has gone on far too long. You're right to be angry.'

Unreasonable, yes, but his niceness just pissed her off more. She extricated herself from his embrace and slapped at his grabbing hands until he got the message and backed off. 'Of course I'm right to be angry! Like I need your permission? I can open my own jars and get mad when I want to. That fucking stupid thundertwat you married is lucky I didn't pop her one right in the eye for that comment about how she forgot. Like you two divorced yesterday. She. Is. Poison. Cancer. She's gonorrhoea! A pustule on the anus of a syphilitic maggot! I hate your ex-wife. Because she is useless. Utterly. What an offence to femininity she is.'

He tried not to laugh, she could see it. She clamped her teeth together and left the room.

He followed her into the en suite bath. She ran a brush through her hair and he watched as she did it, like a cat watching a bird. He crowded in as she brushed her teeth, touching her, sliding his hands over the curve of her ass and kissing her neck.

'Get off.'

'I'm trying, darling Kate. But the women in this house keep trying to stop me.'

She spit into the sink and rinsed her toothbrush, barely holding back a snarl. 'If I were you right now, I wouldn't call attention to Pickles who is now officially also too stupid to knock on a closed door. Even that cat who lives next door to you, the one who walks into walls and stuff? Yeah, that one can figure out how to knock on a door, but, somehow, Eve can't. Thank God the girls got your intelligence.'

He snorted a laugh and continued to eye her as she dotted lip gloss over her lips. With a sigh, she moved past him to pull on socks. He'd given her a beautiful ring for Christmas – one he assured her was just an *I love you* ring until she was ready to admit it was an engagement ring – and she smiled briefly as the stones caught the light just right.

'I knew you liked that ring.'

She turned and kissed him quickly, dancing back out of his reach. 'Doesn't mean I still don't want to hit you and your dumbass ex. But of course I love it. Who wouldn't love a ring this gorgeous?'

He nodded, seeming partially satisfied, but he still eyed her and she considered how she'd get out the door without him springing on her and fucking her senseless. He liked to defuse her anger with sex, which she normally didn't find problematic, but, in this case, she didn't want it. She needed that anger right now.

'What do you need lip gloss for? You look very pretty. All fresh faced but also with an air of *I'll cut you if you mess with me*, which you know how hot I always find.'

'I'm going into town. I'm not a hundred and fifty, so I like to look halfway decent when I leave the house. At least I don't have to apply my cosmetics with a trowel to attempt the aging-gracefully-moneyed-divorcee-who-hasn't-been-fucked-in-a-year look. I used to think she had her act together, that she'd mellow out when you truly moved on. How wrong I was.'

'*Meow*. Careful, Kate, you know how much it makes my cock ache when you're bitchy.'

'Your marriage must have been a veritable fuckfest then.' She went to the door, but he pressed her against it, his body hard against hers. His eyes sparkled as he looked down into her face.

'*Our* marriage will be.' He slid his hand between her belly and her jeans, down into them until he found her pussy, wet and ready. 'Wet.'

She writhed, jutting her hips forwards, stroking herself against his knuckle. Oh all right, just this one little orgasm and then she'd go off in a huff.

He laughed softly, his lips cruising down her neck as she rocked into his hand, totally in control of the pace. 'Take it from me, Kate. As long as you understand I'm giving it, I want you to take it. God damn you're so hot. Your cunt is so juicy I can hear you fucking your clit into my knuckle.'

She groaned at his words, at the flood of pleasure rolling through her body. A quick rotation of his wrist and it was the pad of his thumb on her clit as he slid two fingers into her, sending waves of pleasure up her spine as she arched.

'Good thing you aren't wearing tight jeans,' he murmured before biting her shoulder.

Almost. Almost. Just a bit more ... until she nearly lost her knees with the rush of climax. If he hadn't been holding her against the door, she probably would have slid to the floor in a boneless puddle.

'Now, we both feel better. You can go into town satisfied and I can remember this as I talk to Eve.'

She sighed, pulling his hand out of her jeans. 'That was a mood killer.' She stomped out of the bedroom and down the stairs, pausing near the front door to put her coat and boots on.

'I'm taking your car,' she called out but of course he was right behind her, holding out the keys.

'I love you, Katherine. Please drive safe. Looks like we had more snow last night.'

'I love you too. I'll be back in a while. I have my phone if you think of something you want me to pick up in town.'

'Just come back to me.'

He looked so vulnerable for just a brief moment, her anger melted. He did love her, she knew that. He had spoken to Eve multiple times. He wanted Kate to be happy.

'That's never in doubt. Even with your needy ex-wife. I'll be back.'

Once Kate had pulled away from the house, Dix turned, anger burning low in his gut. 'Eve? Where are you?'

'I'm right here, Charles. I see she's left and now I'm to expect some sort of warning from you?' Eve swept into the room looking perfectly coiffed. He'd ceased to wonder about what he'd ever seen in her.

She was still beautiful albeit went a little hard with the cosmetics since Kate had become a regular part of his life. But she lacked the fire Kate had. Kate took things head on, much like he did. But Eve had always been passive-aggressive and he'd always let it go.

'Don't start. You're wrong and you know it. First you showed up here totally uninvited.'

'This is my house too. I'll show up when I please and your little girlfriend has no say in that. God, Charles, are you so desperate to have sex with her that you've forgotten about your family?'

He took a deep breath, seeking calm. 'No. You won't. Because in the divorce decree, we share this house and we have a schedule for that. This week is mine. We decided on that last December. You do not have any *right* to come here when it's not your week. I let you stay last night because you put our daughters in the middle and it is unconscionable to me that you will again. You do not use them to get at me, or at Katherine. Or for that matter, at anyone. Only one of us has forgotten about her family, and it's not me. You're leaving. Today.'

'Then you can explain to Adrienne and Kendall just why you're making me leave when we have plans to go shopping tomorrow and the three of us have lunch plans the following day.' She crossed her arms and he realised Eve had totally played him. He was in a place where it would be impossible to get rid of her without involving his daughters.

'You bitch. You manipulative, needy, psycho bitch. How dare you use those girls like that?' It was over. His semi-friendly relationship with his ex-wife had just burnt to ash. In that stroke, adding in all the things she'd done over the last months, he'd lost every last bit of respect he'd ever had for her.

'I'll thank you to keep your language civil.'

'Here is how it's going to go from today on. Listen up and don't interrupt me, I'm on my very last nerve with you right now. First, you will not intrude in my activities with the girls. You will not invite yourself along, period. From now on, we will keep things totally separate. Do not include me in your plans with them either. If this is how you act, I do not want any part in it. Your destructive selfishness when it comes to our children has stunned me. I'm ashamed I ever loved you. You've killed any positive feelings I've ever had.' He held up a hand and shook his head.

'Don't do it. Additionally, you will not step one foot on the third floor where Kate and I are sleeping. You won't needle her or use the girls against her. Katherine is my girlfriend and if I have my way she'll be my wife. That means she'll be part of your daughters' lives and I'm asking you to be a fucking parent and not harm them due to your own failings. She is very good to our girls and she completely respects my role as a father and wants me to put them first. I wish you felt the same. I'm going to be moving to Lancaster but keeping the other house. I'm telling you this because we'll have to work on the scheduling more closely. I'll be in town when the girls are with me for school. That's all really.'

Her mouth dropped open and he fought the urge to laugh.

'You actually expect me to help you expose our children to that woman? That foul-mouthed nasty lawyer you're sleeping with?'

'I don't need your help, thanks. I'm just warning you not to attempt to use them to harm her. Because that would harm our daughters and Katherine. I won't allow it. Don't test me on this thing. Above all, the girls are my top priority, I won't let you use them like they mean nothing. You're welcome to not like Kate, the feeling is quite mutual. But I'm warning you, don't use our children. I *will* take you to court on this. I *will* take them from you if you abuse them in such a fashion. Don't be ugly. Just be their mother and back the fuck off my life. We're not married any more. We're not even friends thanks to your behaviour.' He turned and left her there, not wanting to say anything else to her.

Kate took her time in town. She stopped in at the diner for a huge breakfast and three cups of coffee while she read a novel. She shopped along the main street, choosing a pretty scarf pin for Kendall, a pair of earrings for Adrienne and a very handsome tie for Dix. She then bought a ridiculously huge coffee mug with a moose on it for Leah. She'd give it to her friend, pretend she loved it and wait to see how much effort it took Leah to respond as if it were a fabulous gift.

A few hours later, she finally made her way to the tiny grocery store, stocked up on the basics, grabbed some freshly made lemon curd to go with the French bread she'd make for Dix the following morning when Pickles had cleared off. By the time she headed back to the house, her anger had fled.

She noticed though that Eve's Volvo was still in the drive. It would be dark soon, which did not bode well for her leaving because Kate was quite sure the queen of all misery couldn't bear to drive in the dark with her precious wee special self.

Dix met her on the porch, another thing that didn't bode well. His smile was tight and the tension wafted from him as he kissed her and popped the back of the SUV open to get to the grocery bags.

'You were gone a while.' He hugged her tight and she breathed him in. He kissed her, his mouth owning her just the way she liked most. He tasted like oranges and coffee.

'Mmm, you taste sexy. I worked off all my mad. It took time and some retail therapy.'

'You're going to get it all back, I'm afraid.'

He leant against the car and told her about how Eve had set up dates with the girls to prevent her exile. She absolutely understood why he couldn't make her leave then. Kate respected the fact that he didn't want to harm his girls and the devastation she saw in him was real. She knew it had to have really hurt him to see Eve unmasked that way.

'I'm sorry. Sorry that you had to see her that way.'

He looked surprised. 'You're not mad?'

'Not at you. There aren't words for her. But not at you. You're in a hard place. I understand that. But I'm really not happy at the prospect of another three days with her until they leave before New Year's Eve.'

Her phone rang just then, 'Salt Shaker'. Leah.

'Take her call. Tell her I said hello. I'll bring the bags in.'

4

'I have to get out of here.' Leah paced the narrow strip of bare floor between the twin bed and high polished dresser. The comforter, a quilt neatly sewn with blocks cut from T-shirts emblazoned with school names, sports teams and concerts, brushed her thigh as she passed. She went to the window to look out, and pressed her forehead to the frosted glass.

'Uh oh. Mama Bear too much to handle?' Kate sounded appropriately sympathetic.

If she only knew.

'No. Not at all. Caroline's been great.' Leah twisted to peer down to the driveway, ploughed clear of the feet of snow covering the rest of the yard. 'But, Christ, Kate ...'

'What?' Kate's voice went from sympathetic to concerned. 'What's going on?'

'His dad,' Leah said in a low voice, with a glance towards the open door.

'He's an asshole?'

'No. God, no.' Leah shook her head and twisted the iPhone in her palm, switching hands. She sat on the bed, for a moment, then got up almost at once, too twitchy to relax.

She'd come up here with an armful of sheets and towels, ostensibly to help Caroline with putting away the laundry. In reality, she'd needed a place to get away from Caroline's sunny, bright smile and constant stream of chatter, and the basement room she was sharing with Brandon wasn't going to work. Not after what she'd found when she was putting away a pile of his socks and shorts, freshly washed, dried and folded by Mama Dearest.

'Dude, you're totally freaking me out. Tell me they're not fattening you up for sacrifice or something, please!'

Leah laughed, grateful for her friend's drama. 'No. They've been great. All of them. His mom's really, really sweet, and his dad . . .'

'You. Are. Killing me. What?'

'He's hot,' Leah whispered, looking again out the window where Brandon and his father, both incredibly and stupidly bare-chested, even though it had to be below freezing outside, were playing a game of one-on-one basketball.

'Hmm.' Kate chuckled. 'Well, are you surprised?'

'He's seriously hot,' Leah said. 'And not old. He's way too young to be a dad, Kate, to be my dad, anyway. Shit.'

'He hasn't hit on you, has he?' Kate sounded suspicious.

'No.'

Bill Long, in fact, probably had never hit on any woman since he'd met his wife. The love between them would have been sickly sweet if it hadn't been so unselfconscious. So sincere. And, Leah had to admit, enviable.

'Brandon's dad is what I imagine he'll be like at the same age,' Leah said quietly. She heard a muffled sound through the glass and watched her lover – fuck, her boyfriend – no point in denying that's what he was – and his dad wrestle over the basketball.

From downstairs she heard Scamp bark, followed by Caroline's murmur and the sound of the back door opening. In moments Scamp joined the men, dancing around their feet as they played. It was the perfect picture of domesticity. Of a family.

Of a future.

'It scares the hell out of me,' she said.

Kate was silent for a moment. 'I hear that. But you've dealt with worse, haven't you? What else is going on? C'mon, don't hold out on me. If you're freaking out enough to cut your trip short, something big must've happened. Band Boy didn't buy you a sweatshirt with kittens on it for Christmas, did he? Because I will so kick his ass for you.'

Leah laughed again, wishing the humour would chase away the nausea bubbling in the pit of her gut. 'God, no. They gave me gloves and a scarf. You know, something sort of neutral but appropriate. And bath stuff.'

'Spill it,' Kate demanded. 'I can hear the freak-out in your voice.'

Leah swallowed and sat on the bed again. Brandon's mother had made this quilt from shirts he'd worn as a kid. He'd lived in this house, slept in this room. His soccer trophies still decorated the shelves, his prom picture – so fucking cute, complete with the skinny tie and hair in his eyes, his date a punk-rock girl in a purple gown and Doc Martens – beside them. He had brought her here to share all of this, and she loved him for that.

'I love him, Kate.'

'Dude. Of course you do. Who could resist a guy like Brandon?'

That Kate hadn't called him Band Boy meant an awful lot, and half-forced away the tears of panic clogging Leah's throat. But only half. She swallowed again, hard, against the ball of emotion choking her.

'I was helping Caroline put away the laundry, and I found something.' Leah closed her eyes.

'Something like secret porn-stash something? Or secret ... uh oh. No way.' Kate, Leah's best friend since the eighth grade, had always been able to nearly read her mind. 'Secret little velvet box sort of something?'

Leah, grateful she hadn't had to say it aloud, nodded, though Kate couldn't see her. 'Yes.'

'Let me guess. Not a pair of earrings.'

'No.'

'Well ... I'd tell you I was surprised, but that would make me a liar,' Kate said. 'But were you surprised?'

She hadn't been, exactly. They'd talked about marriage, in that roundabout, vague way that included the future, as in 'someday we'll name our first kid after Marlon Brando' sort of talk. But it had always seemed so far away. Six months hadn't been such a very long time, not when Leah considered the rest of her life. Yet coming here, seeing Brandon's parents, his brothers and his entire family, Leah had no doubt that Brandon had been thinking about it.

'I was,' she admitted. 'Not by the idea he might be thinking about it. But by the ring? Yes. Hell, yes. Shit, Kate. Shitdamnpissfucktits.'

The curse, a favourite since high school, leaked out under her breath and she rubbed at the sudden pain in the centre of her forehead. Downstairs, the door opened. The dog barked. She heard the low, familiar rumble of male laughter and Caroline's fond scolding.

'He hasn't asked you yet, though, right? I mean, you just came across the ring. He hasn't actually gone down...' Kate giggled. 'On one knee, I mean.'

'I'm glad you can make crude sexual innuendos.'

'Sorry.' Kate didn't sound the least bit sorry, but she did sound sympathetic when she spoke again. 'If it's any consolation to you, I'm about ready to wring Pickles' neck for being a total douchetwat.'

Leah, guilty at not having even asked her friend how *that* was going, snorted lightly. 'Ah, good old Pickles. She figure out how to open a jar yet?'

'Are you kidding me? She'll be lucky to have a hand left to open anything with if she doesn't keep them off Dix.'

'But to answer your question, no. He hasn't asked. God. I don't want him to. I need time to figure this out...' Leah trailed off as Brandon called her name from downstairs. 'Kate. I need to get out of here, seriously. I just...'

'So get out of there,' Kate said. 'To tell you the truth, I think I might need to get the hell out of here, myself. How's Vegas sound?'

'Are you serious?'

'Would I lie to you about Vegas?'

Brandon called her name again. Leah stood. 'Yes. I mean no, you wouldn't lie. Yes. Let's go.'

There were details to be discussed, tickets to book. A hotel room to reserve. But for now, this minute, just knowing they were really going to do it lifted Leah's spirits. The knowledge of escape made everything else seem bearable.

Well.

Maybe not another plate of Caroline's homemade broccoli and processed cheese casserole, or another BeDazzled baseball cap.

She disconnected the call and thumbed the controls on her phone to bring up the airline website. In moments she'd checked out the flights. One left tonight, just after eleven. She sent Kate a quick text message to let her know.

Then she went downstairs.

'There you are.' Caroline beamed as Leah came down the back stairs into the cosy, homey kitchen where Brandon and his dad were digging into the huge plate of chocolate cake Caroline must've just finished icing. 'I thought maybe you decided to take a little nap up there.'

'Oh, no ... I was just looking at all of Brandon's memorabilia.' That wasn't an outright lie. She had looked.

Caroline chuckled and poured Brandon a glass of milk, which he took without a second glance from her. 'Nobody would blame you if you took a little nap, Leah. I know you can't be getting much of a good night's sleep.'

Leah, who'd been easing towards the lure of chocolate cake, looked up. Oh, no. Oh, gross. Caroline didn't mean what Leah thought she meant, did she? Brandon's mom did *not* just reference their sex life ... did she?

'I keep telling Caroline we need a better bed down there for guests, rather than that old pull-out. Or heck, finally get rid of all Bingo's junk up there and make that room a real guest room. Now that it looks like we'll need it,' Bill said with a grin that locked Leah's smile tight to her mouth, frozen. 'But then again, I guess you kids might like your privacy, huh?'

Oh, God, no. No. Not him too.

'Dad,' Brandon said, and Leah was sure he was going to tell his parents to lay off the innuendo. 'Pass more cake.'

Her appetite for it had fled, which surely meant the Apocalypse was coming. But, faced with the three smiling faces, she found herself unable to tell them she was leaving. Cowardice tasted a helluva lot worse than gooey chocolate cake, but she couldn't have forced herself to eat even a bite.

'You know what?' she said faintly. 'I am tired. I hope you don't mind if I really do take a nap.'

'Of course not. You go right ahead. But don't sleep too long,' Caroline said. 'We'll be having dinner soon.'

Dinner. Leah's hands went automatically to her belly, still full from lunch. The Longs ate constantly. 'Great.'

'And don't forget the Monopoly tournament later,' Bill added, snagging another piece of cake for himself. 'It's my turn to kick all of your butts.'

Brandon snorted. 'Big talk, old man. But we'll see.'

Leah fled.

It wasn't that she didn't like board games, or cake, or even dinner for fuck's sake ... she did. And she liked Brandon's family. She really did. But it was all so foreign to her, this constant living in each other's pockets, the fond inside jokes, the casual acceptance of her as one of them. More than just acceptance, the full-on immersion of Leah into their family, as if she'd always been a part of it.

Leah couldn't remember when she figured out that she hadn't exactly been considered a bundle of joy, but she felt like she'd always known. Not that her parents didn't care for her, or protect her. Not that they didn't love her. But they were older when she was born, not a miracle baby but a mistake created by false menopause and too much wine. Her parents were as old as some of her friends' grandparents by the time she was in high school. They'd always loved her, and she loved them, but there was no denying that when she'd gone off to college and her parents had finally started to do all the travelling her childhood had prevented that Leah's parents much preferred not having to be responsible for her any longer. Her father always sounded faintly surprised when she called to check up on how they were doing, or to fill them in on her life. Her mother never forgot Leah's birthday but always sent the same gift – a card and a gift certificate to the bookstore. An appropriate and often-times generous gift because of the amount, but not very personal. In their eighties now, Leah's parents were still in good health and still travelling. This Christmas they'd gone to spend the week with friends in London. The one before they'd gone on a cruise. Leah hadn't spent a holiday with her family in at least five years, and the last had been when her parents stopped at her house in Harrisburg for one night on their way to New York City, where they were flying out of JFK to go to Scotland. She loved her parents, but they weren't anything like close.

In the basement she pressed her face into the stack of fabric-softener-scented clothes and shut her eyes, taking deep breaths. The ring in its velvet box wasn't big enough to make a lump beneath the pile in the drawer, but she felt it anyway like it was sharp and poked her in the eye.

It was more than the differences in their families. It was the differences in him. The Brandon at home and the one here. They hadn't talked about downplaying the way things were between them, though she'd wondered what his parents might think if they knew how much time he spent on his knees for her. Seeing his father with his mother, though, she understood they might not have found it as strange as some. On the surface, they couldn't have been more different, Bill the sole provider and head of the house, Caroline a stay-home mother who baked cookies and made all their Halloween costumes from scratch. Yet watching Bill with her, the adoration in his eyes, the way he treated her like a queen, Leah understood a lot of where Brandon had learnt how to serve her.

Nevertheless, he was different here. The laundry for example. At home he'd have washed, dried and folded the clothes. He'd have put them away, taking the time to tuck her panties into the drawer and hang her blouses and skirts on hangers in coordinated rows in her closet. He did it that way because she'd told him it pleased her to have everything done just so, and because it pleased him to do what she wanted. It worked out well for both of them, and she couldn't count how many times she'd come home from work to the scent of dinner in the oven and gone upstairs to run her fingers along the row of clothes, then turned to find him in the doorway with that eminently fuckable grin on his face.

How many times had he gone to his knees for her right there, his big hands sliding up her skirt, finding the bare spots above her stockings? She shivered now, thinking of it. Of the warmth of his breath gusting over her skin when he eased her panties down and worshipped her with his mouth, making her come while she sank her fingers into the thick, dark lushness of his hair.

Her cunt pulsed at the memory. Her breath quickened. And somehow, when she turned to see him in the doorway behind her, Leah wasn't surprised.

'My mom sent me down here to make sure you were all right.' Brandon closed the door behind him.

Then, with the smile he knew never failed to get her wet, he moved towards her. His hand slid down her side to anchor at her hip. His other pulled her close, his mouth finding the sensitive flesh of her neck. Leah's nipples tightened and she bit back the low moan his touch urged from her.

There wasn't anything she wanted more than to push him back on the bed, straddle him, yank his cock free and ride it. She always wanted that with him. Every day she thought maybe the passion would fade, that he would begin to annoy her. And every day she woke up wanting him just as much as she ever had. Fuck, no. Wanting him more.

But this time, when his hand moved beneath her skirt to stroke her, Leah handcuffed his wrist with her fingers. He stopped at once, familiar with her need to be in control. His cock pushed against her through the front of his sweatpants. She could smell him, sweat from the game mingled with the cologne she'd chosen for him, and she had to swallow against another low moan. He looked at her, his head tilted. His smile faded; she could only guess from the look on her face.

'Leah?'

'I'm sorry,' she said, very carefully not saying his name even though it wanted to tumble off her tongue. 'But I have to leave.'

5

'Dix, can I speak with you, please?' She breezed past Pickles and went up the stairs to their bedroom.

He followed her, closing the door before joining her on the bed. 'Everything OK with Leah?'

Best to just get it over with. 'I have to leave.'

He froze and then turned those predator eyes on her. 'What?'

'Not forever. Just for a few days. Leah needs to be away for a bit and so do I. I cannot, *cannot* spend four more days with Pickles here. I'm sorry, I can't. I loathe her. I can't be trapped here, fake smiling at her, pretending I don't hate her to spare the girls. It's ruined my fucking vacation. There's another confrontation brewing and I don't want it to be now.'

'Then we'll both leave.'

She smiled and kissed his neck. 'You're a good man, Charles Dixon. But you have this time with your daughters. This is probably the last time you'll all be here like this for a while anyway. Graduations, going off to college, all that stuff. Just spend the time here and we'll see each other when I get back.'

'How very casual you sound just now. When you get back. Are you planning on telling me where you're going?'

She hated when he put on his nonchalant asshole façade. 'Stop it right now. Look here, buster, your fucking ex-wife shows up here uninvited, she's a total bitch to me, she uses your children to try to drive a wedge between you and I, and what have I been? Totally understanding. I have not taken it out on your children. I have been kind to their mother even though I find her repugnant. I have respected your decisions and your need to put your children first. Don't you dare make me feel guilty for not wanting extra helpings of that fucking baby-voiced bitch and her manipulations. I'm not throwing a fit about it, but I don't have to tolerate it either. I don't want to play happy family with her. I love you and I love that you want to show your daughters what a real parent is. But I'm an outsider here. Your kids shouldn't have to choose and it's just a few days. Don't do this to me, you're not being fair. I, on the other hand, have been more than fair under the circumstances.'

'Just when I'm good and pissed at you.' He pushed her back on the bed. 'I don't want you to go.'

'Pfft. So I should what? Hang out up here? Just pine for you? Or, oh I know, go on sleigh rides with Pickles and the girls. I can giggle a lot, bump into walls. Pretend lots of things are really hard.' She pouted theatrically. 'She's totally stupid and I hate her. But she's the mother of your daughters and so will be a part of your life forever. Which, I gotta tell you, sucks. But, as you're so good in bed and all, I'm willing to tolerate. In small doses. So just keep your hands offa that dried-up old skank and I'll see you in a few days.'

'You're vicious.'

'Totally. And I am hotter. Smarter. And, I might add, a thousand times sexier.'

He buried his face between her breasts. 'Oh, God yes.'

With those magic hands of his, he tore off her jeans and panties as she got her sweater and bra. By the time she looked up again, he was naked and looming above her.

'On your hands and knees. I want you from behind.'

She rolled, looking back at him over her shoulder. Her body thrummed with excitement at his dominance. His raised brow and the way he handled her as he arranged her ass just so told her he knew the effect he had.

She gripped the blankets as his fingers traced the furls of her cunt. 'Head down, ass up. So wet already, Katherine.' He pressed two fingers into her. 'Ready for a fucking you'll not forget? I wouldn't want to send you off to some mystery locale with your BFF without satisfying you.'

Kate laughed. 'Shut up and fuck me already!'

She planned to tell him she'd be in Vegas, but not the exact hotel. She loved Charles Dixon beyond distraction but he was a bigger control freak than she was and, if he knew, he'd show up and try to manage things. As it was, she wasn't sure just yet herself. She'd made a few calls after she'd hung up with Leah so hopefully they wouldn't have to stay at the stinky bedsheet inn five miles off the strip or anything.

Dix looked down at her, at the way her hair had fallen free of the pony tail she'd had it captured with just minutes before. Her skin was flushed, her breathing had shallowed and she thrust back at his fingers, clearly wanting him as much as he did her.

He hated the idea of her leaving. It felt as if they were giving in to Eve and her emotional blackmail, but he understood why Kate wanted to. Still, it made him cranky. Made him want to mark her.

He gave in to that temptation, leaning down to bite and suck hard on a super-sensitive spot on her hip. She'd see it each time she got dressed, know who gave it to her. Primal, yes. Caveman even. But he felt better and her little breathy moan told him she was just fine with it too.

Just a few months earlier, he'd have been worried she'd take off for good, but he knew she'd be back to him. He knew she was his and so that part wasn't a concern. But he just didn't want her to go.

'I want to tie you to this bed and keep you here. I should feel like an asshole for saying it but I don't.' He removed his fingers from her cunt and replaced them with his cock, slowly working into her heat.

He loved fucking her this way, loved watching the retreat of his cock, wet with her juices and then the press back in, the stretch of her cunt around him. It beguiled him, the way she fitted around him so perfectly.

She pressed back again, impatient for more and a slow smile crept across his face. He took his time, keeping her just on this side of climax. Because he wanted to. Because he felt petulant and needy and because he could and he knew, in the end, it would be even better when she finally came.

'I know what you're doing,' she gasped out, slightly muffled by the blankets beneath her.

'Fucking you?' he teased. 'Darling Kate, you're brilliant.' Oh, well, that was a bit more sarcastic than he'd intended.

She levered up and he felt the tug around him signalling that she'd begun to play with her clit.

'Impatient? Can't wait to be out the door?'

'You're such a dick. I don't want to fuck you angry.' She pulled forwards, moving free of the cock he'd had inside her. He grabbed her ankle and flipped her, covering her with his body. 'Don't be an asshole,' she said in an angry growl.

'I can't help it, Kate. I *am* an asshole. I don't like that you're leaving even though I understand why you're doing it. Give me a break. I'm not used to being told no. You're the only one who ever does. It's good for me. Everyone says so.' He gave her his best boyish grin and she rolled her eyes.

'You can't just charm yourself out of everything. I'm not your mother or Pickles. And I know how to masturbate so I don't need you to fuck me if the price is you being a prick.'

She writhed against him and, God help him, he wanted her even more. 'I know. But you love me, flaws and all.' He chanced a quick kiss and she didn't bite him so he kept on. 'You're wet, I can feel it against my cock and belly. Let me.' He grabbed a nipple between his teeth and she moaned. He kissed down her belly, across her hips and down between her thighs.

Spreading her labia wide, he took a long lick. Juicy, salty-sweet, her taste seduced him nearly as much as her surrender did. He dove in, loving her softness, the slick furls of her pussy, loving the way she thrust her cunt against him, demanding what she wanted. He didn't waste time or draw it out; he knew he had to work his way back from his fit of pique earlier. That was Eve's fault too, damn it.

He ate Kate's cunt like there was no tomorrow, grinning against that slick flesh as she cried out her climax. He'd make her yell a bit more before she left too.

Muscles still jumping, she still felt his cock slide back into her cunt as he settled in on top of her. God, he was so good at this, he knew her so well, knew her body and her heart, knew how much she was charmed by him, even when he was being an absolute shit.

He thrust slow and very deep, grinding himself just right. She opened her eyes and found his face so very close to hers. Sighing, she gave in and smiled.

'Thank you,' he murmured, dropping down to kiss her. She drew her tongue over the seam of his lips, tasting herself, loving the way he groaned, knowing it turned him on.

'You should thank me,' she said back, teasing.

'I should, I agree.' He meant it, she could see it in his eyes and it shot through her. Their connection had ceased to frighten her, instead it brought a depth of satiation she'd never experienced before. He held on, but not so tight she couldn't move or breathe. But this little demonstration of his masculinity, his dominance, the mark he'd left on her, even the little fit of temper, it turned her on to know she could bring such emotion from a man as cool and collected as Charles Dixon.

He sped his pace, bringing her knees up to his hips, changing his angle of entry just so. He pinned her to the bed with his body and brought an intensity of pleasure as the tightness of her cunt drew around her clit, bringing pleasure so intensely sweet she had to close her eyes to fall into it.

'I want to hear it,' he demanded, his mouth close to her ear.

'You want *her* to hear it,' she said back, gasping as the tendrils of climax took hold in her gut.

'I want it, it's mine. And yes, I want her to know it's you I'm here deep inside. Always. Even when you're not here, I want her to remember the way you sound because you're mine.'

'I'm such a freak for being turned on by that,' she mumbled and he laughed.

'My favourite kind.'

No one else was there except Pickles so why the fuck not?

Orgasm rolled through her then and she let it, grabbed it and opened herself up to it fully. Kate was pretty sure she was loud enough for the neighbours half a mile away to hear but she didn't care. At that moment, he asked it of her and she wanted to give it to him.

He'd sulked the entire time she packed. It hadn't taken her very long, she was used to being portable from the weekends spent at his house anyway. But she knew the minute he left the house, she'd have to have a talk with Pickles.

When Dix had gone out to load her stuff in his truck Eve had smirked one time too many and followed it up with, 'I'd appreciate it if you'd take more care when screaming when my husband is fucking you. My daughters don't need to be exposed to a porn movie every time you visit.'

Katherine had taken a very hands-off approach to the woman up until then. Mainly she didn't care enough to engage but it was also about trying very hard to respect the mother of Dix's kids. But they weren't there and the time had come to make things very clear to Pickles.

She turned very slowly and took a deep breath to keep from throttling Eve. 'Fuck you, Eve. Your daughters aren't here and he's not yours, he's mine. He hasn't been yours for a very long time. He's. Not. Your. Husband. Nine years now you've been divorced. Stop pretending like I'm the one who's threatened here. I'm not. You're no competition for me. He didn't want you then and he doesn't want you now. If I scream the rafters down while he's fucking me, it's none of your business as long as your children aren't here. And we both know how good he is in bed.' Kate smirked and grabbed her coat.

'I've been nice, I've tried to respect what has to be a difficult time for you. But you're using your children to hurt the man I love and that's where I draw the line. I used to think you were a dynamic and successful woman, but now I think you're pathetic. Any woman who harms her children so cavalierly deserves nothing but derision.'

'I don't know what you're talking about.' Eve's voice had gone thready.

'Bitch, please. You know exactly what I'm talking about. But that's between you and Dix and those girls. I'm going, but let's be clear that it's because I can't stand your baby-voice and put-upon helplessness another minute. I can't stand to look at you knowing what you're doing to both your daughters and Dix, who may have been a shitty husband, but we both know he's a stellar father. Lastly, don't cross me. Don't confuse respectful with soft and helpless. I don't need to manipulate teenage girls to get what I want. I *have* what I want.

We're done here. You got me? You want to go to war? Bring it, you self-centred twat. I eat bitches like you for breakfast every day of the week.'

Eve had gone very pale and her mouth opened and closed over and over as she struggled with a come-back.

Kate just laughed. 'I know. I hide my light under a bushel, don't I? You thought, since I never slapped the fuck out of you like you deserved, that I was worried or a pushover. You were surprised this morning, but you still underestimated me. Don't do it again.'

She turned, heading to the door, and heard Dix on the porch. She wondered how much he'd overheard, but he didn't say anything about it as he helped her into the passenger side and they drove off.

He was silent until they got near the airport. Pouting, she knew. She let him because she understood it and because she respected him enough to let him work his shit out.

'I can't believe you're not going to tell me where you're staying. That really pisses me off, Katherine.'

Didn't mean she was going to tolerate this little tantrum when it spilt onto her lap though. 'Stop it. I told you, I don't know where we'll be staying yet. I'll let you know when I find out. You have my cell number. You have Leah's cell number. It's not like I'm running off forever.' He looked like a four-year-old who'd had his lollipop stolen and God knew she shouldn't encourage this side of him. She kissed his forehead and smothered an urge to smile.

'I'll be calling. You'd better be back here soon. I want to be with you on New Year's Eve. That's just four days from now. You promised me we'd be together.'

'I did and if you think over the time we've been together you won't be able to name a single time I've broken a promise, so stop sulking.' She nodded. 'Now my plane is going to leave without me so I need to get moving.'

'You gonna tell me what you and Eve spoke about before we left?'

'I have to say I'm amazed you waited this long. We just had a little bit of a chat. I'm sure you heard at least part of it when you were listening on the porch.'

The flash of his teeth in the darkened car told her she'd been correct.

'I'm not a patient man where you're concerned. I have no moderation. Don't be gone long.' He hauled her over and kissed her soundly.

'How could I go without kisses like that?' She brushed her thumb over his bottom lip. 'I love you, Charles Dixon. Good luck fending Pickles off while I'm gone. You know she's going to try to seduce you or whatever it is women like her do.'

He sighed. 'I blame you for leaving me. You know I'm going to lock our bedroom door every night, right?'

'I know I like that you called it *our* bedroom. I'm gonna bust her lip if she touches your cock. Tell her that. I don't share. Well –' she winked at him '– not with Pickles anyway.'

He opened his door, pulled her bag from the back and met her on the sidewalk, his self-assurance replaced by sadness. 'Don't be gone long. I love you and I'm sorry Eve has driven you away from our vacation together. I don't know what else to do.'

'You're doing all you can do. After this is over, you're going to have to set some rules with her but at this point you're stuck. Now, I have to run. I'll call you.'

Vegas was a good thirty degrees warmer as she got off the plane and headed to baggage. She checked her phone and the message she'd been hoping for was there.

Even better, Leah was waiting at the baggage carousel.

'Hey, dude.' She hugged her friend and laughed. 'Someone took a Xanax.'

Leah looked caught between laughing and crying. 'Kate, they call him Bingo.'

Horror roiled through her. 'No! Oh my God. Wow, I'm having trouble here. I mean, I'm caught between wanting to giggle and the need to pet you and give you a lolly. OK, we need to get my bag and head to the hotel, stat.'

'It's ... they're all so *nice* and wholesome. And I'm in their basement defiling him. Defiling Bingo.'

Kate wisely held back a laugh. 'Sounds like a porn movie. Come on, I heard back from my friend. We're spared the scratchy sheets motel experience and instead we'll be enjoying a muthafuckin' penthouse suite at the Palisades.'

Leah's brows rose.

'They had a cancellation he said. I got him out of big trouble two years ago so we won't be paying full price. Let me regale you with tales of Pickles on the way over. We can rip her to shreds and you can tell me about Bingo's family when you're ready. We have late dinner reservations.'

'Awesome.'

'My friend at the hotel said in the message that there was some sort of convention going on here in Vegas, but didn't say what. We can flirt with dentists or architects or whoever has freaking conventions in Vegas right after Christmas.' And just not think about ex-wives and moving in together or anything else life altering. No, it was time for shopping, drinking, eating and some pampering. She'd deal with her life on the plane ride back home.

6

Brandon didn't realise how much he'd hoped Leah would be at home until he walked into the house and found it disappointingly dark and cold. He flipped the switch and lit the kitchen in the harsh blue-white light from the old, sputtering fluorescent fixture he kept meaning to fix. He paused, listening for a telltale footstep from upstairs, but only silence answered him.

Shit.

He climbed the stairs two at a time anyway, but the bedroom was as dark and cold and unwelcoming as the kitchen had been. Brandon leant in the doorway and let the breath whoosh out of him in a sigh. He went to the bed and fell onto his back to stare at the ceiling.

He closed his eyes, exhausted. It had only been a day since Leah had left his parents' house. He hadn't slept much since then, not even on the flight home, and normally flying knocked him out like a right hook from a prize-fighter.

'I have to go,' she'd said, and he'd seen right away she meant it.

He hadn't tried to stop her. Not when she refused to look at the ring he'd bought, or when she packed her things and apologised to his parents for having to cut her visit short. True to her personality, Leah hadn't offered an explanation, just a simple, straightforward statement that she'd had a lovely time, but she needed to go.

He hadn't tried to stop her when she got out of the car at the airport, either, and, though it had just about killed him to watch her walk away and disappear into the crowd, he hadn't followed. She'd told him not to, and Brandon very much wanted Leah to understand he would always do his best to do what she wanted.

After all, it wasn't as though he didn't understand why she wanted it.

Brandon sighed again and turned his head to look at the closet doors, hanging open. Inside were Leah's clothes, rows of skirts and blouses, colour-coordinated. She didn't like dry-clean-only fabrics and she also hated laundry, so he'd taken over the chore. Even now, alone and knowing she'd walked out on him, thinking about pulling the clothes warm from the dryer, folding and hanging them, all while knowing Leah was due home shortly and would be happy to reward him for his efforts . . .

'Fuck,' Brandon groaned as his dick stirred.

Now wasn't the time for this but he unzipped anyway. Pulled out his cock and stroked it to full hardness with Leah's goodbye ringing in his mind.

'Don't come after me,' she'd said seriously from her place in the passenger seat. She'd been staring straight ahead to the traffic merging into the airport parking lot. 'I need some time to think. Will you think about me when I'm gone?'

'You know I will.'

She'd looked at him then, her smile a little sad but her eyes glinting with familiar desire. 'And what will you do when you think about me, Brandon?'

The game was familiar; his response not so much. 'Wishing you'd come home.'

Her smile faltered and her gaze had fallen to his lap. 'I'd rather have you fuck your fist and pretend it's me.'

'I can do that, too.'

She'd touched his cheek. Looked into his eyes. 'Then do it.'

Then she'd left the car, and here he was, prick in his palm just the way she'd said it. He pushed his hips upwards, feeling the bed sink beneath him. In another minute he was close, just from thinking of her smell and the way she felt around him when she came. Brandon slowed, stroking, eyes closed as pleasure mounted.

Somewhere, Leah would be thinking of him doing this. Pleasure shuddered through him and he bit back her name, held it tight on his tongue. Breathing, finally, he opened his eyes again. He could come here, on the bed, but something held him back.

He thought of nothing more until he was under the shower's hot water. He bent to let it pound his back and shoulders, then pushed his face beneath the spray. One of the first commands she'd ever given him was to jerk himself off in the shower and, no matter how many he'd taken since, he never failed to remember that.

She owned him, and he was fine with that, because he wanted to be owned. Leah was the one still uncomfortable with it, no matter how many times he tried to show her there wasn't much he'd refuse her. There was nothing, in fact, he ever had, and, even though he could imagine a few things she might ask that he'd balk at doing, he also knew she wouldn't ask him. He knew Leah understood him well enough to never push him beyond where he wanted to go ... but she didn't know she did. Or didn't want to admit it.

His cock, still half-hard from his musings on the bed, stirred again. Brandon stroked it once, twice, until it tapped his belly when he let it go. Then again, slower this time, leaning into the water. One hand on the wall, head bent into the spray, eyes closed.

Leah's mouth was tighter than his grip. Wetter. When she sucked his cock she never failed to move lower, tonguing his balls as she used her hand to stroke.

Brandon groaned.

He'd been jerking off for a long time, and yet it didn't matter that he knew his own body well enough to make himself come within minutes. Every time was different. This time his cock grew almost painfully hard, his balls throbbing, as he pushed into his fist.

Thinking of Leah did that. Remembering the heat of her mouth on him, the play of her fingers on his balls. She liked to tease him close to the edge and ease off. She never made him beg, oh no, that wasn't quite the way she liked to play. She liked to bind his hands, though, so he couldn't touch her. She liked to make him crazy by forcing him to watch while she sucked him and played with her clit.

Leah liked to bring them both to the edge, skating so dangerously close he swore there were times he came dry a couple times before he finally shot. She liked to bring herself close, but she hardly ever finished herself. That was reserved for his mouth, his hands, his cock.

A few weeks ago he'd come home from work to find a straight-backed chair in the middle of the bedroom floor. A belt, the old one, not the one she'd given him for Christmas, looped over the back of the chair. He was instantly, almost painfully hard.

Leah, who never made much of latex and vinyl, had appeared in the bathroom doorway. She wore a sheer black bra with tiny red bows at the straps and a matching pair of panties so tiny he'd scoffed at the price tag when he bought them, but paid it anyway. He'd left them for her in the drawer the last time he put away her laundry. She looked gorgeous in them, but he hadn't expected anything less.

'Take off your clothes, Brandon.'

He had, slowly, giving her a show. Naked, he sat on the chair, the wood cool under his ass and the straight back pressing the knobs of his spine. He'd put his hands behind him, and when she looped him bound with leather, he'd closed his eyes and breathed deep to steady himself.

Brandon widened his stance, one hand still on the wall, the other on his dick. Hot water cascaded down his back, down the crack of his ass to tickle his balls – not quite as good as Leah's tongue dancing along his skin, but pretty fucking good. He groaned, then bit back the noise even though he was alone and the rush of water covered it up anyway.

Leah liked to see how long he could go without making any noise.

And Brandon liked – no, *loved* – giving her what she liked. Why was it so hard for her to see that it was all right? He groaned loudly, through the pleasure. He rolled the head of his cock beneath his palm, then stroked down. He bent his knees a little, easing the ache he knew he'd feel later if he wasn't careful.

He wasn't doing this because he couldn't help it, or couldn't control it. He wasn't standing in the shower beating off because he was so overcome with horniness he couldn't stand it. He was fucking himself right now because he couldn't fuck her, and because she'd told him he would do it while he thought of her, and because, even though he knew she'd never know for sure if he had or had not, he wanted to make Leah happy.

More than happy. He wanted to give her everything she wanted, to be everything she needed. Brandon wanted to please her because he loved her . . . and she loved him, dammit, he knew it. Even if it scared her to admit it, he knew she did.

He couldn't hold back any longer. Orgasm shot through him, tore him apart. Left him hollow. He breathed hard, the shower's heat leaving him woozy. He switched the water to cold and stood, stoic, as frigid needles stabbed him. Then he got out and scrubbed himself dry so fiercely his skin turned red.

Wrapping the towel around his waist, he stalked to the bedroom and paced. She'd said not to follow her, and it had been his instinct to obey. Not only because that was the dynamic of their relationship, but because, no matter how much he loved her, Brandon wasn't going to chase after a woman who didn't want to be with him. If she didn't come back to him, he was better off without her.

Except, fuck it. He would never be better off without Leah. She wasn't better off without him, either, and the sooner she admitted it the better off both of them would be. There was only one person who'd know where Leah had gone. Kate. Brandon dialled her cell number and got her voicemail.

'Kate. It's Brandon. I . . . could you call me, please?'

Shit, he sounded as corn-fed and aw-shucks as he knew Kate liked to tease Leah he was. Too late, though, saying more would only make him sound like a desperate asshole. He disconnected.

Kate would know where Leah was, but who would know where Kate was? Brandon dialled another number, one he'd never had need to use before but which Leah had programmed into his when they got matching iPhones.

It rang only a couple of times before a male voice said, 'Hello?'

'Dix? It's Brandon.'

'Band Boy,' Dix said after the barest pause, amusement thick in his voice.

Brandon gritted his teeth and slapped a hand to his forehead. 'Don't call me that, man. C'mon.'

'Sorry.' Dix laughed. 'Couldn't resist.'

Brandon scowled. 'I'm trying to reach Kate.'

Dix stopped laughing. 'Why?'

'Because she knows where Leah is.'

Brandon liked Dix well enough, though he didn't know him as well as he knew Kate. The four of them had gone out a bunch of times to dinner, sat at the same table for things like Leah's company holiday party, stuff like that. He'd met Kate first, though, and had spent more time with her. Had even had a few conversations with her without Leah or Dix around. Kate wasn't his buddy, but he thought she liked him, at least thought he was good enough to be dating her best friend. He wasn't really sure what Dix thought about him, but he was pretty sure Dix knew the sort of relationship Brandon and Leah had.

'I'll give you credit, kid, you held out longer than I thought you would.'

'It's only been a day.'

Dix snorted. 'I didn't wait that long to figure out where my woman went.'

'She told me not to try to find out,' Brandon said and braced himself for Dix's laughter.

Dix only cleared his throat. 'Ah.'

'I know why she left,' Brandon said. 'I was going to ask her to marry me. She got a little . . . freaked.'

Another beat of silence and then Dix growled, 'Damn, what's with those two, anyway?'

'Do you know where she is? Leah, I mean.'

'She's with Kate.'

Brandon snorted. 'So, where's Kate?'

'Vegas.'

Of all the places in the world Brandon might have guessed she'd go, that was the last. Leah had once referred to Vegas as a 'playground for deviants'. He'd assumed she was being derisive. Maybe he was wrong.

'I'm not waiting for her to come back,' Brandon said. 'I want her to see I'm serious about this. I'm not just going to sit back and let her run away every time something gets scary.'

'Dammit, kid . . .' Dix laughed again. 'So. Let's go.'

'Wait. What?'

'Vegas,' Dix said. 'You and me. Let's go get them. Besides, Vegas is a helluva lot of fun.'

7

Kate definitely didn't look at Leah. If she did it would be over and the laughing would begin and that would not be nice. No. Not at all. Instead she tried to pretend it wasn't odd at all to ride in an elevator with a guy in a latex body suit wearing a feather mask and a cape. And a rather large red hat.

Kate had mental rules about certain things. Women over thirty-five shouldn't wear leather mini-skirts. No one should wear reinforced-toe panty hose with open-toed shoes. Not ever. And anyone with an ounce of body fat shouldn't wear a purple latex body suit. Much less with feather masks, capes and big red hats. It was like bad taste exploded all over him. Still, he seemed rather nice, and he held the doors for them as they approached the elevators.

'So, are you here for the con?' Cape guy asked.

'Con?' Leah sounded so very calm, like she had discussions with men in masks and capes every single day.

'FetCon? It's a sex and fetish conference down at the convention centre. You two should come by,' Cape boy's friend – the one on the end of the leash snapped to the spiked collar on his neck – added. Seriously, a collar was one thing, but spikes? It seemed so very right out of a catalogue and poserish.

Kate nodded and smiled, giving her very best blank lawyer face. 'Thank you for the invitation. Our schedule is pretty full.' She was all for letting your freak flag fly. Whatever got you off as long as everyone consented was just fine. Who was she to judge? She liked to have sex where people might see. She had her own kinks, so she assumed everyone else did too. However, it seemed to her that not being a stereotype would be good too. But hell, she didn't know these dudes so what did she know? They could just like spikes. Or something.

'Something for everyone. Not just straight people.'

'Oh? Well, good. We'll keep it in mind.' Kate smiled brightly.

Two more stops and the elevator's inhabitants grew more colourful. After the guy with the cheek piercing and the split tongue got on, a woman in a fishnet cat suit and knee-high boots joined them for several floors.

'Love the boots. Where'd you get them?' Kate asked.

'I got them online. I live in Prairie Hawk, West Virginia, we don't have any lifestyle-gear stores around.' She rattled off a website name and Kate made a mental note. The boots were beyond awesome and Dix would most certainly enjoy any evening she wore boots like that and nothing else.

Kate and Leah managed to hold it until they'd gotten inside the gargantuan suite where they both dissolved into laughter.

'Why do I get the feeling cape guy was headed off to some secluded country manor? Philip Glass would be playing on an endless loop through the surround sound while *Eyes Wide Shut* was on big screens all through the place. Everyone would proclaim loudly just how edgy and kinky they were. I did like those boots though. Verra sexy. She works in the cat-suit-type thing. Guy in a cape was a fetish fashion disaster.'

'Purple latex pants are hard on any body type. This is why I don't go to any clubs or even tell anyone I like to top Brandon. I'd die if anyone imagined I wore a cape.'

'I'm imagining it right this very moment.' Kate studied Leah from toes to head. 'Jaunty. Mysterious. Frankly, you're way hotter in latex than elevator dude. Capewise? You do have a t-h-thing for Superman,' Kate said through her laughter. 'I'm going to pee my pants if I don't stop laughing. God, just like in that book Mike gave you for your birthday a few years ago.' This brought on a renewed laughing fit.

'If I made Brandon wear a collar, which I absolutely will not, not ever, I'd *never* make him wear one with spikes.'

'The spikes would look all wrong on him. He's too big for that. Gah! I feel perverted now. He's like my little brother or something. Please don't make me imagine Brandon in a collar and latex. I can't take it.'

'Neither can I. But I can imagine him dressed like Superman.' Leah raised her brows. 'Mmmm mmm.'

Once the laughter had died down, they walked around the place, before depositing their bags in each of the spacious bedrooms. 'Holy shit, this place is so swank I feel like a hick walking around with my mouth open.'

Leah tossed herself on the couch and they looked out over the fountains below and, beyond that, the lights of the Strip. 'Not bad at all.'

'OK, so the deal is, I don't have any dress-up clothes because I was at the lake house with Dix. I have lingerie and jeans and sweaters. I need to shop. I wonder if it's too late?'

'Doubtful. Maybe we can get you a latex body suit.'

'Har. No one wants to see that. Anyway, while I love you to pieces, you know my rules. If I think I'm too old for leather, I'm certainly too old for full body rubber or latex. I wonder if it makes you sweaty? Hmm. Anyway, let's shop, and then come back here, get ready for dinner and go from there. I feel the need to spend some dough on pretty clothes.'

Dix had had about enough of his ex-wife. When he had a dream about killing her the night before, behind his locked bedroom door, he knew it was time to get out of there. Brandon's call had been just the push he needed.

'Charles, why are you leaving us?' Eve asked as he pulled his suitcase to the front door. She actually pouted and tried to touch him but he took a quick step back. Kate had been right, Eve had put on the works the moment he arrived back from driving her to the airport.

'Eve, stop. You're all due to leave tomorrow anyway and you've got them all scheduled up for social stuff without me so there's no need to be alarmed.'

'Mom, I feel bad for Kate. I want Dad to go and be with her for New Year's Eve. You should see if she'll marry you while you're there,' Kendall suggested, grinning as she gave him a hug. 'I know you love her, Dad. I'm sorry if we made her feel bad,' she added quietly.

'Kate wouldn't want you or Adrienne to feel guilty for spending time with your mother. Ever. She went to spend a few days with her best friend and I'm going to join her as we'd planned. We'll talk when I get back, all right? All three of us.'

Adrienne looked torn. She didn't really like Kate much, but that was more to do with Eve than anything else. He felt for her, but she was sixteen, she'd have to make her own mind up. He'd always put them first, but he had a right to be happy too. He wasn't asking them to move to another state, he wasn't missing school events because he was fucking some young chick. Kate fit into his life without harming his role as a father.

'I just think you should be with your family right now, Charles.' Eve fluttered her lashes.

'Mom, give it a rest. We have cookies to bake and movies to watch. Dad just gets in the way anyway. Go on or you'll be late for your flight.' Kendall tiptoed up to kiss him and he thanked her softly as he hugged her.

'Girls, I love you. Call me if you need to chat. I'll see you next week.' Without another look at Eve, he kissed the girls and headed out, free and off to get his woman.

'*This* is what your inside hotel connections could get us?' Dix stood outside the window where the hotel clerk waited to check them in. The Penny Pincher motor court was so far off the Strip it was just a memory off in the distance.

Brandon sighed. 'It's right before New Year's Eve in Las Vegas, Dix. It's the best we could get on short notice. Hopefully we can upgrade tomorrow. It's just one night. This place probably is cleaner than the fancy places on the strip.'

Dix took another look around and doubted that very much. But whatever, it was just one night and it was already late. They'd sleep and wait for Brandon's special hotel connections to try to find where the women were. Kate had cleverly dodged his questions about what hotel they were staying in. At the time he'd just been happy to hear from her and he hadn't even realised she had talked him around her exact location. Then he'd hung up and it hit him. Sneaky woman hadn't answered her phone since and she'd left him a voicemail when he'd been on the plane flying out. He was so going to get her for this when he found her gorgeous ass.

'One night please. A double.'

The clerk, who was a hundred if a day, looked at him and then at Brandon. 'Hourly? You need condoms and lube?' He hauled a bunch of sex toys onto the cracked, sticky-looking counter and winked at Dix.

Brandon made a choked sound but managed a pretty dignified-sounding, 'No thanks. Just the room for the whole night.'

'We don't got no doubles. Just a single with a queen bed. You want extra towels, that's ten bucks more.'

Dix sighed. Unfuckingbelievable. He shoved fifty dollars through the small slot and got a key in return. 'Come on then, the sooner we go to sleep, the sooner we can wake up and get the fuck outta here.'

The lobby smelt like a porta potty at a three-day music festival, on day three. The ambiance was not spoilt by the presence of the hooker sitting on the plastic-covered couch with his skirt hitched to his thighs, his balls hanging free from the hole in his fishnets or the smeared lipstick bleeding into a face needing a shave quite badly.

'Hi there, sweet thing,' he crooned at Brandon. 'You two looking for some company for your party? I'd do you both for free.'

'I do appreciate the offer and all, but we're good. You might hurt someone with that beard though.' Dix winked as they headed to the stairs, where the scent of vomit joined the medley of urine and spunk.

'Some people like that, sunny Jim,' he called back good-naturedly. 'You two change your minds, I'll be here a while. These shoes are killing my feet.'

'They're very nice shoes,' Brandon said as they moved towards the second floor.

Once they got into the room, Dix, who instantly decided there was no way he was taking his shoes off on this carpet, turned to Band Boy. 'Nice shoes?'

'No harm in being nice. Gross, this room is, um . . . wow.'

'If, by wow, you mean disgusting and ridden with filth, I wholeheartedly agree. I'm not sleeping on that floor so you're stuck sharing with me unless you want to chance a fungal infection from that carpet.'

Brandon looked down, his lip curling. 'I've seen a lot of hotels. Old ones, small ones. But this one is . . . I can't imagine how it stays in business. I'm going to sleep in my clothes.'

'I hate to break it to you, but I don't think all of you is going to fit on this bed.' Dix sighed. 'I need a drink before I can sleep here. Come on, we can go grab a bite and a drink or five. The locks are the only thing in this room that look well taken care of.'

'As long as you don't plan on eating or drinking anything in here. We'd have to take some antibiotics for that I'm pretty sure.'

Dix laughed. He liked Brandon and agreed with Kate that he was a good match for Leah. There was far worse in the world than to be stuck in this shithole with a guy with a sense of humour and a glass-half-full sensibility.

'Is that your phone again?' Leah asked after taking a sip of champagne.

'Yes. It's Dix. Oh I like that colour.' Kate admired the polish Leah had on her toes as the woman doing her pedicure applied it.

'Hmm. He's not a man to be put off. I'm surprised he hasn't come to beat down the door.'

'He probably would have if he knew where we were. He knows I'm in Vegas, just not the hotel. I know I need to tell him. Hell, I need to figure out when I'm going back because I promised him we'd spend New Year's Eve together. But I haven't been this relaxed in ages and it's all snowy and cold back home.' She sat back and drank her own champagne.

She could totally get used to this treatment. But for the moment . . . She picked up the phone and called him back.

'Sorry I missed you. We're getting beauty treatments. How's Pickles? Has she endangered your virtue yet?' She looked across the spa to catch sight of a woman in a rubber dress and sky-high heels. The fabric around her nipples was cut out and the rings danced merrily as the attendant applied top coat to her fingernails.

'By the way, there's a sex convention here in Vegas right now. Some of them are hot, some not. It's awesome to see so many people owning their kink though. You'd be in heaven, so many fake breasts and chicks in latex, you wouldn't know where to look.'

'Where are you, Katherine?' Oops, he did not sound pleased.

'Getting treatments, I told you. Um, the name of the place is –' she looked around '– El Sol Day Spa. El Sol, clever.' She knew she was pushing his buttons, but it amused her. 'I was just telling Leah that I needed to think about coming back so we can be together on New Year's Eve. Did we decide my place or yours?'

'Surely, darling Katherine, you can hear the strain in my voice. I'm not pleased. Where. Are. You?'

'I'm not sure I want to tell you when you ask that way.'

Leah laughed and openly eavesdropped.

'This is me, annoyed. You owe me a very long blow job.'

'Puhleeze, your ex-wife barged in when we were having sex. If anyone is owed a blow job, it's me. I was nice and relaxed from my massage and now that's gone at the thought of her. I'm going to look at plane tickets and I'll get back to you. We'll do it at my place because it has a doorman and Eve can't barge in. Tell her I said hello.' She stabbed her finger on the screen and smudged her polish.

'You did not tell me you were having sex when Pickles barged in.'

Kate sighed. 'It's unfair of me to blame him. Ugh, oh my God, Leah, I want to run her over with my car. I hate her. Every time I see her I think to myself, What the hell did Dix see in this cow? She said she'd forgotten I was there.'

'Yikes. And here I thought I had it bad.'

'Well, you did. Bingo? By the by, will you be wearing that swell BeDazzled puppy sweatshirt out to dinner tonight?'

'You're a bitch when you drink champagne.' Leah snickered. 'Do you think I have to keep it? You know, bring it out when they visit and stuff?'

'So you've accepted they'll visit? You've accepted you and Bingo have a capital-F future then? You know you want to marry him, Leah. He's young and eager and, yes, he makes me want to ruffle his hair. If I could reach it without standing on a chair that is. But he's a good dude. He loves you. He accepts you and respects your space. He *gets* you – in and out of bed. He has a job. He's not a dick like Mike. He'll apparently grow into a hot older man like his dad. And you'll have a lifetime supply of doilies and BeDazzled shirts. Lastly and most importantly, he doesn't have an ex-wife.'

'Marriage? It seems like such a big step. I do not appreciate that he planned to do it there. He should have done it in private. He should have discussed it with me first!'

'You know he did it because that's how he thinks. He wanted to make a statement to you about how important you are to him. I bet asking women to marry them at Christmas with the family is important down in Hooterville. If you weren't ancient, he would have given you his Four H pin or whatever the fuck.'

'Hooterville, ha! You're going to hell for making me laugh about this.'

'You can sit at my table in the cafeteria.'

They paid and went outside, relaxed, mildly intoxicated, still full from an awesome sushi lunch and all prettied up. Kate hadn't been so manicured and facialised in a while. Her roots were done, her pores were sparkling clean, her skin was soft and she smelt good. She wished Dix were there to get an eyeful.

Once they got in the cab heading back to the hotel, Leah got back to the subject. 'We're already living together, why isn't that enough? And you're one to talk. Dix wants to live with you and you keep putting him off.'

'Of course I am. I *would* live with him if he didn't have the whole daughter situation. I can't be the slutty, selfish girlfriend who makes him think with his cock. I love him, Leah. He's patient and kind, he thinks about what makes me happy. He loves to give oral sex and he's damned good at it. He even had dinner with my parents at Thanksgiving! But I don't want him to put his kids aside for me. I couldn't live with that. He adores them. He's a great, involved father. It's only two more years. We can deal with it that long. I'm actually trying to see if I can take some of the cases further out of the city. There's an entire division that deals with Lancaster and the surrounding environs. If I can do that three days a week, it might be a reality that I can move in with him and keep my place in the city.'

'Have you told him about this?'

'He only recently began the let's move in together thing. He suggested we move to Lancaster which makes it halfway between our jobs and we each commute. Which is great but it doesn't get at the situation with his daughters still going to school. While I don't mind *him* commuting an hour, why should they give up the house he's lived in for all these years?'

'Because they're old enough to deal with that. For God's sake, they're not eight years old. You said they were with Pickles most weekdays anyway because she was way closer to the school and their jobs.'

'Back to you. I just think you should take a chance on Bingo. He's worth it. He's like way hot and stuff. He folds your laundry *because it makes you happy*. Christ, Leah, what man does that? He's like ... well, listen, if he were five or six years older and not your boyfriend and Dix wouldn't kill me and I didn't love him and all, I'd nail Brandon myself.'

They got out and let the doorman get the door for them as they sauntered through the lobby, through the atrium and back towards the elevators.

'Whore.' Leah laughed as they rode up to their floor.

'You know it. So when are you going to call him? He has to be worried.'

'I know. After dinner tonight I will. Maybe I'll go home when you do.'

They got off and walked around the serene, luxuriously appointed corner and what should they see but Dix and Bingo looking like they slept rough and very unhappy.

Kate stopped, sheepish. 'Um. Guess you found where I was staying.'

Mouth in a hard line, Dix took the card key from her hand, opened the door, handed it to Brandon who looked equally pissed off, and turned back to Kate.

'Which one is yours?'

She pointed to her room. He swatted her ass and pushed her along the way. She cast a look over her shoulder at Brandon and Leah before Dix slammed the door and menaced her.

'No offence or anything, but, one, you look like you slept on the floor of a Greyhound bus and, two, why are you here?'

He stepped towards her and she wrinkled her nose. 'There's a three, you smell like pee. Did Bingo have an accident or something?'

He threw up his hands and began to laugh. 'Damn you, Kate. Why can you always disarm me? I'm supposed to be mad at you. Bingo? And why the fuck do you look so good? Being away from me means you turn into some fucking supermodel?'

She shoved him towards the bathroom. 'I wouldn't have had four glasses of champagne if I knew you'd be here. Bingo is apparently what Ma and Pa Kettle call Band Boy. If you tell him, I will have to kill you before Leah kills me so keep that to yourself. Get out of those clothes and into the shower. I can't say I've ever had a thing for homeless, urine-stinky men, even ones who can blow me until I scream.'

She brought back a glass of champagne just as he was getting out of the shower.

'Thank you.' He drank it in two swallows, put the glass down and hauled her to him for a kiss that left her tingly, shaky and breathless. 'That's better. I looked like I slept on the sticky floor of a Greyhound bus because we spent last night at the ever so lovely Penny Pincher motor court about five miles from here with hot and cold running hookers with two-day beard growth and fishnet stockings in the lobby. By the way, he offered us a freebie. They had hourly rates. Brandon's feet hung off the end of the bed. Which crinkled from the plastic lining on the mattress. My skin is still crawling. And here *you* are staying in the motherfucking penthouse suite at the Palisades! Why do you look so good? You smell like mango. Your hair is all soft and straight. Your breasts are very fetching in that blouse. What the fuck have you been doing?'

'A guy I saved from a very nasty legal situation a few years ago works here. They had a last-minute cancellation. It's swank, no? I look rested because I am. I slept until eleven the last two mornings and I had breakfast served at the table out there while Leah and I leafed through magazines. Yesterday we shopped and lunched and went dancing. Today we had a spa day which included a massage, a facial, skin treatments including mango body butter, a manicure and a pedicure. Oh and I got my hair done. In between those things, we had sushi for lunch and flirted with servers. I also masturbated three times for no other reason than I could and I knew Leah wasn't going to burst in without knocking and pretend she forgot I was in here. Why are *you* here? And most importantly, is Pickles with you?'

'You test me, woman. You wouldn't tell me where you were. I wanted to be with you. You promised me this entire winter break and I'm here to collect. Take those clothes off.'

She grinned. 'How did you find me?'

'Bingo has hotel connections. My God, your tits look good.' His hands replaced her bra and she arched into his touch.

'I have a suggestion.'

'I'm all ears and erection.'

'We owe each other a blow job, let's start with that first.'

8

Brandon said nothing as he watched Dix and Kate disappear into the bedroom. Without waiting for Leah, he stalked into the other bedroom. Her breath had left her at the sight of him in the hall and hadn't quite returned. She took a moment to run a hand over her hair, soft and smooth from the special conditioner they'd put in it at the spa. Then she followed him.

Leah wished she was wearing high heels instead of soft ballet flats. A skirt and a tailored blouse instead of the yoga pants and T-shirt. She wished she'd pulled her hair into a bun or a braid, something tight and controlled. Because the way Brandon was looking at her right now made her feel anything but in control.

She closed the door behind her. He took a step towards her and, though she hated herself for doing it, she stepped back. His eyes flashed. Those big hands, the ones that knew every inch of her, curled into fists. He looked angry, and she didn't blame him.

He took another step towards her and this time she managed to stand her ground. Brandon would never hurt her. Leah lifted her chin, meaning to say something, anything that would break the awful silence between them, but his mouth stopped her words before they made it off her tongue.

His hand slid beneath the weight of her hair and held the back of her neck. The other went to her hip, pulled her close, ground her against his groin. Fuck, he was hard, and she moaned into his open mouth before she could stop herself.

Leah broke the kiss and pulled away. Not far. With each word her lips brushed his, and she knew in another minute she would have to taste him again.

'I told you not to come after me,' she breathed, still pinned against him by his grip.

'I didn't listen.'

'How did you find me?'

His half-smile didn't quite erase the glitter of anger in his eyes. 'I made a few calls. Asked some friends who had friends who knew people.'

'You went to a lot of effort,' Leah said.

Brandon's hand tightened on her hip then slid around to cup her ass and grind her just a little bit harder against the thickness in his crotch. He opened his mouth, but said nothing, just gave a small shake of his head that made the hair fall over his eyes. She liked it that way, though he preferred it shorter.

'Did you really think I wouldn't?' he asked in a low voice, dark and deep.

Surprised at the tone, she tried to move away but Brandon's grip held her tight. Her hands went to his chest to push at him, but he was like rock, immovable. 'I told you not to.'

'And I do whatever you say. Right? Isn't that right?'

Leah blinked and pushed at him again, but Brandon held her fast. She straightened her back and shoulders. Lifting her chin, she fixed him with the sort of steely glare that had lesser men quaking, but Brandon didn't quake.

'That's the way I like it, yes,' Leah said in a cool, even tone. 'Brandon.'

Heat flashed in his dark eyes. Under her palms, his heart thudded just a little harder. A slow, sweet spasm clenched her cunt and she bit her lower lip to keep from breathing out a gasp or a sigh.

He tilted his head just a bit, though, and looked deep into her eyes. 'And I always give you what you want,' he murmured without looking away from her.

His tongue wet his bottom lip and Leah leant in, just a little. Brandon didn't kiss her. He watched her, instead.

The moment froze between them, and once again Leah found herself grabbing for the threads of her control. Dammit, this was why she'd had to leave him in the first place, to take some time and get her head on straight. Away from those dark eyes, the head of thick dark hair, those big, big hands . . .

'Why do I do that, Leah?'

She opened her mouth but found no words, just a soft sigh. Brandon took his hand from her hip and captured one of hers. He slid it down his broad chest, hard with muscle under his tight T-shirt. When her hand skated over the knot of his nipple, Leah bit down on her bottom lip again. Hard.

Brandon forced her fingers to curl over his crotch. The heavy bulge of his cock pressed her palm through wash-worn denim. He shifted under her touch, pushing himself harder into her hand.

'Feel that?' He bent to whisper in her ear, saving her the sight of his face. Saving her control. Because, as long as she didn't have to look at him, she could pretend she wasn't the one ready to drop to her knees. 'Feel how hard I am for you? I haven't slept in days, Leah. Have barely eaten. I haven't done a damned thing but think about how I was going to find you, even though you told me not to. And then when I get here all I can think about is how much I want to get inside you.'

Leah swallowed but didn't try to push him away. Brandon moved her hand up and down along the length of his erection inside his jeans. He took a quick moment to let go of the back of her neck and reach between them to undo the button and zipper, and another to slide her hand inside. Her hand slipped over soft cotton. His fingers curled, forcing hers to grip his cock through his boxer briefs. His breath stuttered when he moved her hand along his hard cock.

'Feel that.' His voice had dipped low again, though not in anger.

'I feel it.'

'That's for you.' He spoke directly into her ear, each word hovering on a soft puff of breath that tickled her lobe.

Brandon nuzzled her neck just beneath it, and Leah's nipples tightened to poke the sheer lace of her bra. His hand moved hers. Up, down. His cock thickened under her touch. He shuddered when he took her hand and moved it under the waistband of his briefs to touch his bare skin. His cock, let loose from the cotton prison, sprang free, and Leah's hand closed around him all the way. Her other went to his shoulder, gripping tight, because God help her she needed the support.

Her knees had gone weak.

He pressed his teeth to her skin, not quite biting. A shiver rippled over her entire body and culminated between her legs where the lace of her panties had gone damp and tugged at her swollen clit with every shift. She thought he chuckled but the sound was immediately swallowed by his groan as her hand moved up and over the head of his prick.

He was still moving her hand, and Leah let him. She well knew how to get him off with her hand, her mouth, every piece of her, but for now she was letting him move her fist over his shaft at whatever pace he set. His long, strong fingers kept hers held tight to his flesh as he used her hand to jack himself.

Leah's fingers dug deeper into Brandon's shoulder. His free hand grabbed tight to her ass as he cocked a thigh between her legs. The pressure on her cunt sent another gasp from her throat and, when she sagged, his teeth skidded on her skin. Her head fell back and Brandon's mouth covered her throat with kisses. His tongue stabbed at her skin as his lips sucked, gently, then harder when she rocked against his leg.

And all the while he kept up the stroke-stroke of her hand in his, over his cock. He was rock hard now, his cock thick and hot. By now she would've taken over, ordered him to get on the bed, at least, so she could ride his face while she sucked that beautiful penis, but Leah couldn't move. Mesmerised, hypnotised, held in place by his hand on her ass and his mouth on her throat. Anchored to him by his hand on hers.

'Whose prick are you stroking, Leah?' His voice had gone lower than low, now. Guttural, broken by shuddering breaths.

'Yours.'

His hand squeezed her ass as his thigh rocked against her. Leah's clit pulsed and she ground on his leg without shame. Fuck control. Fuck who was in charge. This felt too good, too big, too delicious to deny herself.

'No,' he said, surprising her.

She'd have stopped stroking but his hand kept moving. She tried to pull away but couldn't. Brandon stepped up the pace, his hand moving faster. His hips moved. He was getting close.

'It's yours,' he said without a trace of irony, no hint of facetiousness. 'This is *your* dick, Leah. It belongs to you.'

He pulled away to look into her eyes. His hand pushed hers faster. Harder. A tiny line appeared between his eyebrows and his lips pressed into a thin line. She knew that look. He was going to come, and she couldn't stop him.

She didn't really want to.

'This,' Brandon said through clenched jaws, his hand squeezing hers around his cock, 'is yours.'

She started to shake her head, thinking she would find some words to protest this statement of ownership she didn't want to admit had her hungry cunt begging for more. The look on his face stopped her. His gaze dropped for just a second to his leg and her body against it, then moved back to her eyes.

'Say it,' Brandon told her. 'I want to hear you say it, Leah. Own it. Own me.'

She tried to deny it. She didn't want to own him, like he was a piece of furniture or a jacket or a car. And he knew that, damn him, just as he knew that forcing her to say it would make real what was also already true.

Brandon pumped his hips, forcing his cock into her fist. 'Say it, Leah. I want to hear you say it. Right . . . now.'

'Oh, yes,' she said finally, and her hand moved on its own. Up and down, palming the head, adding a twist that made his entire body jerk. 'Yes, Brandon. This is mine. You . . . are mine . . .'

He came with a long groan. Heat spread over her palm as he filled it. The smell of his arousal flooded her senses. Her own breath sobbed out of her as she gave him what he wanted.

What they both wanted.

Pleasure had blocked Brandon's brain and made him stupid but only for a minute or so. He'd heard what Leah said, and what she'd given him. He opened his eyes, his breath still harsh in his throat, and looked down between them. Her grip had eased off just right, but he was still holding her tight against him. Leah's eyes had gone heavy lidded, her mouth soft.

Part of him wanted to bask in the afterglow of what had been a pretty hot orgasm, despite the circumstances. The other part, the sneakier one, wanted to take advantage of the situation. He kissed her before she could pull away and get that look on her face again, the one she'd tried hard to give him when she walked into the bedroom. Part of him, the one ruled by his cock, loved that look, because it meant she was about to get all disciplinary on his ass. He was trying hard not to think with his prick at the moment, though.

She opened to him, which told him a lot and eased his mind. He'd been a little afraid he'd pushed her too far. She sighed into his mouth as he used both hands to hold her under the ass. She wrapped her legs around his waist as her arms slid behind his neck. Her tongue stroked his.

Maybe, he thought a little incoherently as she clung to him, this wasn't going to be so hard after all.

He took her the two steps to the bed and laid her down. Leah always made love the way she did everything else, as though she knew exactly what she were doing every step of the way. Now, though, she looked a little lost. A little fragile in a way that didn't make her seem weak. She could never be weak.

They lived together. He did the laundry, she paid the bills, he cooked when she didn't want to and ate what she made when she did. Sometimes she liked to tie his hands behind his back with a belt and sometimes she liked to blindfold him, and mostly all the time she liked to leave him long, intricate lists of tasks and chores she wanted him to perform. And he did them, usually half-hard and thinking about making love to her, because he wanted to. They didn't talk much about what this meant or how it worked. It just did.

'Brandon –'

'Shh.'

She looked surprised, then that softness came over her again and she leant back against the bed to pull her T-shirt over her head. She offered herself to him, and he took her. He loved the sound she made when he hooked his fingers in the waistband of her pants and slid them down her thighs and past her ankles. She wore the tiny, pretty panties he'd bought her for Christmas, the ones she swore she wouldn't wear in his parents' house but had packed anyway.

He kissed all the places he knew made her sigh and wriggle under his mouth. 'Baby, you smell so good.'

'Day spa,' she whispered, arching as his mouth traced a path over her hip and across her belly.

She cried out softly when he kissed her clit through the lace, then again when he slid her panties down and put a finger inside her. His cock tried valiantly to stir, but there was no way he could get hard enough to make love to her right now, and there was no way he was going to wait to make her come. He needed to feel and taste her orgasm now, within moments.

'You taste good, too,' he murmured and licked her gently.

Leah arched again, pressing herself against him. She was so wet already his finger slid in and out without resistance. He pressed gently at the knot of nerves just behind her pubic bone and she sank her fingers into his hair.

'Oh, God, Brandon . . .'

'Yeah,' he said against her flesh as he licked and sucked, as he pulled back to nibble at the inside of her thighs until she bucked her hips and demanded with her body he return to her core. 'I'm going to make you come all over me.'

He smiled when she let out a familiar, sobbing gasp and she yanked his hair so hard he almost winced. Almost. Brandon slid his hand beneath Leah's ass to hold her to his mouth as he kissed her into climax. She rode his tongue and fingers without mercy until at last he felt the tight walls of her pussy convulse around him. He eased off, then moved back in, stroking and sucking, paying close attention to the tensing and relaxation of her muscles. He could bring her off again in a minute, if he played this just right, and he intended to do it all just right.

She cried out again, lower this time. Her clit pulsed as her pussy gripped his finger. Slick heat coated him and he buried himself in her scent and the feeling of her, as his cock stirred and thought about getting hard again.

He eased off when she let out a small noise of protest, then slid up her body to kiss her mouth. He gathered her close, aware that he was still mostly clothed and she was mostly not. After a minute she pushed him off her and he thought she might get up to go to the bathroom, but instead she curled up in the curve of his arm. Silent, she kissed his ribs.

Brandon ran a hand over her hair, waiting for her to speak. He had a lot to say, but he could wait. Leah's breathing slowed. Exhausted, he let his eyes slip shut.

'I should be angry about you coming here,' she murmured finally, 'but I guess . . . you should be mad that I left.'

'I'm not mad you left,' he told her without opening his eyes.

The bed dipped as she shifted. 'You're not?'

'I'm mad you left without telling me where you were going. Or why. Though I know why, Leah.' He felt her looking at him, but kept his eyes closed. God, he was tired. Brandon yawned until his jaw cracked.

He felt her fingers running through his hair. That would put him out for sure. He knew he should fight it so they could talk, but, after no sleep for a few days and last night with Dix on a bed that crackled whenever either of them moved and was a good six inches too short, Brandon had little resistance.

'You look awful, baby,' she said quietly. 'Where did you stay last night, behind a dumpster in a cardboard box?'

'Penny Pincher,' he said through another jaw-cracking yawn.

Her fingers stroked through his hair, over and over, and along his scalp, just the way he loved it. The tension of the past few days threatened to ease out of him and he fought it, only because he half-suspected Leah of trying to put him under so she could avoid a confrontation.

'You can stay here,' she said.

The invitation forced his eyes open at last. Brandon sat up. He took her hand and kissed it, then kept it close. 'You never answered my question.'

He knew her well enough to know she wouldn't misunderstand. When she sighed and refused to meet his eyes, though, Brandon let go of her hand. He got off the bed and started making sure he was put together enough for public viewing.

'Where are you going?'

He looked at her. 'Back to the Penny Pincher.'

'But ...' Her eyes narrowed. Leah got off the bed, too. 'I'm sorry. I'm not ready to give you an answer.'

He nodded as though he'd expected that, and he guessed he did. It stung, but he wasn't surprised. 'I'll have my phone with me if you change your mind.'

She blinked rapidly. 'Brandon!'

'Shhh,' he said. 'Don't. OK? Just ... don't say it, Leah.'

'You don't even know what I was going to say.'

He loved her smile, even now when he thought maybe they were on the verge of breaking up. Especially now. 'I do. You were going to say you love me but you just can't marry me.'

'I –' She stopped herself and then shrugged, looking away. 'It's a big step.'

'I know.' He did know, that was the kicker of it all. He'd never wanted to marry anyone before, and now he did. Everything had changed, he wasn't quite sure how, just that it had.

She sighed and pulled on her shirt and pants. 'You look like hell.'

'I told you. I haven't slept. Haven't eaten ...'

'You poor thing,' Leah said softly, yet with her tone somehow filled with pride. 'I know how you get when you don't sleep or eat.'

He laughed. 'OK, I had a burger last night.'

'Ha. I knew it.'

'But no fries,' he told her. 'And only a single.'

Leah raised an eyebrow. 'Wow ... you must really have been upset.'

'I was,' he told her, joking cast off. 'Why would you think anything else?'

She leant in to kiss him, lingering, then slid the ball of her thumb over his lower lip after the kiss. She looked deep into his eyes. 'And here you are.'

'Here I am.'

She was quiet for another half a minute, and that was fine. He could give her that. When she kissed him again, Brandon let her. He even kissed her back.

'I can't say yes,' Leah said.

The look in her eyes made him want to flinch, but he kept very still.

'Not right now,' she said. 'I just can't. I'm sorry.'

He already knew her list of reasons. He was too young, she made more money, they hadn't been together long enough, he hadn't met her parents. She had met his, which had freaked her out and, as much as he loved his parents, he understood why. He understood all about Leah. He could see her excuses ticking through her brain, one after another, but, when it came right down to it, Brandon knew there was only one reason, one real reason why she wouldn't say yes.

'I meant what I said earlier, and I'm not ashamed of it.'

'I'm not ashamed.' She sighed and reached for his hand to pull him closer.

Brandon kissed her slowly and thoroughly, then got off the bed. He wanted more than anything to get the hell out of that rat-trap motel, but he knew this was one of those now-or-never situations. He pushed the hair out of his eyes and straightened his back.

'I love you. I love being with you, and I love what we do. I'm not ashamed of any of it, and I want to spend the rest of my life doing it. With you.'

He could see her struggling.

'I like what we are together,' he said.

'I like it too. I love it. I love you. But I need some time to think about this.'

He nodded again. 'OK. Well, I'll be at the Penny Pincher. Call me.'

Her eyes narrowed again. 'You're really walking out?'

'I'm really walking out.'

She crossed her arms, one finger tapping against her elbow. She was trying to give him the face, but, though Brandon most always gave Leah what she wanted, this time was different.

'On the way up to this floor,' he said, 'Dix and I rode in the elevator with a man dressed like a zebra. Full-on latex and vinyl costume. Hooves. Ears. A mane. He had pink and purple stripes, he weighed about three hundred pounds. And he was totally living that moment, Leah. That guy ... he was absolutely overjoyed to be walking around dressed like a zebra.'

Her mouth tipped on one side. 'Please don't tell me you want to dress like a zebra.'

'No. My point is, he was happy to be what he was. He was OK with it. More than that, he was proud of what he was.' Brandon paused. 'I feel that way when I'm with you.'

He took a few steps towards the door. 'I know you can't say yes right now. But can you tell me that you're not saying no?'

She nodded. 'If I told you to stay right now, would you?'

He nodded after a second. 'Yes. If that's what you wanted.'

'But you really think you should leave.'

'Yeah. I think I should.' He could stay. They'd make love again. She'd cuddle up to him all snuggly and contented and put off their conversation again and again.

'Then leave,' Leah said with a lift of her chin. 'Go, if you think you have to.'

He nodded one last time, wondering if he were being the biggest douche in the world, or if this meant too much for him to give in right now. He back-stepped towards the door, watching her as he went. She didn't look away. She wasn't crying, at least. He couldn't have handled that.

'That guy,' Brandon said in the doorway. 'He knew who he was. Well, I know who I am, too.'

'I know who you are, Brandon.'

'And you know who you are. So why can't we be those people together?' he asked her and waited for an answer he could see she tried, and failed, to give.

'I'll call you,' she told him.

He wasn't sure he believed her, but there wasn't much choice for him to do anything but go.

9

She moved so they lay side by side instead of the traditional sixty-nine with her on top.

'Me first. I know how much you prefer one-at-a-time oral.' His voice held a smirk but also gentleness. Good sweet Clay Aiken she was a goner.

'I like to be able to enjoy it when you're eating my pussy and I can't with my face hovering over your cock and trying to balance and you know how I feel about you on top. I don't like balls in my face.'

He laughed then, relaxed and very sexy. 'Then come on up and sit on my face.'

'So romantic.' She sat up and turned around, bending to kiss him because he was there and how could she resist that mouth of his?

'A man's mouth on a woman's cunt is very romantic. Her taste, the way she feels, the trust, all of it makes me want you more. No one smells like you, tastes like you. I'd do almost anything for you and your cunt.'

He said it with the corner of his mouth up in his normally sardonic smirk, but the words had a softness in them, a tenderness that felled her even as they freaked her out. Like what would he do? What a dangerous, slippery slope of girl issues that one little statement held.

Instead of thinking about it further, she did as he asked, scrambling atop him and fitting her cunt over his mouth. He gripped her ass, holding her in place just how he wanted and she found her balance, holding the newel post of the headboard.

She closed her eyes and fell into the way his mouth felt. His hands were strong and sure, she knew she wouldn't lose her balance. He wouldn't let her. And that was a whole different level of fear and excitement.

Two more years, she could wait and then they could move to the next level. His daughters would be out of high school and things would be easier.

Oh Christ, the thing he did with his bottom lip against her clit, rolling it up and against the underside, following it then with his tongue. A sound dragged from low in her belly as her hips rolled forwards. Her knuckles whitened as her hold on the newel post tightened. Her skin was super sensitive, the air caressing it, his hands burning into her flesh, his mouth warm and wet as he devoured her. Her breath stuttered as she drowned in pleasure.

Need to grind her cunt into him warred with control, control that floated away like ash as she came, shattering around him, her head falling forwards.

He moved from beneath her, licking his lips, loving her taste. She was warm and relaxed, the way she went after climax. He laid her back and she opened her eyes slowly, looking at him with a lazy smile.

'You're so good with that mouth of yours. Sexy.' She stretched and he watched as her breasts jiggled, offered to his gaze as her back arched.

'Glad you approve.' He grinned as she sat up, her hair fell forwards in a sweet-smelling curtain.

'I'm going to suck your cock now.' She arranged pillows and he sat back against them while she got on all fours and bent over him. He loved to see her this way, her ass swaying as he watched the show. Her mouth taking his cock over and over. So fucking pretty.

She sucked slow, wet and hard. The perfect combination. Each time she pulled up, she left his cock shiny, darkened as she brought him closer to the edge. One hand fisted at the base of his cock, angling him so she could suck him better and the other braced on his thigh, her nails lightly digging into the muscle there.

'Darling Kate, you look delightfully debauched there with a mouthful of my cock,' he murmured, running his fingers through her hair. That contradiction lured him. The way she was in court or at work, buttoned up, cool, sharply professional, versus the way she was with him. Sexual, adventurous, not afraid to ask for what she wanted or to demand it. He loved the hidden facets she only showed to a few people. His secret dirty girl. Dix liked that. A lot.

He liked it even more when she took him so deep he felt the back of her throat and his toes curled.

Gulping, he managed to croak out some encouragement but, for the life of him, once he'd said it, he couldn't remember what the fuck he'd said.

She toyed with him for what seemed like hours. Sweat beaded on his forehead and he couldn't seem to stop moaning. He was adrift in a sea she'd created. She was his only way back, his anchor.

'You're a very bad, or rather good, girl. Christ, Kate, take pity on me and let me come,' he begged.

She pulled off, licking her lips, and he felt it like a phantom touch.

'Pity? Oh my sweet Charles, I have no pity. I'm a lawyer, remember? What I have is this, umm, what do I call it?' She played with her clit as she pretended to think, fisting his cock and sliding it up and down as she did.

'You're evil,' he gasped as she brought him right up to the edge and then, holy God, straddled him and slid down his cock hard and fast.

'Evil and making you come,' she agreed, as he came hard and fast as she surrounded him with her cunt. That hot, sweet place he'd dreamt of since the moment she'd left the car and headed into the airport three days before.

He tossed her to the bed and kissed her thoroughly. 'Why, hello there, counsellor. And how are you today?'

'A lot better now. My darling, Dix. It was only three days.' She tried to hide her indulgent smile but he won it anyway.

'I'm greedy when it comes to you.'

She made one of those little snuffling noises to indicate her amused annoyance and damn him if it didn't turn him on. Rolling her pretty ass out of bed, she sauntered into the bathroom and back out again some moments later.

She crawled towards him on all fours. Up the bed, just the way he liked it. All to please him and he loved it.

'Greedy. Pffft. Dix, it was three days. You're like a toddler who's had his candy taken away. I was coming back to you well in time for New Year's Eve.'

'You left because of Eve. I missed you. You promised me this time. And I didn't want you to go away mad. This bed ... Christ, Katherine, I slept on a plastic-covered cootie mat last night with Bingo. You were here with Egyptian cotton sheets?'

'I was. It's a rather superior hotel bed, I will say that.' She smiled up at him as she snuggled into his side. 'I'm very relaxed right now, Charles. Don't fuck with my mood. I wasn't mad at you, still not. Don't make me change my mind.'

His phone rang – the girls' tone. Kate sighed and rolled over, digging through his pants to hand it to him.

'Hello?'

'Oh, Charles, I'm so glad you're safe. You didn't call and I worried.' *Eve.*

'Is there a problem with the girls?'

'No. But you didn't call back after I left a message last night and I was worried.'

Kate growled and moved to stomp away in a huff so he stopped her with his leg over her body, ignoring the slap she delivered to his belly.

'Don't use Kendall's phone if it's not an emergency. For fuck's sake, Eve, I'm here with Katherine. I told the girls I'd arrived safely.'

'But you didn't tell me.'

'Eve, what the hell is wrong with you? Do you need a CAT scan? Did you hit your head? Stop this. You're embarrassing yourself and me too. Just. Stop.' He flipped the phone shut and met Kate's gaze.

'*Now* I'm getting mad. Again with this woman. Let me guess, she put the make on you the moment you returned from taking me to the airport.'

'Doesn't matter. I'm with you. You know that. She knows that. Let's order in, I'm starved. Then we will have sex again.'

'Leah and I have tickets to a ... thing. A show. I don't know what her situation is with Brandon just now and I don't want to run off. In the meantime, we can definitely order up some snacks. I'm sure the room service at the Penny Pincher was less than fabulous.'

'A machine at the end of the hall with a three-inch-thick sticky film over the entire surface. Whatever was inside you couldn't see it through the glass. What kind of show?'

She picked up the phone and ordered some food and turned back to him. 'Now, what are you going to do about Pickles?'

'When are you going to move in with me?'

'In two years when your daughters are out of school and they won't need you as much.'

'I can be their father and live with you. Come on, Kate, this can be managed.'

'And I can be the girlfriend who takes Dad away. Special. I don't want that. I don't want to be your underline and I don't want to be the reason your children feel you're abandoning them. It's not fair. Not to me and not to them. Certainly not to you. It's two years. I'm not going anywhere. Why are you so pushy about it right now?'

'Because.' Before he could explain, the food arrived and she pulled on a robe. He snorted, took the robe and went out to take care of it.

He shoved a few of the little sandwiches into his mouth and put the tray down and moved back to the bed where she looked pissed off.

'Back to Eve for a moment. She is up your ass all the time which means she'll be up mine if we live together. I don't like her. In fact, after this little series of stunts she's pulled, I can safely say I hate her. Hate. I only hate like three people. I'm not having any holiday dinners where she's invited. I don't want her in my home. This is a big reason not to move in together since you all seem incapable of celebrating holidays without her. I'm not Mrs Brady and she totally hit on you and not for the first time.' She sat up, crouching and looking at him closely.

'What does it matter? She's not a threat to you. And we don't have to have her at our house for holiday dinners. I expect there will be times when we'll all have to mix. When the girls graduate, weddings, that sort of thing. Well, not *our* wedding of course,' he amended quickly.

'OK, first of all, that "not a threat" thing? She used that and I don't like it. Not from her and not from you. The thing is, I don't think you'd cheat on me with her. If I did, I wouldn't be with you. I asked you a direct question. Has she hit on you?'

'Yes. Have people hit on you? Come on, I see the way men look at you all the time. Why are you making a big deal out of it if you know I wouldn't cheat on you? Not with her. Not with anyone.'

She took a deep breath. 'Don't. Don't you dare condescend to me. I am not your intelligence-impaired ex-wife. Can you actually sit there and compare random guys asking me out to the woman you've had children with hitting on you? You have a history with her, a life with her. You've shared some of the most intimate and important life events with her. Of course that bothers me!'

Kate got off the bed and began to get dressed in short jerky movements.

'I don't know what to say. Katherine, I love you. I want to share my life with you. I can't change my past. I can't deny that Eve was important to me once. But it doesn't matter that she throws herself at me, I'm not catching.'

'You're missing the point. Oh my God! Seriously, Charles, you are a smart guy, I'm laying it all out here and you're giving me this shit?'

He got up and tried to hug her but she slapped his hands away. 'I love you, damn it. This is ridiculous. You're acting irrationally. You say yourself that you know I won't cheat. I'm begging you to be with me and you're pissed? I'm missing the point.'

'Because you *want* to miss it. The point is, Charles, she's a person who is tied to you forever. In a way I cannot be. She's part of what's the most important thing in the world to you – those girls. And rightfully so, they're good kids, you've done a great job. But you act like I'm crazy to be bugged by the fact that she's totally disrespectful to me by repeatedly trying to fuck you when she knows you're with me. And yet I'm supposed to just tolerate it like it's no big thing. Well, buster, it *is* a big thing. I don't like it. I hate it as a matter of fact and what I hate even more is that you'd compare that level of disrespect to some random guy at my firm asking me out for drinks.'

Oh.

'You're right and I'm sorry. She's been like this for so long I just tend to ignore it and let it be background noise. Because while, yes, she's the mother of my children, she's not what you are. She can play her games, but I don't want her. I want you. Every minute of the day I want you. I wake up wanting you, I go to sleep wanting you. I used to think I was done with kids but I look at you and change my mind. Don't freak on me here, Kate,' he said quickly, noting her body language.

'I'm not freaked. Not really. It's not like our future is in doubt. We're together and I get that. But like whoa serious, you need to deal with her. I've already told her off, but your daughters are in the middle so I can't do much more without harming them too.'

'So move in with me. That's the best way to solve this issue.' He backed her against the bedroom door and nuzzled her neck. She moaned softly and gasped when he found his way between her thighs. No panties and a skirt. His idea of the perfect Kate outfit.

She opened and hitched a long lean leg up at his hip and he took her invitation, angling his cock quickly and driving up and in as she came down. He thrust hard and fast, sweat building on his spine, on his forehead. Kate held on to him, open to his body, her gaze locked with his. Taking her this way was intimate, more than soft and romantic. The frenzied need she stirred inside wasn't something he was used to, even now after he'd had her time and again. He needed her and she gave herself to him. With her eyes open, meeting him thrust for thrust. That was something of a wonder to him.

'Make me come, Dix.'

'My pleasure.' He pressed her harder against the door, pinning her with his body. This changed her angle and she moaned, grinding herself on him. The swollen knot of her clit pressed against the stalk of his cock, slippery and hard. 'Is that enough for you?' he asked teasingly in her ear as her cunt fluttered around him.

'It's never enough. You could crawl into my body and stay there forever and I still couldn't get enough. I need you.'

'Christ, you undo me,' he murmured before nipping at her neck.

She made that sound, the one that unravelled everything within him when he heard it. Deep and low, a desperate, pleading sound as if she were willing her orgasm to manifest and then the tiny intake of breath as it did, like she was surprised.

The heat of her, the wet of her, the clamp of her pussy around his invading cock drove him on, drove him as the slap of his body against hers lured, as the rising scent of her body married with his. Sex and lust, need, craving and desire, and love too. She fit him in a way he'd never imagined. In every way, Katherine was his match, exciting and comforting.

He grunted as his cock shot, unloaded deep within her as she writhed through the echoes of her climax.

In the background, as his knees buckled and they headed to the floor, he heard the front door open and close and then his phone rang.

'My God your ass is stellar,' she said as he crawled to where he'd tossed his phone.

'I'm glad you approve.' He looked at the screen. 'Uh oh, it's Bingo.'

Kate regained feeling in her legs and moved into the bathroom to clean up and set her clothes to rights. When she came back out Dix was sitting on the bed, eating the food they'd had delivered.

'What's up?'

'He's going back to the Penny Pincher. He's giving Leah space to think.'

'Go on after him. He's not a moron, but he probably needs a friend right about now. I'm going to talk to Leah and see if, between you and me, we can't get these two crazy kids back together. Take him to a strip club or something suitably guy-bondy type. If you get a lap dance, do not return to me with feminine goo on your pants or I will maim you. Only my feminine goo is acceptable on any part of you. But who am I to refuse a stripper such a face?'

He stood up and smirked, kissing her hard. 'And you'll be where?'

'Thunder From Down Under. Hunky Australian dudes taking clothes off, undulating, all that jazz. We have tickets and they're non-refundable. What can I say? I wouldn't want to waste the money. I'm all about value.'

He laughed. 'I do like lap dances, but I like the one you gave me at that little club in Philly two months ago. Your goo is far more preferable. But hell, I like to look at strippers and it'll give Bingo an outlet. God, I've got to stop calling him that. The rule goes for you too. I don't want any male goo on you.'

'I don't think they do lap dances but I'll keep that in mind. Now go.' She pressed her key card into his hand. 'You're more than welcome to sleep here, in this luxurious bed, servicing me.'

'Let's hope I won't have to endure a sympathy night at the Penny Pincher again.' He pulled his shirt back on and stepped into his shoes as he ate the last bit of food. 'We're going to hash out this moving-in-together thing when Leah and Brandon have worked this through.'

Before she could argue, he swatted her ass and left.

Smiling, she wandered over to Leah's door and tapped. 'Leah? Girl, I hope Bingo didn't wear you out, we have Australian strippers to ogle,' Kate called through the closed door.

Leah opened up. 'I'm ready.'

'Good, you can tell me why poor little Bingo went away upset and why Dix is going to have to take him to a strip club.'

'He'd better not bring him back with anything itchy.'

They both laughed as they got ready for their night on the town.

10

'Those can't be real. Are those real? Those can't be real.' Laughing through her astonishment, Leah put a self-conscious hand on her chest. 'Good Lord, they're bigger than mine.'

Kate, drink in hand and eyes shining with laughter, had to catch her breath before she could speak. 'All real and covered with enough oil to fry a basket of fries.'

The man gyrating on the stage had stripped down to a fringed loincloth, his long hair held back from his face by a leather headband. His broad, muscled chest gleamed under the barrage of disco lights as the music thumped. And then he did it again, the trick that had so astounded Leah. One, two, one, his pecs jerked in time to the bass beat. He never stopped grinning.

Leah finished her second margarita and leant back in the comfortable padded booth Kate's connections had scored for them. 'Damn, that's impressive.'

The show had barely gotten under way, but already the screaming audience had been whipped into a frenzy by the totally cute emcee with the sexy Australian accent. The place was packed, wall-to-wall women, and not a one of them had to wave a dollar bill to get a stripper's attention. Thunder From Down Under didn't work that way. You paid to get in, you sat back and enjoyed the show.

'I sort of miss the dollars,' she confided to Kate. 'I mean, they say that something like twenty-five per cent of the dollar bills in circulation have spent some time in a stripper's G-string. Besides, stuffing money in a guy's jock is so . . . tactile.'

Kate guffawed and slapped the table, then jerked the platter of nachos towards her to grab up a chip dripping with cheese and salsa. 'You'd better slow down on those drinks. You're starting to rationalise touching strippers again.'

'As if that needed rationalising!' Leah waved at the waiter, a cute young thing in a pair of black dress trousers and a bow-tie, and nothing else. 'Another round!'

Then they had no more time for jokes, because the show began in earnest. And sure, it was a group of buff, toned and tanned men all greased up and shaking their moneymakers to 80s pop tunes, but what wasn't there to love about that? Leah sipped at her third drink and sat back to enjoy the show.

'Dix is so much hotter than any of these guys.' Kate shoved away the empty nacho basket and pointed to the stage, where a trio of dudes dressed like firefighters were bumping and grinding. 'So's Bingo, for that matter.'

'*Brandon*,' Leah said firmly, because the name Bingo made her want to laugh and cringe at the same time, 'is super-duper way hotter than that.'

Kate lifted her glass. 'We are fucking two of the hottest men on the planet. You do realise that.'

Leah clinked her glass to her friend's. 'Hell, yeah!'

'Although that one on the end is pretty fucking delish,' Kate added, pointing to a short-cropped blond in a pair of ball-hugging denim shorts. 'I could do without the plum-smugglers but, holy shit, does he have a nice belly.'

'I'm not into blonds so much, but yeah. Nice.'

Kate snorted and rolled her eyes. 'You're not into blonds. No kidding.'

'What's that supposed to mean?' God, it felt good to laugh.

'It means you have a type.'

'Pfft.' Leah nodded towards the stage. 'And you don't?'

'Nothing wrong with it,' Kate said, then paused, looking at the stage. 'Now that one. That guy, he's your type.'

The song had ended and a new guy took the stage. Leah looked. Tall, lean, dark hair with emo bangs covering one eye. From this distance she couldn't be sure, but she thought he might have blue eyes. He wore a pair of black suit pants and a white button-down shirt, a tie pulled loose at his neck.

'Hell, yes,' she murmured, watching as the emcee pulled a woman up from the front row and seated her in a spinning office chair. 'Can I tell you how happy I am we're back here in the non-VIP section?'

Kate laughed. 'What, you're not interested in going home covered with baby oil?'

'Not even.' Leah watched as the cute guy, just her type, twirled the woman on the chair and danced around her. 'And I already told you, if Dix brings home my Brandon covered in – Oh, shit.'

The action on the stage had taken a surprising turn. Leah had been expecting the dancer to shake his stuff in the woman's face, maybe reach down and yank off his tearaway pants and sit on her lap. Standard male stripper moves. But this guy . . . this guy in his naughty-schoolboy outfit, had just dropped to his knees, pulling at his tie, sliding open the buttons on his shirt to reveal a bare sleek chest with a line of dark hair disappearing down his belly into the waistband of his trousers.

'He's got body hair!' Kate crowed. 'Wow!'

Leah swallowed a rush of saliva, tasting tequila and lime. 'Yeah. That *is* just my type.'

Kate shot her a look. 'Like I said. Nothing wrong with it.'

The scene on the stage was overblown and bordering on ridiculous, but nevertheless Leah felt a rush of heat as the dancer rubbed his cheek up the woman's leg, only to pull away and arch back, thrusting his groin into the air as the emcee encouraged the woman's friends to egg her into unzipping his pants. When she did, the energy level in the room ratcheted up another couple hundred notches until the air practically vibrated from it. Or maybe that was all the screaming, Leah thought as the woman reached for the stripper's crotch and gave them all what they clamoured for.

Kate woo-hooed along with the crowd, and a moment later Leah found the voice to join her. The waiter brought more drinks. The guy on his knees got up so the woman in the chair could pull his pants down around his ankles for him. After that, the moment was lost when he started to re-enact the famous underpants-dance scene from *Risky Business*, but Leah kept her eyes on the guy as he finished his strut, planted a kiss on the woman's cheek and left the stage.

Nothing wrong with having a type, hell no. Wasn't it better to know what you wanted, what you craved, than denying it? Or worse, never finding out? Leah sat back again against the padded booth, watching the next set of dancers, one of them in a pair of fishnets and a wig, rock out to the 'Time Warp'. How could anyone not love a bunch of half-naked men with good senses of humour?

Her phone lay dark and silent in her bag, but she reached for it anyway and slid a finger across the touch screen to unlock it and check for any missed calls or text messages. Nothing. She put it on the table where she'd be able to see if something came in, just in case.

'Brandon checking up on you?' Kate teased.

Leah shook her head. 'No. I'm sure he and Dix are busy right about now.'

She frowned, imagining a set of huge tits and a tiny, tight ass in a thong bouncing on Brandon's lap. Women paid attention to him all the time. Hell, they couldn't walk into the grocery store without him turning heads. But there was no threat from a stripper, no matter how naked or covered in glitter she might be. Or how big her tits. For strippers, it was just a job. Right?

'You're not worried, are you?'

The music had died down a little bit while the emcee chattered, getting them ready for the second half of the show. He was talking about some sort of picture package available for sale after the performance. Leah shook her head. 'No. I trust him.'

'I trust Dix too,' Kate said. Then she frowned. 'Did I tell you Pickles came on to him?'

This put everything into proper perspective, and Leah drew in a breath. 'No! Well, I'd say I'm shocked, but I guess I'm not. What a bitch.'

Kate sneered. 'I tried. I tried to put myself in her place. Dix is an awesome man, how would I feel if he didn't love me?'

Leah nodded as they both made growling sounds when the dark-haired pirate came on stage and undulated around a young woman in a tight T-shirt with BRIDE emblazoned across her boobies. Boobies she now was busily exposing and shoving into the face of the oiled-up pirate as she tried to grab a handful of cock.

Leah sniffed. 'Her mother must be proud. Anyway, they've been split up for a long time. While it's nice and all for you to be understanding, that bitch needs a smack.'

Kate shrugged and downed her drink. Wow, she was tipsy. It was a good thing Eve was thousands of miles away or she *would* have gotten a smack.

She snickered. 'I'm done with her. I told her off, but she doesn't care. Dix says he told her off too. I believe he did. But like I said, she doesn't care. She can't possibly think she'll win him back. She couldn't do that before I entered the scene.'

'Maybe she just wants to drive a wedge between you.' Leah shrugged, and Kate was comforted by how much her friend saw in people.

'Her latest is to use the girls and Dix is really upset. I feel bad for him, you know? Holy shit, you could bounce quarters off his ass.' Kate nodded her head back to the stage where pirate boy had pulled off his skin-tight pantaloons and made a slow, sensual circle with his hips. 'Christalmighty, I'm having impure thoughts about a boy I'm probably old enough to have babysat for.'

'That hip action is impressive,' Leah said, rapt.

They were both silent a while as they watched the grace and blatant sexuality the pirate guy brought out of his body. A flex, a shimmy, it was more than just shaking his cock. He owned it, owned his sexual lure, clearly revelled in the power he had over this room of women. The cocky smile, the coy look through his hair as he glanced back over his shoulder – the man was all about that moment on stage and while it was fun to giggle, there was a definite depth of pleasure emanating from him. Pleasure at being happy in his skin. Leah needed that with Bingo, er, Brandon. And truth be told, Kate knew she had to figure out how to get that with Dix. How to move past this current Pickle-sized hurdle and embrace their future. They'd worked through her reluctance regarding dating a co-worker and now they had even bigger things to deal with.

'What's his plan then? Has she said things about you to the kids?' Leah broke away from the scene on the stage for a moment to look at Kate.

'She hadn't before this latest little stunt. But...oh wow, a threesome.' Three of the dancers got on stage and did a sort of unified grinding thing. So totally homoerotic and what girl didn't like that? 'Whew, guh, wow. All hunks all the time. Yannow, I can watch men crawl all over each other all day long.'

Leah snorted a laugh and they clinked their glasses together as they continued to watch the show and the roiling wall of women who grabbed any male who came within grasp.

'Oh holy shit, that thing...' Leah's voice wandered off as they both watched pirate boy jump up on a table and pour two bottles of water over his body. In the lights his skin glistened blue as the water sluiced down over a very defined chest and belly. 'He's so wet. I should be disgusted but I'm not. I feel dirty.'

They both laughed. Kate's sides already ached from all the laughing they'd done since arriving in Las Vegas. They'd both needed this trip.

'Uh huh. Really dirty. He has nipple rings. That's really fucking hot but only in context. Like on guys like him. On Dix, it would make me laugh. A tat? Now that would be hot.' Kate shifted, squeezing her thighs together a bit.

'We need to get the pictures with them afterwards.' Leah's statement was decisive and Kate nodded. Leah loved strippers of all kinds and she *was* Kate's best friend. What sort of friend would refuse a photo op with the fine young pirate? She snickered. Yeah, right. It was all about Leah.

'I can see you blaming this all on me if photographic evidence leaks out,' Leah said.

'Hey, I will not hesitate to throw you under the bus. Remember when those Borg things came at us at the Star Trek Experience at the Hilton? Bitch, please, you're Borg meat and you'll slow 'em down so I can get away. If Dix sees a pic of me looking all stunned by that flat hard field of twenty-two-year-old stripper ass? It's all you. You made me and shit. I'm a pawn, an innocent.'

'Cold. So very cold.'

'Totes.'

'Back to Pickles.' Leah made a circular motion with her hand, telling Kate to get on with it.

'So until her arrival at the lake house she hadn't said anything to the girls, but I think that might change. I don't want to put him in the middle. That's the one thing I've always promised myself. I demand he give me all of himself, yes. But they come first. He's a father first and I respect that. It's one of the things that makes him so sexy. He loves his daughters and they love him. They trust him, Leah. They simply know he will be there for them and he is. I can't get in the middle of that. She's trying to put me there and I know it's hurting him. I don't want to be the source of that sort of conflict for him. It hurts me that Eve would try to use those girls to harm him. That's just so fucked up.'

Leah took a deep breath. 'She's a douchenozzle. And we hate her. But you can't let her win. Katherine, this woman cannot best you. She's a complete and total idiot. You're Katherine Edwards and she's Pickles. And from what you've said, Dix's daughters love their dad, he loves them and they're certainly old enough to spot bullshit. Why let her do this?'

'Whoa! Wow, is he double-jointed?' Kate blinked as she and Leah goggled at the stripper on the stage. He fell into the splits and did some back bendy deal. All emphasising a body he had to spend hours every day on. And still, Dix was the man who brought her nipples to a point and her cunt wet and hot.

'He's um, wow. I think he needs a spanking for getting too close to that woman there. Is that allowed?'

Kate smirked as Leah's eyes widened when emo boy came out and fell to his knees again. Type indeed. Types made the fuckin' world go 'round and thank heaven for 'em.

'He's obsessed with moving in together. I keep telling him we can wait.' Kate took another sip of her drink as she watched the scene on stage unfold.

'Why? You're being dumb. Wow, just, wow. Look at granny go! She's gonna grab a hank of that long stripper mane and paw his wangdoodle too. I hope I'm still as horny when I'm her age.' Leah nodded towards the very elderly woman one of the long-haired blond strippers made the mistake of thinking was safe and got too near.

'Teach him to assume just because a gal is up there in years that she's not spry enough to check to see if that bulge is peen or tube socks. And I'm not dumb. I'm practical.'

Leah stood up quickly, grabbing Kate's arm and heading stage left. 'Show's over, picture time.'

Kate laughed. 'You gonna see if it's peen?'

Leah rolled her eyes. 'Pffft! I'm not touching strange, sweaty, random cock. I could get a cold sore.'

They'd been at Studio 54 the first night they arrived and had been in line in front of two extremely drunk dudes from New Jersey who claimed to be stockbrokers. Later, inside, they'd stumbled upon one of them making out with a woman who had practically unhinged her jaw and was licking his tonsils. It had been a stunning sight and they'd both stood and stared for long moments, dumbfounded by sharing such a face-eating kiss with a stranger. Leah had finally summed it up in her very Leah way by saying, 'He could totally get a cold sore.'

'Here's my thing,' Kate said as they stood in line for fifteen-dollar Polaroids, 'I like sweat on a man. Clean sweat. Like when he's been working in the yard or working out. Or after sex when the sex is mixed with the sweat and layered on his skin.' She shivered, thinking about that spot on Dix, just where his neck met his shoulder. Nothing tasted better than a long lick up to his ear after they'd fucked.

Leah snapped her fingers. 'Snap of out of it. Jeez you two. I have to work with him and it's just weird imagining the two of you going at it.'

'Whatever! Anyway, but random sweat on a stripper who has just had eleventy billion women grind their cooters on them? Ew.'

Leah's lip curled. 'Gross. Oh, we're next.'

'I'm not sitting on that one's lap,' Kate said, indicating the very young, very thin one on the end who looked like he was about to cry. 'I'll break him.'

'He might need that,' Leah joked. 'Let me handle this.' They were motioned on the stage where the dancers were arranged and Leah did what Leah did best. Bossed the fuck out of those men and they snapped to it like they always did. Leah was very handy as well as pretty awe inspiring at times.

'Kate, you back there next to the pirate and the big blond one. I'll sit right here.'

Kate followed directions and found herself sandwiched between two slices of hot dude and Leah sat down on the lap of the one sitting in the front row opposite the scared one. As one, the two friends threw up the devil horns and grinned when the photographer said beefcake.

Good times.

11

Dix leant back, puffing his very fine cigar as he watched two women on the stage just beyond and raised above the main floor dance to pretty typical strip-club music. Nice tits on the blonde, but the brunette's were too hard. He liked breasts, but not if they looked like they could give you a concussion.

Kate's breasts were perfect. He grinned around his cigar. Not many women would have told their men to go off to a strip club. Not that he'd ever do anything with anyone else, much less a stripper. But Kate's confidence in herself and in him was damned sexy.

She'd given him a lap dance at a strip club she'd taken him to in Philly. Had lifted her skirt and ground over his cock until he'd nearly lost it. The lights and music had buffeted them while her heat seared him through his pants. Women had been on the stage, crawling on all fours, nearly naked, but as he'd flicked a glance here and there, his real attention focused on her exposed ass as she rode him.

Yes, Katherine was a thousand times sexier than any of the women they'd watched that night. Because she knew herself and him too.

Bingo was mopey, but still watching the parade of hot, gyrating sex bombs up on that stage. Dix had considered getting them a VIP table in one of the rooms, but that might go too far and he didn't want Brandon to feel like he was betraying Leah any more than Dix wanted to be alone in the dark in a tiny room with a woman who didn't give a fuck about him as she slid her cunt over his cock. Goo indeed.

It was time to forge ahead in his plan to sleep next to his woman in a luxury hotel suite rather than that roach trap of a motel. 'So talk. Mindy is up next and according to the guy at the table next to us, she can do that upside-down-pole thing. That takes super thigh muscles. Usually makes for a very nice ass.'

'Talk about what?' Bingo's mouth went all sullen, frowning, and he slouched even more.

Dix opted for a sip of Scotch before returning to the cigar. 'Bingo, let's get this straight. You love Leah. And from what I can see and what I've heard from Katherine, Leah loves you. The question is . . . for fuck's sake, just smoke the cigar. It's good.'

Brandon sent him a narrow-eyed glare, but allowed Dix to light the cigar. He took a few puffs. 'You don't call me that unless you're my mother. And this *is* a very good cigar.'

'Fair enough, *Brandon*. OK, so the question is, why the hell are you even considering another night in that roach-infested piss-hole when you could be in a bed with thousand-thread-count sheets next to a naked woman? A naked woman who loves you.'

Brandon sighed and took a swig of his beer. 'Sometimes you have to do what's right for the long run even if it sucks hardcore short term.'

Dix understood that. Some things were worth risking everything for. Because without them, nothing else mattered. Like this living-together thing. Damn it.

'Christ, kid. Sorry! Habit.' Dix held a hand up as Brandon grunted his way. They'd sort of bonded over the last two days. He liked Brandon and Dix believed without a doubt that the guy was a good thing for Leah. 'I understand and I agree that sometimes you need to make a stand. Wow, the splits upside down. Impressive.'

'Her breasts don't move. I like her hair though. I bet those shoes hurt.'

'Those aren't walking shoes.' He loved toweringly high heels on a woman. Kate wore them out to dinner a lot. Again because she knew he dug it. She told him, her body pressed to his, her mouth against his ear, 'I didn't buy them to walk, Charles. I bought them to make my ass look nice and to make you hard. Money well spent, I'd say, given the cock bruising my belly through your pants right now.'

She was so sexy, his perfect match in every way.

Why the fuck was he in this place, in the semi-dark with a

hundred other men watching women they'd never actually touch without paying when he had a woman back at a luxury hotel who was more than willing to let him touch her wherever he wanted?

'Why did Kate leave?'

Turn about and all that. 'My ex-wife showed up at the lake house. Wedged herself between me and Kate. Manipulated our daughters to keep herself there. Kate got upset. Pissed off at Eve, frustrated at me.'

'Not to be totally obvious or anything, but it has to be bigger than that. Kate's levelheaded. She's talked about your ex before. I have no doubt Kate can hold her own. Unless you did something with your ex?' The look Brandon gave Dix was decidedly unfriendly and, even as he was offended, he liked that the other man felt protective of Kate.

'Please. You've seen Kate, why would I want anyone else? Anyway, I want to make the next step. I want us to move in together and she's using this situation to keep that from happening. Hell, I want to *marry* her, but I know she will want to wait at least another year for that. I know we can make moving in together work if she'd just let go of whatever Eve thinks. I'll handle my daughters.'

He hadn't meant to say all that, but it was nice to get it all out anyway.

Brandon took another long, appreciate puff of the cigar. 'I was going to ask Leah to marry me. She saw the ring in my suitcase and ran.'

'Not to be obvious or anything, but pot, meet kettle. Obviously she didn't run because you wanted to marry her. You're already living together and she seems very happy when I see her. Which is several times a week at work. So you want what from her now?' Dix looked up to see the new stripper on stage start shaking her tasty ass to Fergie's 'London Bridge'. 'I think I'm going to start talking over all my relationship problems while watching strippers shake things. It's oddly relaxing.'

Brandon snorted but his gaze was locked on the woman on stage as he spoke again. 'I want an answer from her! She's not the only one of us who knows what the other one needs. I know what she needs and how to give it to her. She just won't . . . let me.' The last was an aside but Dix got a clearer picture of Leah and Brandon's home life and he reminded himself to goad Kate about it. Clearly she'd been holding back.

'How did you ask her?'

Brandon and Dix cocked their heads sideways as the woman on the stage bent and undulated around the pole. Once they left the club Dix planned to get his ass over to Kate's and ravish her ten ways till daylight. He hoped like hell he and Kate could broker a peace deal between Brandon and Leah so he could sleep in that huge bed with a beautiful woman instead of that dump from the night before.

'Is that even possible?' Brandon murmured.

'Dunno, but I'm gonna think on a way to ask Kate to try it.'

Brandon looked at him and then laughed. 'She'll cut you if you suggest it tonight after being here. That might be entertaining to watch.'

Dix chuckled. 'She can be pretty vicious. But that's part of the allure.' He met Brandon's eyes. 'Isn't it? Tough and strong but soft underneath?'

Brandon nodded and puffed the cigar. 'But it's not everything. Sometimes you have to take a stand.'

Dix agreed and he tended to think that's what he needed to do with the whole living-together situation. He'd been making some tentative plans, working schedules around to see what was realistic. He'd get Kate high on endorphins from climax, bring over chocolate and some expensive champagne and at her weakest, most relaxed, he'd press his advantage. Sure it was sneaky, but this was war and his opponent was wily.

'What are you going to do about your ex?' Brandon asked, bringing Dix out of his thoughts.

'That's a good question. I've made it clear I'm not interested. Hell, I made it clear for years. I divorced her! We never had sex after I left. But now every time I'm near her she's all over me like a cheap suit and you can imagine what Katherine's reaction to that is.'

'Sounds like you need to not be around her.' Brandon shrugged like it was easy.

'I wish it were that easy. Fuck. Maybe it is and I just need to be harsher and not worry if my daughters see. I just wanted them to understand that you could still be united with someone when it came to important things like raising children.'

'Haven't you done that already? You've been divorced for nine years.'

Huh. So Bingo wasn't so naïve after all. Maybe the kid had a point.

A lovely thing, young enough for him to have fathered, cruised past and positioned herself between them. 'Hello there. You two want a lap dance? Private room?'

Dix smiled slow and sexy. He had no plans to have any pussy but Kate's grinding on his cock but that didn't mean he couldn't flirt. He was in love, not dead, and God knew he loved to look at women of all shapes and sizes. This one was easy on the eyes in every way. 'Darlin', you're mighty tempting, but I'm going to have to pass on the lap dance and the private room. I'd be happy to buy you a drink for looking so good though.'

She smiled and he stood to pull a chair out for her.

'Thank you.'

In short order the twenty-dollar drink showed up and Dix paid for it.

'I'm Tiffani. Where are you two from?'

He bet it was with an 'i' she probably dotted with a heart. Most likely one of three Tiffanis who worked there. Her real name was probably Julie or something.

'Harrisburg, Pennsylvania. I'm Brandon, this is Charles.'

Well, lookie there, Bingo knew how to handle himself with a stripper.

Brandon was used to staring down at the tops of girls' heads rather than having a face full of boobs. It was a little distracting, but he managed to look at the stripper's face and not just her tits and the pasties dangling from her nipples. Not that that he didn't look at all. She had a very nice pair of tits. But somehow, unlike the many times in his past when he'd gone out to clubs with the goal of getting his hands on a woman like the one in front of him, all he could think about was how bad her feet must hurt at the end of the night.

'Hi, Brandon. Charles.' Tiffani drawled their names, drawing out the syllables and rolling them around on her tongue. She pouted. 'Sure I can't convince you to take a private dance? Hell, boys as handsome as you, I'll do a twofer.'

Brandon looked at Dix with a raised eyebrow. 'That's quite an offer, Tiffani.'

Dix grinned. 'Sweetheart, you're entirely too generous.'

Tiffani put her hands on her hips, determined, it seemed, to entice them. 'Two full songs. Both of you. Same price as one song, one guy.'

Dix snorted laughter and shook his head. Brandon tried hard to think about why she was so insistent when there was a club full of high rollers itching to stuff their cash into her pair of very tiny thong panties. Tiffani huffed her bangs out of her eyes and stared him down.

'There's a fetish con in town,' she said finally, when neither Dix nor Brandon looked like they were going to take her up on the offer. 'Most of the people who'd be in here ready to spend their money getting sexed up are out there either doing it, or watching it, for free.'

Brandon looked at Dix, who shrugged. Great. 'Thanks, man. Make me be the bad guy.'

Dix sighed and dug for his wallet, pulling out another twenty. 'Listen, sweetheart. We're under strict orders not to get anything here that's waiting for us at home.'

Tiffani sighed and plopped down in the chair across from them, then plucked the twenty from Dix's grasp and gestured for the waitress. 'I won't tell your wives. Believe me, sugar, ninety-nine per cent of the guys who come in here are married, and most of them don't leave without at least a woody.'

'No doubt,' Brandon said, looking around.

Dix snorted again. 'Some of us, sweetheart, are a little beyond the Sears and Roebuck underwear catalogue level of hard-on.'

Tiffani gave them both a hard grin. 'No kidding.'

Brandon didn't have a clue what that meant. 'Huh?'

Dix curled his fingers and pumped them around an imaginary dick. 'Back in the day it's what most guys first jerked off to. The Sears catalogue underwear section.'

Brandon, three beers settling in his stomach, guffawed. 'Get out of here.'

'It's true,' Tiffani said with a nod. 'If you do a survey.'

'I can't think of any reason to do that,' Brandon said. 'But seriously. Sears?'

Dix wadded up a cocktail napkin and threw it at him. 'What was it for you? Don't tell me you went straight to *Playboy.*'

'Victoria's Secret,' Tiffani said.

Both men turned to look at her.

'Not me. Mine was a poster of the New Kids on the Block.' She rolled her eyes and jerked her thumb at Brandon. 'Him. Victoria's Secret, am I right? Snuck it out of the mail before your mom got it? Went up to your room, got the trusty bottle of hand lotion, went to town, am I right?'

Brandon swallowed a gulp of beer. She had him pegged. He could still remember the smell of the perfume sample mixing with cocoa-butter tang of the hand lotion. His prick stirred a little at the memory. 'Um . . . yeah.'

Tiffani held up her hand to Dix for the high-five, which he gave her after a moment. 'I knew it!'

'It's almost the same thing,' Dix said.

The waitress brought them all another round of beers. Tiffani didn't leave. 'So, why are you two sitting here not getting hard-ons if you've got such hot stuff waiting for you at home?'

Dix jerked his thumb at Brandon. 'This one's taking a stand.'

Tiffani's eyes lit up and she leant forwards, creating a truly impressive wedge of cleavage. 'Oh, yeah? What's going on? Your woman trying to rein you in? Keep you on a short leash?'

Dix laughed aloud, then shot Brandon a glance and toned it down. Brandon didn't care what Dix thought he knew about him and Leah. 'Nothing like that.'

'Well, which is it?'

'I want to marry her, and she's not sure.'

'Ouch,' Tiffani said with what sounded like genuine sympathy. She turned to Dix and nudged him with the incredibly high heel of her shoe. 'What about you, Trouble?'

'Why am *I* trouble?'

It was Brandon's turn to laugh. 'You've got the same problem, man. Sort of.'

Tiffani raised an eyebrow that looked drawn on. 'What the fuck is wrong with them? Are they mental? What? I mean, a girl like me can't find a nice guy, and here you two sit telling me your women won't marry you?'

'Crazy as hell, huh?' Dix said.

Tiffani polished off her beer and stood. 'Crazy as fuck, Trouble. Crazy as F.U.C.K. Well, unless you gentlemen have changed your minds, I've got to get back to work. Though I gotta tell you, maybe if you came home smelling like pussy you might get somewhere with your women.'

'Oh, I'd get somewhere. A wooden box and a hole in the ground,' Dix said.

Tiffani gave Brandon a sly glance. 'How about you?'

He almost said yes, wondering if he came home smelling like body spray and sex if Leah would change her mind or if she'd instead be so angry she wouldn't forgive him. And while the idea of getting a rub-off from a stranger was just filthy enough to make for a great one-handed fantasy, he was pretty sure it wouldn't be so great in reality.

'He's thinking about it. Be a good friend and convince him,' Tiffani said.

Dix shrugged. 'Far be it from me to stand between a man's lap and a stripper's ass.'

Brandon shook his head. 'The offer's really tempting, Tiffani, but no, thanks.'

'Fine. But if you want me, the offer stands until midnight. Then I gotta go one on one, house rules. And don't take Brandi over me, either. You will go home with something on your pants, and it won't be hand cream.'

Gross.

'It's not like that with us, you know,' Brandon said when they left the club and waited outside for a group of leather-clad fetish-con folks to pass and leave room on the sidewalk.

'Like what?' Dix was giving them all an eyeful, particularly the woman in the full-coverage vinyl cat suit, her face covered by a mask with a zippered mouth.

'Like what just passed us by.'

Dix looked like he meant to say something, thought better of it, then nodded. 'Look, kid. Whatever works for the two of you isn't my business. You know?'

'I know.' Brandon grinned. 'Just like it's not my business that you and Kate like to fuck almost in public.'

Dix choked a little. 'Damn it.'

Head swimming, Brandon thought the four beers had been fine, but the final shot of Jack had probably been sort of stupid. He was big enough to hold a lot of alcohol, but not on the almost-empty stomach he'd been sporting since this crap with Leah had stolen his appetite. Hell, he and Dix had only had a basket of bread, a fourteen-ounce steak, potatoes, salad and a helluva-good shrimp appetiser . . .

The belch lurched out of him long and hard, and he had to thump his chest when it was done.

'Don't worry. Leah didn't tell me. You know about the exhibitionism thing. I overheard the two of them talking. Pretty hot, getting it on in public.'

'Yes, very hot.' Dix grinned, probably at the memory. 'You're slurring your words and weaving. Christ, kid, you're sloshed.'

'Not,' Brandon said. 'Let's go to that bar in New York New York. Something Irishmen. Or something.'

Dix looked around as another crowd of extravagantly clothed conventioneers passed by. 'Shit. It beats the fucking Penny Pincher. Which I am not going back to, by the way, you can have that vermin-ridden bed all to yourself if you're gonna be proud.'

They moved through the crowd, which parted pretty easily for them since they weren't dressed like everyone else. They got their share of stares, though. At the bar, they found a booth in the back, Dix checking his cell phone while Brandon ordered a round of shots.

'*Slainte*,' he said, raising his glass.

'May your life never be hard and your dick never soft.'

The liquor burnt Brandon's throat and belly. A couple, not wearing fetish gear but obviously in town for the convention, slid into the booth beside them. The woman, a tall brunette, wore a black fitted dress. The man with her wore a simple white long-sleeved T-shirt under a black one and a pair of jeans. But what caught Brandon's eye was not the way the couple looked so adoring at each other, or how their fingers linked across the table.

It was the collar.

Braided leather, plain, it could be nothing else. It fit tight to the man's throat. As Brandon watched, the woman reached to adjust it against the man's skin.

'Fuck,' he muttered, and looked away.

'What?' Dix looked over. 'Oh. Well.'

Brandon ran a hand through his hair, then rubbed his eyes. 'It's not like that, either.'

'Hey. I already told you ...'

'I know. But it's like ... shit.' Brandon looked around, noticing other couples in various levels of costume. 'Everyone thinks a guy who likes to let the woman lead is a pussy. I'm not a pussy.'

He said it a little too loud. Turned heads. Dix looked uncomfortable for a moment.

'Nobody said you were.'

Brandon pointed at the couple next to them. Shit, that last drink had been a little too much. 'Leah doesn't like any of that stuff. Those games, she calls 'em. The pomp and circumstance, is what she says. She'd never put a collar on me, because I'm not a dog.'

Dix looked amused. 'No more shots for you.'

Brandon lifted a finger, trying very hard to make his point and knowing he was probably failing. 'Even if sometimes they call me Bingo, which is NOT my name-o.'

Dix laughed and Brandon joined him. Dix shook his head. 'Listen, kid, I can't pretend I get it, but if it makes you happy and makes her happy, who the hell cares about anyone else?'

'I guess it doesn't make her happy, or she'd have said yes. Man,' Brandon said, aware he was not too drunk to want to explain but a little too sloshed to make sense. 'Shit. Well. Whatever. I told her what

I had to say, and if she doesn't want it I guess that's it. Nothing else to do about it.'

Dix still looked amused, but before he could say anything else, Brandon's phone rang. The ringtone, a clip from Portishead's 'Glory Box', didn't sound too loud compared to the bar's raucous atmosphere, but the photo of Leah told him it was her. He thumbed the touch screen immediately, listening. He didn't have to say anything. Leah said it all.

'Get over here, Brandon, and fuck me until we both can't stand.'

He ended the call and sat back against the seat. 'She says she wants me to get over there right now.'

Dix raised a brow and set his glass down. 'And?'

The Penny Pincher had looked a hundred times worse after seeing Leah's suite. Not only that, but after a few hours of fake tits in tiny bras and tight, tanned asses jiggling in glittery thongs, Leah looked a thousand, no, a million times better.

'Fuck taking a stand,' Brandon said.

Dix clapped him on the shoulder. 'Well, kid, there's not a damn thing wrong with being a booty call. Let's get out of here.'

12

Kate must've answered the door, because when Leah came out of the bathroom after brushing her teeth and washing her hands – she didn't want to greet Brandon with nacho breath or stripper oil on her fingers – he was standing in the doorway.

'Well, hello.'

Part of her had known without question he would come at her command. Part had wondered if she'd pushed him too far, finally, and if he'd rebel by not showing up. The uncertain part had been bigger than she wanted to admit, because at the sight of him, Leah let out a low, slow breath of relief.

'Did you have a good time with Dix?'

Brandon smiled. Fuck, she was such a sucker for that grin. He shrugged out of his jacket and tossed it to the floor. Her gaze followed it, then looked back to his face. Oh, she was in over her head this time. And she totally didn't care.

Off came his buttoned shirt to follow the jacket into a heap on the floor. Brandon tilted his head to look at her. 'Should I be doing this to music?'

Oh how much she loved him, for something as simple as a tossaway line of self-deprecating humour. Leah laughed, more relief sweeping through her. Things were going to be OK.

'No. I've had enough of that tonight.'

'You sure?' He swivelled his hips. 'I could put on some Lil Wayne. Rock your world.'

'Come here, Brandon.'

He did at once, stepping up against her, his hands on her ass and rubbing through the denim of her jeans. 'Yes.'

She'd taken off her shoes and had to stand on her tiptoes to find his mouth. He tasted of beer and smoke and whiskey and Leah retreated a little even as his lips followed hers. 'What did you and Dix get up to?'

Brandon nuzzled her neck as his hands caressed her rear. 'Decadence. Naked women, booze. Cigars. Oh, and before that, we had ... steak.'

His tongue slid along her throat and Leah let her head fall back to give him free access. 'My God. No. Not steak. How can you come here and face me after that?'

'I feel so dirty,' Brandon said against her skin as his hands roved higher and pulled her closer. His teeth pressed her skin and Leah held her breath, her nipples tight and her cunt throbbing.

Leah wasn't much into punishment, even for play, and truthfully, there'd been few enough times Brandon had failed her in any way major enough to warrant something like that. She laughed, though, low and throaty, and pushed back from him even though denying him access to her body was just as bad for her.

'Naughty,' she told him just to watch his eyes flash. 'If you're so dirty, maybe you should clean up.'

Her gaze flicked to the open bathroom door. It wasn't a bad idea. The smell of the club still clung to her clothes and she was pretty sure the seat of her jeans had oil stains on them. Besides, the bathroom in this suite was orgasmic.

'Huh,' Brandon said with a quirk of his mouth. 'Maybe you're right.'

Leah took a couple steps back, watching him, but his long arm snaked out to grab her wrist and draw her back to him. He kissed her, not hard, but thoroughly. His tongue stroked hers, and she stifled a moan, her eyes fluttering closed.

He started walking her towards the bathroom, step by step, breaking the kiss just long enough to reach upwards over his shoulder and pull off his T-shirt. Leah's feet hit cool tile as her hands found Brandon's warm, bare chest and tight nipples.

She tweaked one and it hardened further under her fingers. She had to taste him, her desire sudden. Urgent. She kissed his chest and licked his nipple, then skidded her teeth over his flesh. His hand cradled the back of her head as she looked up at him.

'I want to suck you,' she breathed against his belly, where the muscles jumped at her touch. 'But first. Shower.'

He looked that way and let out a long, low groan of pleasure that made her laugh and straighten.

'Brandon!'

'Look at it,' he said, awed at the glass brick and waterfall showerhead. 'Steam jets, Leah. And it's so big.'

'Big enough for you, baby, I know,' she teased. 'You won't have to crouch down. But I might expect you on your knees.'

He kissed her again. 'I think I could live in a shower like that.'

'Take off the rest of your clothes,' Leah told him. Her heart skipped as her voice lowered and he responded by sliding his tongue over his bottom lip. 'Turn on the water first so it gets hot. And let me see you get naked for me.'

He nodded and turned on the faucet, then stepped out of the spray to face her. Leah, still fully dressed, leant her ass against the marble countertop. Her jeans, which should've felt way too tight anyway, considering the buffet meals she and Kate had consumed, rubbed insistently between her legs as she crossed them at the ankle. Watching him. Knowing he got off on this as much as she would.

As steam started swirling from behind the glass brick, Brandon reached over his shoulder to pull his T-shirt over his head. He threw it to the floor without looking at it. He wore leather work boots without laces or a zipper, shoes she'd have had to sit to pull off, but Brandon didn't falter, just stood on one foot at a time to yank them off.

'I am so impressed,' she murmured. 'You didn't even lose your balance.'

'I'm tricky that way.'

'Uh huh.' Heat bloomed in her belly and lower down. Leah shifted and the seam of her jeans pressed her clit. She wore cotton boy brief panties, nothing especially sexy, but the soft fabric felt damp on her pussy, and no wonder. Watching him strip for her, at her command, had her hot and wet.

Brandon put his hand on the button of his jeans and paused, gaze locked on hers, before he tugged it open. He notched his zipper down.

Click, click, click. Then he hooked his fingers into the denim and shoved the jeans down to step out of them. His black cotton boxer-briefs hugged his package. He looked like an underwear model.

'God, your legs are seven miles long,' Leah said, admiring his tight calves and thighs, covered with crisp dark hair. 'Did you get taller in the past few days?'

He laughed. 'Why don't you come over here and measure me, find out?'

'Take off the briefs, Brandon.'

He did, slowly, and stood before her totally naked and sporting an erection that made her crave the taste of him again. He didn't stroke it, perhaps waiting for her to order him to do it. That thought sent another bolt of desire through her.

'Did you do what I told you to do? While I was gone?'

His smile faded a little and she wanted to take it back so neither of them were reminded of the reasons she'd left in the first place. But then he nodded. 'Yes. You know I did.'

'Let me see you,' Leah breathed. 'Show me how it was.'

He hesitated for only a bare second before stepping into the water. The glass bricks distorted his figure, but didn't block his groan of sheer pleasure as the hot water surrounded him. Leah slid open the buttons of her blouse as she moved forwards to stand in the shower's walk-in doorway. Brandon, facing the water, had put his face directly under the spray to let the water sluice over his body.

'We need a shower like this,' he said.

'Show me,' she repeated.

And he did. First a slow, downwards stroke, almost thoughtful. Like he wasn't sure what he meant to do. Then another. Then he widened his stance and jutted his hips forwards, just a little, to let the water hit that beautiful cock as he started to stroke it in earnest.

Leah took off her shirt and draped it over the edge of the sunken whirlpool tub, big enough for two, just past the shower. Her jeans came next, less gracefully but faster than Brandon had doffed his, but then she didn't have an audience, either. His eyes were closed, lost in the sensations of his hand on his cock.

Leah stripped out of her bra and panties as she watched him shift the pattern of his strokes. She loved to watch him jerk himself off – it was intimate and sexy and she always learnt something new about him – but she also loved to be the one to get him off. Whether it was with her hand, her mouth, inside her body, or if it was just from the power of her words as she talked him through it, Leah liked that power over him. Craved it, as a matter of fact.

She was so lucky, she thought, as Brandon opened his eyes and looked over his shoulder to watch her watching him. That she'd found a man who could give her what she wanted and be so comfortable with it. More than comfortable, as turned on by it as she was. She was so fucking lucky, and what had she done but almost squander it? And why? Because she was worried about . . . what?

Nothing.

She had everything right before her that she'd ever wanted and everything she'd ever need. Leah stepped into the shower and reached around him to twist the faucet for the aromatherapy jets, and soft steam scented with lavender hissed out. Another fiddle with the faucet and the second showerhead began to spray, along with the row of pulsing massage jets jutting from the wall.

'Wow.' Brandon's voice had gone hoarse with pleasure. 'Just . . . wow.'

Leah laughed and pressed herself against him, her cheek on his back. She reached around to cup his balls. 'Don't stop.'

He'd paused at her touch but now his hand took up the stroking again. But Leah was no longer satisfied with watching Brandon make himself come; she had to help him along. 'Turn around.'

He did. His cock rubbed her belly as they kissed, tongues tangling around the rush of hot water pouring over their faces. Lavender swirled around them as he ground against her wet slick skin. Leah found his cock with her fist and pumped it gently before reaching to the towel rack along the back of the shower wall and throwing down a thick soft washcloth.

'Ah . . . God.' Brandon sounded strangled as she got to her knees in front of him and engulfed him with her mouth. His hand found her hair and stroked it back from her face.

His body shielded her from most of the spray and the cloth buffeted her knees from the shower's rough tile floor. She could spend an hour here, sucking and licking and tasting and stroking ... but she didn't think she could last that long. He probably couldn't, either, not based on the familiar noises leaking from his throat or the way he was pushing into her mouth.

God, she loved sucking him. For all the times Brandon spent on his knees, worshipping her, there were just as many moments Leah found herself at his feet. She licked his shaft now, then sucked gently at the head while she cupped his balls. Her thumb stroked backwards, along the seam of his sac, and he widened his stance automatically to give her free rein to anyplace she wanted to touch him. Fuck, she loved that, too, that he was so open to anything she ever wanted ...

'Wider,' she said from around his cock.

He obeyed, putting one hand to the wall to steady himself. His other hand rested lightly on her head. Water spattered on the back of her neck as she took him down her throat, working his cock with her lips and tongue and just barely scraping her teeth along the shaft as she moved. Her fingers played along his balls and perineum, toying with his ass.

He grunted. His cock throbbed. He was close, maybe a minute or two away from coming, if she kept this up.

'Towels,' she told him.

He knew just what she meant. The towels, decadently thick, fell as Brandon jerked them off the rack. Leah spread them quickly, making sure not to block the drain. She turned onto her hands and knees and looked over her shoulder at him. 'Now.'

He got behind her, his hands on her hips. Sometimes fucking in the shower could be a problem, but not tonight. Leah was so slick, so ready, he slid inside her smoothly. She cried out as he filled her all the way to her core. In this position the water rained on them both but didn't threaten to drown them. Leah put her head down to the cushion of soft terrycloth and pressed her ass higher, harder against him.

'Fuck me,' she said, her voice shaking.

He moved inside her, slowly at first though she knew he had to be craving speed. Delicious friction built as she matched his rhythm.

His cock skidded across her G-spot, and when he reached around to press his fingers to her clit, Leah's body jerked.

It was all perfect, the timing right. He knew how to move, how to touch her, and all she had to do was let go and let him. He thrust deeper as his fingers circled. And he spoke to her, a long, low stream of words designed to push every single one of her hot-buttons.

Leah had had countless orgasms in her life, each different and miraculous, and every time her body filled with that ecstasy, she wondered how she might stand it. If it would not, indeed, splinter her to pieces. But now, this time, with Brandon urging her towards climax, all she could do was revel in being torn apart.

She came saying his name. His hoarse, low shout told her he'd joined her. Brandon stroked deep inside her a few more times, then slowed, then stopped. The water beat down around them, sounding much louder now that she wasn't blinded and deafened by desire.

Leah stretched as he withdrew, her body tingling in all the right places. Brandon helped her to her feet and kissed her under the spray. Leah laughed, light-hearted and loving it.

'Someday we'll take a shower together and *not* have sex,' she said.

'I hope not,' Brandon replied seriously.

Actually, she hoped not, too. She told him so as he soaped her back, and she told him about the older woman at the Thunder From Down Under show. He told her about the strippers who could hang upside down by their thigh muscles as she washed him in return. And then as the water rinsed them free of suds, he kissed her again.

He led her from the shower and dried her with a fresh soft towel. Pampering her. He took her to the bedroom and bundled them both between the sheets, where Leah settled back between his legs, against his chest, while they watched very bad late-night television and Brandon combed her hair carefully free of every tangle.

They talked, too, about everything. And nothing. And Leah once again thought how simple it was to talk to him, how he understood her even when she didn't make sense, and how she didn't need to ask him to know what he felt.

When they made love again, slower this time, the pinkish light of morning had begun seeping in around the blinds. After, he pulled her against him, spooning, and, though Leah knew there was more to say, there would always be more to say to him. And also, if she were the smart woman she pretended to be to the rest of the world, she'd give Brandon the time to say it.

Brandon knew the sound of Leah sleeping as well as he knew everything else about her. So when her breathing slowed and her body went limp in his arms, he stopped talking. He pressed his face into the softness of her hair. He nuzzled her neck. He smiled to himself when she murmured and shifted, pressing herself against him even in her sleep. They hadn't talked about marriage, but that was OK. Tomorrow. Or the next day. Hell.

He was willing to wait.

13

'Well, hello there, stranger.' Kate smirked at the handsome, sexy and tipsy man standing in the doorway after she'd let Brandon pass.

'God, you look good.'

'After all those enhanced, gravity-free breasts and flat bellies? Do tell.'

'Meh. They were all right. But you, now, *you're* something to write home about.'

She laughed, sliding into his arms. 'That so?'

'So.'

His hands roamed over her body as he brought his mouth to hers for a kiss. He tasted of whiskey and cigars, of sex and utter decadence. Everything in her tightened for a moment as she moaned softly.

'You wore this to the strip club?' he asked as the palms of his hands stroked over her ass as he delved under her skirt.

'I had "winter at the lake house" clothes when we arrived. I went shopping. This stuff was expensive. I'm wearing it to get my mail.'

He laughed, his mouth finding the hollow of her throat. 'I'm not complaining. In fact, I just had a flash of you in that club we were in, giving me a private dance.'

A shiver wracked her at the thought.

He stilled as she telegraphed how hot she thought that was. 'Let's go.' He pulled her from the room and she grabbed her bag on the way out the door. Once downstairs they grabbed a cab out front and headed a bit away from the Strip to some strip club, oh scratch that, they were *gentlemen's* clubs now. Pffft, right. Gentlemen giving women twenty bucks to grind on them was right up there with opening doors for them and paying for dinner.

Men got to admit it was hot, why couldn't women? Well OK, not so much the grinding part. Kate didn't have any desire to pay a stripper to grind on her, but the idea of sex being so blatant the way it was at a club like the one they were going to was appealing in some sense. Not every day appealing, but certainly sexy. Whatever, it connected to that part of her that liked to be looked at and objectified on some level.

Just thinking about it made her tingly. She scrambled onto his lap and went for his lips. He met her kiss with a groan of pleasure as he held her to his body. The strength of his hands, splayed on her back, drove her insane. It was so good with him. Better than it had ever been with anyone. Each time he touched her she craved him more.

She pulled her hair loose and it slid around his face, curtaining them off. His breath was hers as her tongue slid through the softness of his mouth.

'Your cunt is so hot,' he said into her mouth and she drew in a shaky breath.

'Uh, we're here,' the cabbie called out as they came to a halt.

Kate grinned and got out when he opened the door. What the hell? She wouldn't see any of these people ever again and, hello, it was Las Vegas during a fetish convention!

The smile and looks she got at the door and as they walked through the club drove Kate's inner bad girl. There were other women there, but this was not their world. Not as viewers and participants, but as objects to be viewed. There was power in that, the beat of it vibrated through her along with the bass from the music.

Dix kept his hand on the small of her back. Possessive. A note to the others to look, but not touch. He couldn't keep his eyes off the sway of her ass, of the peek as her skirt moved to expose the creamy expanse of upper thigh. He caught the press of her nipples through the thin material of the bodice of the dress, the curve of her cleavage called to his mouth.

'Over there.' He motioned with his head to a table off in a far corner. Discreet, but not totally hidden.

A secret smile touched her lips as she put on another woman's skin. That woman who got off on being seen. He liked that part of her, small enough to be hot, easy enough to thrill, and all his.

She sat when he held her chair out, the hem of that already short skirt sliding up dangerously high. She leant back, crossing her legs slowly enough to send him a peek of the heaven between them.

One of her brows lifted as she realised where he was looking. Even better, she trailed her fingertips along the exposed, pale flesh, up her body, over her nipples until they both sighed. When she caught her bottom lip between her teeth his cock hardened to the point of pain.

Like he'd stop her. Christ, she was sex on fire right there, the low lights casting shadows in all the right places.

A waitress came by, bending low, but Kate looked too. How fucking hot was it that his woman appreciated all forms of beauty? Not that the server had anything on all that long-legged, feline sensuality reclining just to his left.

'While we wait for those ridiculously expensive drinks you're totally going to pay for, do you have any cigars left?' She leant towards him to be heard over the music and he nearly swallowed his tongue at the perfect view of a round, hard nipple.

'Darling Kate, anything you want is yours.' He patted his jacket pocket down and found a cigar.

Kate watched him avidly as he trimmed the cigar and lit it for her.

'I don't know what it is about it when you do this sort of guy stuff,' she said, leaning forwards not to take the cigar from him but to take his wrist and take a puff while he still held it. 'It's just so sexy.'

'Goddamn, woman. I want to eat you up when you're like this. Well, to be honest, I want to eat you up all the time. But right now you're . . .' He paused, searching for words but settled for a shrug and licking his lips.

She sipped her drink, her leg slowly moving back and forth along with the music as she watched the dancer on the stage. And then her hands were on her tits, weighing them.

'I think having them as big as hers would be uncomfortable. I hear you lose nipple sensation with implants. I'd never want that. This place isn't that bad. Did you have a lap dance? I forgot to ask.'

'Don't forget to breathe when you're talking. No. I'm saving my innocence for you. By the by, just how much did you drink at that club?' he asked, amused.

'Enough to mock, but not so much as to get mean. It's a fine line. And it wasn't a strip club. Look at her up there. You can see the lips of her pussy. These ladies get nekkid all the way. The guys at the show tonight didn't show peen. They undulated around. Pretended to be gay, some pretended to be straight. But they kept their tight boy shorts on. Or their tiny Speedo dealies. Whatever. Anyway, none of them was you. None of them made my body tingle just thinking about that thing you do with your tongue when you're licking my clit. That little flutter you do.' Putting her drink aside she stood and moved to stand in front of him. The body part in question right at mouth level. 'Sends me over the edge. Every. Time.'

He skimmed his palms up over the muscles of her calves, higher, grabbing two handfuls of her ass, hauling her forwards to inhale. The sweet spice of her pussy met his senses. Around them, the lights flickered and something slow with a heavy bass beat pounded. She tunnelled her fingers through his hair and when he looked up, her head was tipped back as her body was offered up to him.

One of his hands slid up her belly and she opened her eyes and tipped her head forwards to look. So much desire there, raw, on the surface. It snagged her, caught her breath and pulled a gasp from low in her gut.

'No one like you,' Dix murmured. 'And you're all mine.' His soft laughter caressed her skin and she shivered.

'I want to see your face when I slide my cunt over your cock.' She lowered herself over his lap slowly, rolling her hips to underline what she'd just told him. Sensation jarred her, jangled her nerves as she ground her swollen, wet pussy over the edge of his cock through his jeans.

'And I want to see your face when you come. Right here in the open with all these men watching you. They are, you know. There's a table just to my left, two of the men are looking at you, looking at your nearly bare ass as you rub yourself on me. And they can't have you. They'll go back to their rooms, or maybe even get a lap dance and think about you.'

She dug her fingertips into the chair above his shoulders, her breath hitching as orgasm began to ride through her system. She was going to come right there as he watched her, as others watched her and fuck if it wasn't hot.

'When did this exhibitionistic streak – *oh, Christ, that felt good* – develop, darling Kate?'

'In the parking garage that day with you. With your fingers in my cunt. Even though we nearly got caught. It – oh my God . . .' She had to stop, pushing climax away for a bit longer.

'You're going to kill me.' The strain in his voice was clear. 'But it'll be a beautiful death after I embarrass myself by coming in my pants like a fourteen-year-old after touching a nipple for the first time.'

She laughed, swooping down to kiss him. 'I doubt you were as old as fourteen. I'm sure you were groping girls years before that.' Another kiss to the spot between his eyes. 'I love you so much. I love this. I love that I can be all that I am with you.'

The levity on his face softened, changed, deepened and the corresponding tug in her belly, in her heart made her eyes burn.

'Pretty, darling Kate, you're everything. I want you with me all the time. Can't you see that?'

She nodded.

His thumbs brushed the seam where thigh met body and she stuttered a breath. 'Touching is extra.' She smirked down at him and began to ride him again.

'Since I can't grope you, I want you to imagine my mouth on you. Licking your nipples, biting them until you gasp. Kissing down your belly. Spreading you wide and licking your pussy. Slow at first until you beg. I like hearing you all impatient and demanding. I like it even more when that dissolves beneath the need to come and you whimper for it.'

Kate liked that too. Liked it when he tortured her until, when he finally made her come, it hit her so hard everything inside her went molten and time seemed to stop just a moment until it all hurtled over her, submerging her until all she knew was him.

But she didn't have the patience for that. She wanted to come. Heard the men nearby murmuring, heard the movement of the people all around them, knew there was a woman on the stage undulating, emanating blatant sexual promise. And here she was delivering it.

'I'm so fucking hot for you. I want to slam you back to that table behind us and fuck you right here and now.'

She levered forwards, grinding harder, moving on him to angle the pressure where she wanted it and putting her tits right in his face. A guttural sound broke from her lips when he laved over the curve of her breast, wet and warm.

With her mouth near his ear, she murmured, 'I'm going to come now, Charles. Wet and hot, my clit against your cock through your jeans. Oh, God yes. I'm imagining your mouth on me, your hands all over my body as I, oh . . .' And it broke, hard and fast, sweeping through her as he whispered back, straining up to meet her body, to keep the pressure where she needed it to prolong the climax.

He took her mouth again, fiercely, possessively. He owned her in that moment. Hell, he had since he showed up at her hotel room well over a year before and she'd let him in, knowing they'd fuck.

His taste filled her until she nearly overflowed with it and yet she held on to him, let him plunder her. He finally tore his mouth free. 'Goddamn, I've got to fuck you or I'll die.' He stood and when she didn't walk fast enough, still drunk with endorphins and that kiss, he simply picked her up, taking her from the noise of the club and outside where he grabbed a cab. All as she remained tucked in his arms.

She perked up a bit in the cab on the way back to the Palisades and then at the Concierge desk where she found four tickets to a very swanky New Year's Eve party being thrown at one of the most exclusive nightclubs in town.

He looked at the envelope as she chatted about the party and then took the keycard from her other hand. 'Yeah, nice. Here, move so I can get the door open.'

Once they were in the suite he hustled her towards her room and slammed the door. The look on his face was feral as he tore the clothes from his body. She stepped to him, gently moving his hands and took over.

'Let me. Let me take care of you like you take care of me.' She kissed over every bit she revealed as she undressed him. Licked across tight nipples, dragged her nails up his sides and down across his lower belly.

His cock was hard. So hard it tapped his stomach, the head glistening with pre-come. Irresistible. She licked over it, tasting the salt of his body and he jerked in response before hauling her up to her feet.

'I will be happy to come in your mouth another time. But now, I want to be inside your cunt when I blow. This lap dance will be the way I was imagining back at the club.'

He sat in a nearby chair and tipped his chin in her direction. She reached back and flipped on the iPod she had plugged into portable speakers and hit the *fuck me* mix. While he watched she stepped out of her panties and approached him.

She stepped one foot up on the chair, opening herself up, showing him what he did to her. Idly he reached out to draw a fingertip through her pussy, up around her clit, still sensitive, and then up to her mouth where he smeared her honey on her lips.

Straddling him, she rubbed her bare cunt over his cock, also bare, until he gave a frustrated half-growl. Licking her lips, she rose up enough to grab the base of his cock, angle him just so and sink down hard and fast.

'Yes. That's the motherfucking way. Sink that cunt down onto me, darling Kate.'

Such a beautiful, cultured man, such a gorgeous face and what a filthy, dirty mouth. She loved it.

Dix watched, felt as she undulated on him, rolling her hips, keeping him deep inside her pussy while the music played. First one strap of the dress slid down over the shoulder and off, then the other until those marvellous breasts were bared.

'This time, I'm touching.' He rolled and pinched her nipples until her inner muscles clenched and fluttered around his cock. Until her eyes blurred and he watched a bead of sweat roll down her neck.

He was close. So close he very nearly just went into the bathroom at the club and rubbed one out to relieve himself. Instead, he'd waited as she'd curled into him on the cab ride back. Her body heavy and relaxed against him. The heady scent of her pussy had tickled his nose as his cock throbbed to the beat of his pulse.

'I want you to come inside my cunt,' she whispered, her voice taking on that fevered edge he craved to create.

'Finger it for me first.' He reached down and spread her labia. She was slick and dark there, primed. Her clit was swollen and they both groaned when her middle finger slid around it. Her pussy tightened around him, seizing as she pleasured herself as it pleasured him to watch.

'I'm not taking my time, Dix. You feel so good.' Her eyes dropped to half mast, stoned with pleasure. Greedy. So greedy and it only turned him on more.

'Good. Because I'm really close.' And she did that thing. That thing where she moved in tight circles, pressing down against him to keep him deep, using his cock to stir within her. The wet, superheated walls of her cunt surrounded him, caressing, stroking, until she started to come and that nearly impossible to resist clutch became unbearably good and he lost it. Hurtled into climax with her, holding her tight, down against him as it kept on, wave after wave, until he nearly slid from the chair.

He managed to get them both to the bed where they lay quietly, regaining their breath. She wriggled from the dress, sitting up to toss it in a nearby chair, turning the music off while she was within reach.

'If I go to sleep, please feel free to wake me in a few hours with sex,' she mumbled, turning her body into his. Burrowing into him, her head finding its place, pillowed on his biceps, fitting just beneath his chin. Right where she was meant to be.

'I love you, Katherine.'

'Mmm, me too.' She snuggled in, her nose snuffling into him, making him smile at how silly and tender she made him feel even as he was ready to fuck her again. Even as he wanted to tie her up and keep her with him and simply make the choice to move in together at last.

He'd bring it up when they woke up. New Year's Eve was in a few hours. He'd fuck her, bathe her and feed her, maybe not in that order, but those were the things she found most relaxing. While he had her relaxed, he'd go in for the kill and close the deal. He was just as driven as she was and there was simply no way they were going back home without her promise to move in with him.

Especially if she doled out lap dances on a regular basis.

14

Brandon only snored when he'd been drinking or was exhausted. Now the buzz-saw rasp vibrated the bed between them. Sort of like an aircraft taking off. Verrrrry relaxing. Even though he had his head buried in the pillow and the covers yanked over his head, she could hear him. Leah never understood how he could stand sleeping like that, and it made her nervous, like he was going to suffocate in the night and she wouldn't know until the morning.

God, if she couldn't bear to trust the fact her lover was going to wake up safely every morning, how would she ever handle having a child with him?

This thought drove Leah out of bed, even though the soft sheets and Brandon's warm, naked body were both tempting enough to keep her there for a few more hours. Taking her cell phone, she went to the bathroom, closing the door carefully behind her so he wouldn't wake. Leah had no doubts Brandon was in desperate need of a few more hours' sleep.

This bathroom was bigger than her living room, which wasn't saying much, since Leah's house was what she liked to think of as cosy. Which meant small. Sometimes Brandon knocked his head on the doorframes, it was so tiny. It wasn't a house they could live in forever, that was for sure, especially if they had kids.

That thought, the second so close and hard on the heels of the first in the bedroom, forced a breath out of her. She clutched the cool marble of the countertop and splashed some water on her face and the back of her neck. Then, budget-be-damned, she took a bottle of diet Coke out of the minifridge under the sink – a minifridge in the bathroom, of all things! The one room where food should never be stored! Las Vegas was pure decadence, and Leah was ready to go home.

Back to her small house where nothing was ever out of order and everything had its place, including Brandon.

Leah twisted the top off the bottle and drank back the sweet bubbly liquid with a grunt of pleasure much like she imagined heroin addicts made when they took their first hit of the day. The stuff was poison, but, damn, did it taste good. She wiped her mouth and set the bottle on the counter and looked around the bathroom again, at the shower where they'd made love the night before and the giant soaking tub she could easily imagine fucking him in later today.

Leah had spent a lot of years being responsible for herself, and she didn't bear a grudge against her parents for making that happen. She liked who she was because of how she'd been raised. She was satisfied with her relationship with her parents because even though it wasn't close, it was genuine, with both sides having no false illusions about what the other wanted or was able to give. But now, for the first time since her high school prom date had stood her up to take the school slut instead, Leah felt herself reaching for something and regretting that she'd never get it. Not from her mother, anyway, who'd be happy to listen to her dilemma and even offer advice, but who would sound a little confused as to why on earth Leah would bother asking.

Leah thumbed in a number that was familiar even though she'd only had to call it a few times. It rang and rang, and in the half a minute before it was answered she panicked, wondering if she'd miscalculated the time difference. If she was making a huge mistake.

'Hello?'

'Caroline? It's Leah.'

'Leah! Hello, hon, how are you?' If Brandon's mother was pissed off, she wasn't showing it.

Leah pulled out the low chair in front of the bathroom's vanity and sat. The tray of sample-sized, high-end beauty products rattled and she reached to still the shaking bottles with the flat of her hand. She knew she should say something or look like an even bigger idiot than she had when she'd left Iowa with hardly any explanation.

'I'm in . . . we're in Las Vegas.'

'Oh, yes, I know.' Caroline laughed. 'Bingo called me when he got in so I'd know he was all right.'

Caroline paused, then continued before Leah could speak. 'I told him he didn't have to do that, you know. I'm glad he did, of course. I worried when I heard there was ice down your way, that his flight might have problems. But he didn't have to call me.'

Leah's parents must've worried about her, she thought. Sometimes. Didn't they? Isn't that what parents did? It's what she would be expected to do for a husband and children. Worry about them. Take care of them.

'But how is it?' Caroline continued. 'Bill and I went out there once, oh, it must've been three years ago now. We had the most incredible food there, I came home in my fat jeans and still couldn't button them. I'm sure you won't have that problem, you're so slim. But my goodness, the shows there. Have you been to see a show?'

'Um . . . yes,' Leah said, not ready to spill it about watching naked men gyrate while bathed in baby oil.

Caroline's voice dipped low. 'I thought about going to one of those burlesque places, you know, but Bill and I decided to see Barry Manilow instead.'

Leah laughed then covered her mouth with her hand. 'How was he?'

'Oh, Leah, he is so dreamy,' Caroline said. 'But I'm glad he kept his clothes on.'

Leah laughed again, softer this time. 'Caroline, I'm sorry I ran out on you all. That's why I'm calling.'

'Oh, hon. Don't you apologise for a darned thing. I could tell we were just overwhelming you within ten minutes of you walking in the door. You got that deer-in-the-headlights look. I'm surprised you lasted as long as you did.'

'I did?' Leah swallowed, face heating. 'I'm so sorry. That was so rude of me, I'm sorry.'

Caroline laughed. 'Stop that, right now. Sorry's for when you do something wrong. Not for just being yourself.'

Leah looked at her reflection as she spoke. Being herself around Brandon's family? 'About that . . .'

'Hold on a second, hon. Scamp! Get that out of your mouth! Bill! Can you please come and get the dog away from the baby. He's trying to eat little Prue's crackers! OK, hon, go ahead. You were saying?' Caroline didn't sound stressed by the chaos Leah could hear in the background.

'Is this a bad time? I could call back.'

'No, we're all just getting ready for the big party tonight. The kids are coming over to play games and I guess the men will watch some sort of sports. I've got the Crockpot going and Linda – you remember Bingo's Aunt Linda, don't you? God love her, the woman's seventy and still makes her own bread. Well, she slipped and fell on the ice and we all thought she broke her hip but she didn't, so she's about due to arrive any minute and I've got everyone on standby to get out there and bring her in from the car.'

Caroline's story washed over Leah in waves. A few days ago the words would have drowned her, but now she floated in them, comforted. 'It sounds like a good time.'

Brandon's mom didn't remind Leah she could've been there if she hadn't run away like an idiot. 'Oh, I'm sure it will be. But you must have something fancy planned for tonight. New Year's Eve in Las Vegas, that has to be a pretty big deal.'

'I don't know yet. I guess so.'

Caroline paused. Leah heard the background noise soften. 'I had to go in the pantry just to hear myself think. Make Bingo . . .'

Again, she paused. 'I guess I should stop calling him that. He's a little too old to be my Bingo any more.'

'Oh, he's not,' Leah assured her, but Caroline laughed.

'Leah. I have four sons. Every one of them has brought home a dozen girls to meet me, and I never said a word to them about it, but I could always tell which were the ones who would be sticking around for a while and which would be never heard from again.'

'Which am I?' Leah asked, smiling, because the words that might've sounded like a challenge from someone else, only sounded kind from Caroline.

'You're a keeper.'

'Thank you.'

'You're welcome.'

Leah traced the pattern of gold sparkles in the marble countertop. 'Your son is a very good man.'

'Of course he is. I raised him, didn't I?' Caroline chuckled. 'My sons know how to treat their women, Leah. Just like their dad does.'

Leah swallowed against her rise of emotion. 'Yes. About that . . .'

'Leah,' Caroline said sternly. 'I have three daughters-in-law, and I'm going to tell you something I never said to any one of them.'

Leah's throat closed, so she couldn't answer, but Caroline didn't seem to mind. The silence let her carry on without interruption. Leah braced herself for the bad news.

'You're good for my son.'

Leah blinked. 'You never said that to any of the others?'

'Nope.'

'Why not?' Leah had met Brandon's brothers' wives, all of whom seemed to get along with his family. They all had a handful of kids and all favoured the sorts of jewelled and glittery sweatshirts his mother did. They all seemed to fit together in a way she knew she never would.

'None of them needed me to.'

'Oh.'

'Leah . . .' Caroline's voice softened. 'Brandon will always be my boy. But he's not a boy any more, is he?'

'No. I don't think so.'

'I don't, either. And I'm proud of the man he is. I trust him to make good choices. So if you're the choice he's made, I believe he's making the right one.'

Caroline sounded so enviably serene, and so much like her son, that Leah had to laugh a little. 'I never thought I'd ever be having such a conversation with you, Caroline.'

'But you called me, didn't you, hon?' the other woman asked kindly.

'Yes. I'm not sure why.'

'Because it's what you do when you need some advice. You call your mom. I'm used to it, hon. It's what I do. It's part of who I am. I'm happy to do it for you, too.'

Leah swiped at her eyes though she knew the tears were evident in her voice. 'Thank you.'

'You're welcome. Have fun tonight.'

'I'm sorry we aren't there to celebrate it with you.'

'I told you before,' Caroline said sternly. 'Sorrys are for when you do something wrong.'

Sudden cacophony sounded in the background. 'I have to go, hon. Aunt Linda's here and she forgot her buns. The ones she baked, obviously, not her rear-end, though you never can be sure with Linda.'

Leah laughed, wishing with utter sincerity she and Brandon were there to see that. 'Happy New Year.'

'You too, hon. Give Brandon a kiss from me.'

'I will.'

Caroline hung up and Leah cupped her phone in her palm.

She loved him. What was so hard about that? 'Nothing is the answer to that,' Leah whispered and drank more soda. 'Absolutely nothing.'

All at once the giddiness in her belly was like the bubbles rising in a bottle of cola. She clutched her arms around herself and put a hand over her mouth to hold back her giggles.

Leah went back into the bedroom and slid beneath the covers to align herself along Brandon, who'd stopped snoring. He made a little noise when her hand slid up his thigh to find his cock, half-hard. She gave it a gentle stroke and he stirred.

'Good morning,' she said.

'Mmmmphf.'

'It's time to get up.'

'I'm already up.' He put his hand over hers. 'Feels good.'

She knew what would feel better. Leah dove beneath the covers and slid her mouth over his belly, his thighs. She licked his sac and laughed when he let out a muffled half-yelp. She sat up, tossing back the covers, and looked at him with a grin that felt very, very wicked.

'Hands on the headboard,' she said.

He was wide awake now. He did as she said, though the padded headboard had no place for him to grab. His finger splayed on the white fabric and dug in slightly. His cock was not fully erect and Leah eyed it, licking her lips.

'Delicious.'

She ran her hands up his sides, over his chest. She stopped to toy with his nipples, making them hard. Then she tickled his sides until he groaned and wiggled in protest – but he didn't put his hands down. His fingers just pressed all the more into the headboard's soft cushion.

No matter how many times she had him in this position, or any, it never got old. Just watching Brandon do what she told him to do got her heart thumping and her pussy slick. And yes, she had to know his limits, had to be responsible for his pleasure as well . . . but it was no hardship, was it? When she knew him this well, when he gave her everything she could ever ask for or need, it wasn't difficult at all to do the same for him.

Even if it was for the rest of their lives.

Leah straddled Brandon's thighs and took his cock in her fist. She stroked. He smiled. She stroked him again, slowly, twisting. His smile twisted, too.

'I love to watch you come,' she told him.

'I kind of like it too,' he told her in a thick voice with a hint of amusement.

'Imagine that.' She licked her finger and swirled it around the head of his cock, then captured the slick, glistening drop of pre-come seeping from the slit. He watched her as she tasted it, and his erection throbbed in her hand.

She could make this last for hours, if she wanted. She knew she could stroke him to the edge, then leave him there and know he wouldn't move until she came back, and when she did he'd be as ready for her as he was just now. But Leah didn't leave. She stroked him with one hand as she rocked her clit against the other.

Desire coiled tight in her belly. 'Sit up.'

He did, his arms going around her. Leah shifted to wrap her legs around his waist as she guided him inside her. He filled her so completely it made her want to weep. Instead, she let her forehead rest on his as they stayed without moving for the span of several breaths.

His hands moved up and down her back, smoothed along her spine, then settled on her hips. When Brandon kissed her, soft and sweet, Leah opened her mouth for him. She'd thought upon starting this she'd get him close and ease off, then ride his mouth for a while until she came. But now with him settled inside her, a frantic pace didn't seem to suit.

And she didn't need to command him for Brandon to understand that. He moved after a minute, his hands going under her ass to lift her on his cock as he thrust. Her arms and legs wrapped around him. Her clit rubbed with delicious, perfect friction each time he moved.

And he kissed her over and over, just the way she liked it. Needed it. His tongue stroked hers as his lips nibbled. Leah tipped her head so he could mouth her throat. His teeth skimmed her. Her cunt swelled, hot and slick, and he groaned when she bore down on him with well-trained internal muscles.

The pace quickened as they rocked together. The bed, so soft they sank half an inch into the mattress, wasn't helping this position. Brandon, a hand behind her neck and one at the small of her back to support her, fell back onto the bed and took her with him.

This changed the angle of his cock and Leah gasped when the head of it moved along the tight bundle of nerves behind her pubic bone. Her knees dug into the bed as she leant forwards, their mouths still locked in kisses. All she had to do was lift her ass, just a little, and ...

'Fuck, yes!' She bit out the words, let them fall into his mouth, where he swallowed them.

Brandon thrust harder, every motion smooth and slick and precise. At this angle she didn't have to do anything but let him fuck into her, she didn't have to move or shift. She only had to ... be.

The hand on her ass cupped her flesh, stroking. The other one joined it. He moved her as he moved himself. Their bodies slapped. Her clit scraped his belly with every downthrust and there was no stopping the ecstasy sweeping over her.

'Yes,' she said into his mouth. 'Yes, yes, yes.'

Leah buried her face into the curve of his neck, and Brandon said into her ear, 'You're so hot, and tight and wet for me. I'm going to come so hard. All up inside you.'

Leah groaned and bit him, which made him gasp. 'That mouth ...'

He knew all too well what his dirty talk did to her, at odds as it was from how he seemed the rest of the time. 'This mouth?'

He licked her earlobe. 'This mouth that wants to eat your pussy right now?'

There had to be laughter, even if it was mixed with a gasp of pleasure. Sex was simply too precious and ridiculous at its base not to invite laughter. Brandon wasn't offended when she giggled. He just fucked into her harder.

'Let me taste you,' he told her.

If she moved off him, she thought she might die of disappointment. If she didn't let him get that tongue on her clit, she also thought she might die. Dilemma, dilemma.

Leah moved, sighing as his cock slipped out of her. She put her hands on the headboard, her knees on either side of his head, her clit hovering over his mouth. His lips and tongue found her, licking and sucking. She was out of control in half a second, writhing, grinding onto his tongue. Coming.

Her body jerked and shuddered as her climax coursed through her, but even before she was finished she moved back down his body to sink onto his cock again. She kissed him, tasting herself. A second orgasm lurked, not unexpected except for how soon it would come and how strong it would be.

'Come inside me,' she ordered, looking into his eyes.

His eyes flashed and he gave a small nod. He bit his lower lip in concentration as he thrust faster, but not harder. Still gentle, still controlled, each rubbing the head of his cock against her G-spot.

'Oh,' Leah cried, surprised at the warmth and sensation flooding her. This *was* unexpected, this was different. 'Oh ... God ... Brandon!'

His hands gripped her hard enough to pinch but she didn't care. He was coming, she felt him inside her, pulsing and throbbing even as her own body gave over to the waves of ecstasy flooding her. They came together. The world spun. Leah collapsed against him, breathing hard.

A few minutes later, Brandon's stomach rumbled.

Leah sat up, laughing, and lightly pinched his nipple. 'Very romantic.'

He captured her hand and kissed her palm. 'Sorry.'

'Don't be sorry,' Leah said and kissed him. 'Sorry's for when you do something wrong.'

Brandon blinked, then smiled. 'Were you talking to my mom?'

Ah, she was caught. 'Yes. I called her when you were sleeping.'

He didn't ask why. He kissed her again, then wrapped her in his arms and rolled them both over so they could spoon. His stomach rumbled again, louder this time. Leah laughed.

'I think we need breakfast. The hotel has an amazing buffet. I should go see if Kate and Dix want to go with us.'

'In a minute.'

She gave him the minute, not anxious to get out of bed. His breath ruffled her hair. Leah turned to face him.

Brandon smiled. 'Love you.'

'I love you, too.' She kissed him. 'And Brandon, about . . .'

'Uh uh,' he told her, sitting up. 'Not before I eat.'

She gave him a look that told him she knew exactly what game he was playing, and that she was letting him. 'God forbid you go without a meal.'

He put a hand on his belly. 'You don't want me to lose my strength.'

'God, no. Who'd fuck me so deliciously tonight?'

'Nobody,' he said with that self-confident surety she loved so much about him. 'Not as good as me.'

'Breakfast,' Leah said. 'And later, we'll talk.'

15

Kate breathed in deep and stretched. As she rose to consciousness she realised the whooshing sound wasn't the waterfall in her dream, but the bathtub in the adjoining bathroom. She snuggled back into the comforting weight of the bedding, not bothering to open her eyes just yet.

The scent on the air meant he was in there shaving. She knew his body. Knew he'd be standing, hip leaning against the marble counter. His movements would be slow, methodical as he started up his neck, *whiiick, whiiick*, as he dragged the edge of the razor over that sweet, hard flesh to remove the hair. He'd already have used the electric trimmer to edge around the line of his goatee.

So utterly beautiful and masculine all at the same time. She liked the way he was smooth on the exterior, perfectly groomed and dressed. Even in jeans he looked like he'd stepped from a men's magazine. The man was very neatly put together for such a hedonist. But scratch beneath the surface and he was delightfully dirty.

Because it pleased her, she imagined the width of his shoulders tapering down to his waist. The high tight ass, powerful thighs, long legs and hard calves. She knew he'd be naked, that was his preferred mode of dress when it was just the two of them and she couldn't complain. The skin of his ass to the tops of his thighs would be paler than the rest from all those afternoons at the pool in his backyard. Her tan lines were faded due to the depth of winter. But Dix's skin had a golden tone year round.

The thought of the dark, soft line of hair swirling around his belly button and trailing southwards to his cock brought a shiver. All Pickles had was a memory. Kate had it within reach. It was hers. All six feet of handsome, utterly unrepentant male ready to fuck her or carry her heavy bags was hers. He loved her. Flaws and all. Her life was very, very good.

Happy, she rolled from bed and padded through the doorway to stand and watch Dix shave. 'I kinda liked the five o'clock shadow thing you had going. You looked like a wicked pirate.'

He turned, laid the razor down and moved to her in two long strides. 'I *am* a wicked pirate, darling Katherine. You know I covet your booty. Can I raid you?'

She laughed as he kissed down the side of her neck. 'My sails are unfurled, I'm so ready to be boarded and raided.'

'Get in the bath. I figured the sound would wake you. It's still quiet out there so I figure we've got a while before Leah and Bingo wake up. Maybe we can all grab breakfast.' He paused, raking his gaze up her body slowly. 'After.'

She grinned, pausing to press a kiss to his shoulder as she passed to get to the giant tub. A groan of pure pleasure slipped from her lips as she stepped in and the water enfolded her like a lover. God, she loved hot baths. Showers were for when she didn't have enough time and she just needed to be clean and run out the door. A bath was a treat, a way to press the luxury of stillness into your routine. You didn't need special potions or goo, you just needed a large tub, hot water and twenty minutes. A long hot bath was better than a drink and almost as good as sex. Almost.

'What are you trying to butter me up about?' she asked, allowing herself to float in the water.

'You wound me with your suspicion.'

'Mmm. I'm a sharp cookie. Isn't that what your mother said? I like your mother. She's not nearly as crazy as mine. Plus she doesn't like Pickles, another point in her favour. She told me, your mother, not Pickles, that you were a wily one and to keep an eye on you. Said you got it from your father.'

'I see I was wise to limit the amount of time the two of you had alone.' The water rose as he stepped in and she automatically leant forwards so he could sit behind her. She relaxed again, leaning against the hard wall of his chest.

'Your mom is awesome. Dare I even say, spunky? Yes, spunky.

Kendall is a lot like her. A girl could do a lot worse than to have a grandma like her. She calls me, you know. Your mother.'

'She does? It doesn't surprise me, she does like you and she's always been the sort to go her own way. Should I ask what you two discuss or remain blissfully ignorant?'

'Well, she called after I met her the first time at that barbecue at your house this summer. She said it was to thank me because she was so very polite and all.' Kate laughed. 'But then she just came out and got nosy because we both knew why she was really calling. She wanted to get the low down on me. You can learn a lot about a man by meeting his mother. Thank God you can get past my insane mother to love me anyway. But your mom, she's sharp. And not just because she likes me. Although that in and of itself is a very powerful indicator.'

'I notice you didn't really answer my question.' His voice held amusement, not anger.

'We talk about all sorts of things. She tells me about the stuff the women in her neighbourhood get up to. She likes to chat. I like to listen to her. She makes me laugh. I took her shopping a few weeks back so she could get her holiday presents taken care of. She gave me these baby pictures of you.' The gesture had been as warm as it had been an unmistakable stamp of approval.

'How come you didn't tell me any of this before now?' He began to massage her shoulders with the fragrant soap.

'It was weird to say. I didn't want to come off like I was bragging. It's not like it was a secret. I've told you stuff about it. Like she gave me her recipe for that cinnamon bread you love so much. How'd you think I got it? And your dad stares at my boobs when I go over there, albeit he can be as sneaky as you. You must get that from him.'

His laughter jiggled her a bit. 'He told me it took a while but I'd finally grown into some very fine taste in women. Said I should kidnap you and bring you here to Vegas to marry me.'

She leant back a moment and then turned around. 'You know I love you, right?'

His smile softened even as his hands automatically headed to her breasts. 'Yes. Of course. Don't sound so dire, you're going to freak me out.'

'Am I as totally lame and passive-aggressive as your ex? No. I'm a big girl and quite capable of saying what I mean. Don't be an idiot. Do you think I'd be here with you if I was going to break up with you?'

He used the shower attachment to rinse her off and she soaped him up, taking extra care to make sure his cock was squeaky clean.

'I'm wary. My cock and my heart are in your hands. I've been asking you to marry me and to move in and you keep saying no.'

'You know why I'm saying no.'

He took a deep breath and stood, the sight of him looming over her so magnificently male and pissed off dried her mouth.

'Get out of there.' He handed her a towel after she'd pulled the plug and gotten out. She dried off and reached for her lotion until he made a frustrated sound and pulled her into the bedroom.

The curtains glided open, revealing the glory of the morning.

'Here's how it's going to be.' He turned and her eyes went to his cock. 'You're not going to sway me with that fuck-my-mouth face. Not right now.'

She couldn't help it, she laughed and fell back onto the mattress. 'You make me so happy. Even when you boss me around. I shouldn't tell you that, it'll only go to your head. But you do. Now, what is it you're going to attempt to dictate to me?'

He harrumphed and got into bed beside her. 'You will move in with me. I just made arrangements with a realtor yesterday to find us a house in Lancaster. It's halfway between your job and mine. I told him we needed plenty of bedrooms so we can have an office to work from home and also so the girls can have a bedroom there. You can take the train in or drive.'

One of her brows rose and he met it with a rise of his own. He wasn't going to give up on this.

'You thought you'd just go ahead and do it without even consulting me?'

'Shut up about that. You knew I was near the end of my patience with this. You know what kind of man I am and you stuck around, so guess what, pffft.'

Her eyes widened and then she laughed, kissing him in the hollow of his throat. 'You're lucky I'm so tolerant of your pushy ways.'

That was a good sign, he thought. She wasn't trying to argue with him yet. But he knew how he handled this next bit would sink him or make their being together a reality.

'I know your biggest concern is the girls and, believe me, I appreciate that more than I can say. Especially in light of how their mother is using them right now. So this is what I'm going to do to address that. Right now they are with Eve three weeks of every month during the school year because Eve's place is in the district boundaries and is only half a mile from their school. So in the week they're with me, I'll stay at my old place with them. Just until they're both done with school. On breaks they can stay at our new place because I want them to be used to it and to understand, without any doubt, that you and are together. Yes, before you speak, yes, it will change their lives, but Kate, they're not children, they're smart, well-adjusted teenagers. Seventeen and fifteen, they know I love them, they know they're my priority but they also realise I have a life. You can keep your condo or sell it, whichever you prefer. But I expect you to marry me by the end of this coming year. Counsellor, you may present your rebuttal.' He waved a magnanimous hand at her.

She tumbled him to his back and climbed astride him.

'Pickles?'

He groaned. 'Up until that, this was going in a very nice direction. What about Eve?'

'What about Eve, indeed. I'm going to be painfully and selfishly honest here. I've held my tongue because I love you and I don't want to lose you or to look like an evil bitch. But, if you really do mean to marry me and for us to live together and not wait two more years, I have to get this all out.'

He sat up, leaning in to kiss her. 'I want you to be honest with me. I love you, dumbass. You're not going to lose me. We can work through just about anything.'

She nodded. 'We'll see how you feel when I'm done. It's really all about Eve. Here's my thing, Charles, I hate her. I want to punch her in the face every time I hear her stupid, whiny-baby-helpless-girl voice. She's everything I have to prove I'm not when I'm on a case. She's why women are judged so harshly.'

'I agree. Now fuck me while you're talking. It's much easier to work out a solution with your cunt hugging my cock.'

She rose up and angled him the way she liked and slid down over him. He'd known she was ready, she always was when they were together and goddamn if that didn't make a man puff his chest up a bit.

'Such a multi-tasker. Back to the subject and don't blame me if you can't keep hard because we're talking about *her*.'

He made a face. 'You're the one talking about her, but as long as it's your body hovered over me, and your pussy around me, what the fuck do I care?'

She smiled and he relaxed a bit. 'OK, then here goes. If I'm in, I'm in for real and for good. Which means *I'm* Mrs Dixon, *capice*? I'm your wife and I don't share. That means if I take this step, it's all the way. I don't want to have Sunday dinner with your ex-wife. I never want to have dinner with her and I reserve the right to not go to events when I may have to see her. I don't want her to have a key to my house, I don't want her to ever enter it to start with. I know that makes me selfish but there it is.'

She adjusted herself and stretched above him. He lost his train of thought for a few moments and then remembered she was not only fucking him, but had agreed to both move in and marry him. He tried to keep the gloat off his face.

'Don't think I can't see the gloat in your eyes. But let's hold off on the end-zone dances for a few more minutes, shall we? If we move in together, your girls will lose some of that together time they have with you and her both. This will be because I can't bear their mother. It *will* be my fault that they lose it. They will resent me, how could they not?'

'You're jumping to conclusions as well as getting lazy. Ride me while you're talking. I can live with no Sunday dinners, which you have to admit rarely happen anyway.'

She rose up and slammed her body down on him several times, her breasts bouncing, her eyes sliding halfway closed. He felt her cunt change, slicken, get hotter as she rode. He had no plans to interrupt wherever she was going at that moment. He was putty in her hands, or between her thighs, whatever.

'Weddings, funerals, graduations, these are the events I am willing to deal with her over. Oh and birthdays, but only if there's no way around it. And by deal with, I mean I know she will be there too. It does not mean I'll plan parties for these events with her. I *will not* spend Christmas or Valentine's Day alone if we live together and I sure as hell won't if we're married. I will not sit at her table for Thanksgiving, nor do I want her at mine. This is *non-negotiable*. I don't want her in my house eating my turkey and I'm not going to her place either. I'm not her friend. I don't plan to pretend to be, nor do I want to be. I'll be civil for the sake of your daughters, but that's as far as it goes. Her behaviour this time has just gone too far. I don't plan to call her up to chat and I don't want to hear that voice on my answering machine. By the way, her parents are assholes too, no wonder she turned out the way she did. Same goes for them.'

She took one of his hands and brought it to her clit. 'Hello? You're neglecting me already?'

'What did her parents do and why didn't you tell me earlier?'

'Mmm, there you go, sport, right there.' She leant forwards, bracing her hands on his biceps and slid back onto his cock time and again. This position was so good for her. Every inch of his cock stroked, rubbed and stimulated her. The broad head of him brushed over her G-spot and she controlled the intensity with her movements.

'Look at me.'

She did, not stopping herself from grabbing a kiss as well.

'I want you to come.'

She laughed, arching her back and slamming herself back against him in earnest. With him, the wait, once she let herself go, was never long. He set to flame what had smouldered and that was all she could feel, see, think about.

Those stirrings of orgasm stirred low in her belly and bloomed outwards, flushing heat and pleasure over her skin, through her cells. He filled and she teased herself with his retreat. He played her, stroking her clit between a slippery thumb and forefinger.

'So bold, taking what you want. Sexy. That's the way, damn it, you're so hot and juicy. I'm close, darling Kate, so you'd better get a move on or you'll be all alone. I'm too much a gentleman for that.'

Her nipples slid back and forth against him as she moved; the hair on his chest abraded but in all the right ways. She dropped her forehead, resting it against his chest. That changed the angle of his entry just enough to bring orgasm tumbling through her.

He rolled her so that he was on top, picking up his pace, thrusting hard and deep. She took in the luxury of looking up into his face. The forelock that perpetually seemed to slide rakishly over his forehead. The way the iris in each eye seemed to be swallowed by the darkness of his pupils as he got drunk from fucking. He never did anything halfway, despite how easygoing he appeared to be. He took fucking very seriously, it showed in the concentration just around his eyes, the set of his mouth and at last when he came with a half-shout. He continued to stroke inside her for long moments more until he finally relaxed and flopped to the side, tossing a thigh over her to keep her in place.

'I'm hungry and we didn't really get this whole thing settled.'

'There's some huge buffet. I've never done one before, believe it or not. And we have the important stuff settled. You and I are moving in together and I absolutely agree that you shouldn't have to deal with Eve except on rare occasions.'

'I don't want to be the woman who comes between the father and his daughters.'

'I know you don't. Which is one of the many reasons why you won't. I won't lie, I sense Eve will try to make trouble with the girls. It's going to be rough at first. Maybe we should get married here, that way there's a strong message that you and I are permanent.'

'Your daughters will be part of our wedding. I want to include them in the planning. If we got married without talking to them about it, it would only make things worse.'

'So you'll marry me?'

She shoved him off and stood up, walking on still rubbery knees towards the bathroom. 'Let's not get ahead of ourselves here, Charles. We still have some talking to do, but I'm starved and, um, you've sullied me and I need a shower before we go. I don't want your liquid souvenir to be an uncomfortable reminder of this lovely fuck session.'

He stood up and stalked her as she backed into the stall. 'Oh your love words are so beautiful.'

She began to wash her hair as he used the showerhead just across from where she stood.

'I could have said spunk or jiz. I was being artful. I'm going to have potatoes, bacon, pancakes and perhaps gravy on something. I'll work out when we get back. Now that you've bought the cow so to speak, maybe I'll have gravy with every meal as God intended.'

He laughed and chased her out, fondling her as she tried to get dressed.

'Go be useful. See if Leah and Brandon want to have breakfast with us.'

He caught her in an embrace first. 'Your wish is my command, darling Kate. Then we'll have the rest of the day to play. I need clothes for tonight and at some point, I plan to lick your pussy until you scream.'

A delighted shiver broke over her. 'Mmm! My favourite.'

16

Soft skin. Silky hair. Brandon loved it when Leah wore her hair down, and the way it spread over the pillow when she slept. He loved how it felt sliding over his body. He loved to gather it in his hands and push it away from her face, the way he did now, so he could watch her mouth move on his cock.

Leah looked up at him with her hand gripped tight at the base of his dick and her tongue swirled once, twice around the head before she sucked him gently. Then deeper. Brandon groaned, losing himself in the pleasure of her mouth and hand.

Leah's tongue trailed down to the root of him, then lower, over his balls. Her hand, slick with spit, stroked him harder as she licked a little further back. When she nibbled the inside of his thigh, his prick jumped in her hand. He'd have shot off then, but her fingertip pressed the sweet spot behind his sac and she slowed her stroking hand just enough.

'I love it when your cock gets so hard I can feel your heart beating in it,' she murmured and added a lick and a nibble that made all his muscles jerk.

She'd been sucking him for half an hour, bringing him close and easing off at the last moment to keep him close to bursting. Brandon thought his head might explode if he didn't come soon, but, though he knew he could force it through, he let Leah have her way with him however she wanted. It would be that much better, hotter, if he did.

She sat up, her beautiful hair falling over her shoulders and over her breasts. Her hand moved slowly but steadily. 'Hmmm . . . You look like you're enjoying this so much, I think I want a little bit of it, too.'

Electric desire arced through him. He reached for her, but Leah moved out of his reach. Her hand never slowed.

'Tell me what you'll do for me.'

He licked his lips, thinking already of sinking his face between her thighs, of finding her clit with his lips and tongue and licking her until she came. 'I want to lick you.'

'Mmm,' she sighed and gave a little shiver. Her hand gripped and squeezed, teasing. 'More.'

'I want to lick your clit, Leah. And taste you. I want to fuck your cunt with my mouth,' he managed though by now his voice had gone so hoarse and rough with pleasure it was a miracle he could say anything.

'Oh, yes,' she whispered and shifted so, instead of kneeling next to him, she was straddling his face. Her mouth found the head of his prick and her lips brushed it, her tongue licking, as she lowered herself over him.

Brandon gripped her hips with both hands and moved her over his mouth so his tongue could find her clit, but he didn't move her more than that. Leah would move her body on his mouth, fucking it while he licked and sucked. He groaned when his mouth found her hot, slick flesh. He lost himself in the smell and taste of her.

He couldn't last much longer, but he was pretty sure Leah was close, too. Her clit was a hard bead under his tongue, and her thighs shook. Her moan tipped it for him as he heard it and felt the vibration of her lips around his dick at the same time.

He tried to hold off but pleasure seared through him and heat rushed up from his balls and out of his cock. Leah took it all, swallowing him, and her clit throbbed all at once. Her cunt jumped under his lips, pulsing. She came on his mouth, and he eased off after a second or two. Then, with the aftershocks of his orgasm still rippling through him, he licked at her clit gently, tongue circling, until another wave of shudders moved over her body and she collapsed off him and onto the bed.

They lay in silence, panting for a minute. His hand found her thigh and he stroked it. Leah pushed herself up on the bed to look at him.

'Breakfast,' she said. 'Before I pass out. Before you waste away to nothing.'

She paused to stroke a hand over his hair, and he grabbed it to kiss her palm. 'You're the one who said you were hungry for my cock. I'd have taken you to get something real to eat an hour ago.'

Leah raised a brow and fixed him with a stern look. 'Are you saying this is my fault?'

He grinned and pulled her close for one more kiss. Just one more, a little one. 'Yes.'

'I guess I can own up to it,' she whispered against his mouth, but pulled from his grasp and danced away from him when he reached for her again. 'No, Brandon! No. Breakfast. Now.'

He got up on one elbow. 'Yes, ma'am.'

Her eyes gleamed. She'd told him from the start she'd never make him call her Mistress, and she never had. Ma'am, though Leah would never ask him to say it, always made her eyes flash. He watched her cross her arms and lift her chin, watched her stretch her spine until she looked as regal as a queen. She'd say it didn't turn her on, but he knew it did.

'I'm going to jump in the shower and get dressed. You,' she said when he made as though to follow her, 'will use the sink to wash up.'

Shit. He'd been looking forward to hopping in that awesome shower. He knew better than to protest, though – if he got in the shower with her he'd want to wash her back … and her front … and it would be another hour before they left the room. And his stomach was growling. And, more importantly, Leah was giving him the look that meant she was serious. Arguing with her about it would only lead to trouble, and not the good kind.

'Yes, ma'am,' he said, just to tease her a little.

She smirked. 'And I want you to wear that belt I bought you for Christmas along with the sweater in my suitcase.'

He looked in that direction, not knowing what she meant.

'It's new,' she explained as she disappeared into the bathroom. 'What you had on last night, frankly, Brandon, was shameful.'

He hadn't packed appropriately and had left most of his stuff at the Penny Pincher. He hoped it would still be there, though it would need a massive disinfection. He'd have to head over there with Dix at some point today and check out of that rat-trap and get their stuff.

They both washed quickly and as he pulled the new sweater, black with a fine line of red across the chest, he caught Leah looking at him.

'What?'

She smiled. 'Handsome. I knew it would suit you.'

He looked at the sweater, which was light enough for Vegas at this time of year, and pushed the sleeves up on his elbows. 'Of course you did.'

She always knew. Even things he'd never have thought he'd like, Leah knew he would. It had been true of sushi and clothes and movies and music and books. Brandon had no doubt it would be true of most everything, always.

'And you know, too. Don't you?' she asked as she pinned her hair into a twist on top of her head. 'What suits me.'

He moved closer to pull her into his arms. 'I hope so. I want to.'

She snuggled close. She could be so soft when she wanted. He loved that, too.

A knock at the door pushed her to kiss him and then open it. 'Hi.'

Kate stood on the other side, a hand over her eyes. 'I'm just making sure nobody's naked.'

Leah laughed. 'No, it's fine. Breakfast?'

Kate peeked through her fingers with a laugh, then took her hand away. 'Do they call it breakfast if you eat it at lunch time?'

'I don't care what they call it,' Leah said. 'I'm starving.'

Brandon's stomach rumbled again, even louder.

'Uh oh,' Kate said. 'Better get some food in you, Band Boy, or else you might stop growing. C'mon, I've got some vouchers for the buffet downstairs and my contact hooked me up with tickets to the big party tonight, too. Not that we'd have any trouble finding something fun to do ourselves, but this thing looks schwanky. Black tie.'

She swept Brandon up and down with her look. 'Did you bring your tux?'

Leah laughed as she followed Kate into the suite's living room. 'I didn't exactly bring a gown, either. What are you going to wear?'

Brandon liked to look good but aside from that didn't much care about clothes. He caught Dix's eye, and the other man shrugged. It wasn't likely he'd packed anything black tie, either.

'We'll go after breakfast,' Leah was saying as she took his hand. Her fingers squeezed his. He hadn't been paying attention, and she had to explain. 'Shopping.'

He tried his best to shield the 'I'd rather poke my eyes out with a burning stick' expression, but Leah saw it anyway. She laughed and nudged against him.

'It'll be fun.'

He believed that like he believed in fairies.

Breakfast, on the other hand, he could get behind, especially from the hotel's huge, extravagant buffet. The four of them shared a booth big enough for six. Within ten minutes, every inch of the table was covered by heaping plates of food, mugs of coffee and flatware.

'Where do you put it?' Dix asked him as Brandon came back with another plate of eggs, sausage and biscuits.

'Inside my gigantic dick,' Brandon said with a grin as he slathered butter on his biscuit.

Dix laughed and leant back with his arm across the back of the booth to toy with a strand of Kate's hair. 'Good one.'

Leah nudged Brandon in the side. 'Gross.'

He raised a brow, mouth full of bread and butter. Her hand slid up his thigh to squeeze him gently while he couldn't speak. She gave him an utterly wicked grin that had him stirring.

'Hey, hey,' Dix said. 'Don't get him started, he needs that thing to store dessert.'

Kate sat back, a hand on her stomach. 'God, I'm stuffed.'

Dix leant to nuzzle at her neck. 'Don't worry, darling Kate, I'll help you work it all off.'

Kate shooed him, laughing, but submitted to a kiss a second later. 'Leah, get yours out of here and I'll take mine. Boys, we need clothes for tonight. As much as I'm sure we'd both like to see you show up to the party naked, I think this place has rules against it.'

'And no way am I missing the party.' Leah tapped an advertising card set up on the table. 'Champagne and caviar, a complimentary buffet ... jeez, I hope there's going to be dancing to counter all that.'

'Three dance floors, baby.' Kate pointed at the card. 'Live big band music, a techno rave club, whatever the hell that means –'

'Glow sticks,' Brandon said.

Kate rolled her eyes, teasing. 'Why am I not surprised you'd know that?'

'And damn, I didn't bring my whistle,' Brandon said to poke her back.

'And a classic rock cover band,' Leah finished as she knuckled his side. 'Behave, you.'

Dix waved at the server to bring their check. 'Sounds like a helluva party.'

'It's New Year's Eve in Las Vegas,' Leah said. 'How could it be anything less?'

'I still can't believe you stayed in that hotel.' Leah curled her fingers through Brandon's as they navigated a crowd of tourists ogling the hourly pirate-ship show in front of the Treasure Island Hotel. They'd stopped by the Penny Pincher to get Brandon's luggage and she'd nearly thrown up at the smell in the elevator. Fortunately he'd only packed one small bag and it had been easy enough to transfer to the suite.

'No reservations,' Brandon said carelessly, also ogling the pirate wenches in their skimpy costumes until Leah tugged his hand. 'I took what I could. Glad you let me stay with you, though.'

'No doubt.' It was his expression but felt right on her tongue. That happened a lot lately, this transference of pet phrases and habits. Hell, he even had her checking the NHL scores on her Google Reader, because hockey turned out to be the only sport she could stand to watch with him.

'So. Where do you want to go?'

Leah considered. She and Kate had already plundered a lot of the shops and gone to the mall. She could find a dress and shoes in any of a couple dozen places, but she thought the easiest place to find a suit for him would probably be in the hotel where they were staying.

She'd seen an ad for tux rentals there, and there was no sense in making him buy a tux to wear for only a few hours.

Not that she was going to let that stop her from getting a new dress, of course.

'Let's head back to the hotel. It's that way.' She pointed through the crowd that had started to disperse once the pirate show ended but now had swelled to enormous proportions in exactly the direction they wanted to go.

With Brandon leading, that wasn't a problem. He held tight to her hand and wove them through the crowd, finding the gaps and leading her effortlessly into them so they were barely even jostled. It was because he was tall enough to see over everyone else's heads, she thought fondly as he side-stepped a mother with a stroller, of all things – was the woman crazy?

'I will never bring our child here,' she said as they ducked at last into the lobby of their hotel.

He looked down at her with a smile that widened as she watched. 'Our child?'

She knew he wanted kids, probably a few, but they'd never talked much about it. 'Don't get ahead of yourself. Let's make it through this party tonight before we worry about getting me knocked up.'

He squeezed her hand and looked as though he were about to say something, then just nodded. The tux rental place was in the lower level, close to some of the convention rooms. The ones in use for the FetCon, Leah realised as they rode to the bottom of the elevator and the attire of the guests mingling in the public areas changed drastically from T-shirts and shorts to lots and lots of leather and vinyl.

Leah lifted her chin even as her lip curled. She couldn't help it. Mike had taken her to a convention like this once. He'd wanted her to wear a mask with a zipper over the mouth and a bra cut to show her nipples. She hadn't done it, but she'd gone along with him. She could still feel the collar he'd made her try on.

'Let's find another place,' Leah said.

'No. Wait.' Brandon's hand anchored her and Leah, not wishing to make a scene, didn't pull away. 'I want to check this out.'

'It's a vendor room. With ... demonstrations.' Again, Leah's lip curled. She knew what was inside that room. Booths offering sex toys, fetish gear and all sorts of lotions and potions. Books, movies, adult film stars. Hundreds of people with their sexuality on display not just for the world to see but to shove it in everyone else's faces.

'No,' she said.

'Please,' Brandon asked quietly and waited until she looked at him before continuing. 'I know how you feel about this stuff –'

She'd told him only tiny pieces of her life with Mike, and never about the conventions or the sex clubs.

'But I've never been to something like this,' he finished before she could protest.

Fuck, he was giving her the puppy-dog eyes.

'It's only ten bucks to get in,' he said. 'C'mon, Leah. Consider it an educational opportunity for me.'

Damn it, he knew she couldn't resist that look. 'I would prefer to be in charge of your education, Brandon.'

He grinned but didn't give up. He looked at the door, where a large man in a leather biker cap and vest was taking money for admission. Then he looked at her, amusement glinting in his gaze. And something else, too . . . interest. Curiosity. Arousal.

It was unfair of her to say no, Leah thought as she sighed and nodded and let herself be smothered in Brandon's embrace. It was as unreasonable of her to expect Brandon to not be interested in what other people did as it had been for Mike to be too concerned with it.

'Two, please,' Brandon said at the door and pulled out his wallet to hand the guy a twenty.

The guy took the money and gave them both a serious look. 'This isn't for looky lous, kids. You both over eighteen?'

Leah sniffed. She might get carded every once in a long, long while at a bar, but there was no way she looked under eighteen. 'Of course.'

'How 'bout you, sonny?'

'He is, too.'

The door guy grinned, giving her a different sort of look. 'Pardon me, ma'am. You both go right on in.'

He stepped aside to let them pass through the double doors. Just inside was an entry way created from portable fabric panels hung with drapes of heavy velvet – probably to keep casual gawkers from getting a glimpse when the doors opened. Brandon, still holding her hand, pushed through the hanging material and they both stepped into another world.

The space had been set up much like any other vendor room with booths and a stage set up on one end, currently empty. The difference here was that all the booths were decorated with hanging bits of leather and lace and vinyl, and instead of slideshow presentations and demonstrators in business suits, the vendors all wore typical fetish gear.

Or, nothing at all.

'Wow,' Brandon said after a minute. He had to talk loud enough to be heard over the heavy industrial beat of background music.

Leah breathed in deep, waiting for a wave of anxious nostalgia to wash over her . . . but it didn't. The last time she'd gone to something like this, she'd been forcing herself into a role that didn't really fit, with a man who'd done nothing to make it work. This time, she was here with Brandon, and the sounds, the smells, the sights were all different. Or maybe just she was.

The creak of leather and the sound of a muffled cry of pain turned her head. To their left and just down the aisle, a vendor demonstrating a selection of upscale restraints had cuffed a young woman over a padded bench. The guy demonstrating wore blue jeans, no shirt, his nipples pierced and tattoos covering him all over in a swirl of colour. A bandanna held his hair off his face, and his chipped black nail polish matched the thick black eyeliner. The girl, her mouth gagged by a complicated-looking contraption of leather straps, wore a schoolgirl outfit, the skirt pulled up to reveal white cotton panties. Her ankles had been strapped to the bench legs.

'See how comfortable she is?' the vendor said to the small crowd paused there. 'Felicia can't move or even wiggle, but because of the padding she can stay in this position for hours.'

'Wow,' Brandon said again in a thick voice. 'Umm . . .'

'Let's go this way,' Leah said.

She didn't give him enough credit, she realised as they wandered the aisles, and she ought to know better. He gave off a gee-whiz vibe but Brandon could hold his own. Even here, among the floggers and the handcuffs.

'Hold on.' He stopped in front of a small booth decorated with purple fairy lights.

Leah looked around him to see what had caught his attention. Leather bracelets? She looked again. Oh. Bracelets, cuffs ... collars. She swallowed a command for him to come away from there.

At least he wasn't looking at the near-naked girl chained to a large ring hung from the back of the booth. The girl, on the other hand, was looking at him. She couldn't move very fast since her feet were hobbled, both by her incredibly high stiletto shoes and by the length of chain hooking her ankles.

'Those are very nice,' she said. 'Master Venom creates all his pieces from hand-cured leather. The pieces you see here are all from his Bound collection, which you can buy online or from our catalogue, but all you see at the booth today is on sale at a highly reduced show price.'

She laid out the details in sing-songy but professional tone, and even though Leah rolled her eyes at the title Master Venom, she had to admit the pieces laid out did look to be of high quality.

Brandon let go of Leah's hand to touch a leather strap with o-rings hooked into both ends. 'What's this for?'

Leah watched him look the girl in the eyes as he spoke, not staring at her breasts the way quite a number of other people were. Well, they were kind of hard to miss. But she watched Brandon give the girl his attention ... and respect.

She fell in love with him all over again.

'It's for restraint. Those are for padlocks.' The girl reached beneath the counter to pull out a padlock and demonstrate.

'And this?'

'Male chastity belt,' the girl said. 'This part goes around the testicles, this part around the penis, and the straps go between the legs, over the anus, and hook around the waist.'

'Ouch,' Brandon said and put that piece down at once.

Leah laughed. 'Not for you, huh?'

He made an exaggerated scared face, eyes wide. Leah laughed

again and picked it up, meaning to simply tease him. Before she could say a word, a woman appeared beside her.

'That's a great item,' she said. 'I use it on all my slaves.'

Leah's fingers twitched and she put the chastity belt back on the display board. 'Uh huh.'

The woman wore a black vinyl corset top over which her tremendous cleavage threatened to trap unsuspecting passers-by. Her hair, also black, streamed down her back. Her boots, black, were knee-high patent leather. Her thong, black to match the rest, barely covered her pubis and left her ass totally bare.

She gave Leah the once-over with raised brows at Leah's outfit of khaki capris, white T-shirt and a pretty, pale-green cardigan. 'It cuts down on their jerking off quite a bit.'

'No doubt,' Leah said aloud.

The woman grinned up at Brandon. In her heels she could almost look him in the eye. 'This one looks like he could use some discipline.'

Brandon's laugh caught in his throat, but Leah only smiled. 'Sometimes.'

The woman tapped the chastity belt and gave Leah a wink. 'Go with that one. You can add a section for an assplug that will really keep him in line.'

Beside Leah, Brandon gave out a little strangled groan. Leah waited until the woman stalked away to look at him with a raised brow. Brandon just gave his head a small, helpless shake. Leah grinned.

She tugged the front of his shirt to bring him down close enough to whisper in his ear. 'I would never, never make you do that if you didn't want it.'

'Good,' he whispered back and snuck a kiss. 'Because I think my nuts just crawled up so far inside me you wouldn't be able to find them to fit them in that thing, anyway.'

Leah laughed just as the flap at the back of the booth opened and a small man dressed sort of like a pirate – a BDSM pirate, with a frilly shirt and rings on every finger, came out. He was shoving the end of a burger into his mouth and, as he came closer, the girl who'd been showing off the products dropped to her knees. He wiped his greasy fingers along her hair.

The girl behind the counter was obviously more of a lifestyler than Leah had ever been, because all she did was duck her head.

'Pansy, didn't you help these people?'

'Yes, Master Venom.'

Master Venom sneered and nudged at her with his foot so she got up, but she kept her head bowed. He fixed his attention on Brandon and gave him a large smile. He rubbed his hands together, too. What a cliché.

'What can I help you with?'

'Just looking,' Leah said, as Brandon pointed to a braided leather bracelet woven with silver charms and said, 'I want to see one of these.'

Master Venom looked confused for a second, his beady gaze going back and forth between them. Then he looked at Brandon again, ignoring Leah. 'I can make these with any charm you want. Initials, or a bead symbolising something special for your slaves. Whatever. I can show you what I have.'

Slaves. Leah hated that word. 'What about for someone who's not a slave?'

Master Venom turned to her with a sneer. 'Everyone's either a master or a slave. My name's Master Venom. You'll address me as Master Venom, got it? Now, say, "Yes, Master Venom."'

Brandon took a step back. Getting out of her way, Leah realised. She set her jaw and stepped closer. 'You know, "master" only means something if it's given to you by the other person, not if you demand it. And I don't call anyone master. Ever.'

A small knot of people had gathered, watching, but Leah didn't care. She took a deep breath and faced down the man on the other side of the counter. He was every reason she'd never wanted to be part of the lifestyle and a few reasons she hadn't thought of before.

'Dude, not the best way to sell your products, bitching at the customers,' Brandon said.

Venom turned, his face getting red. He looked at Brandon from top-to-toe, then turned to Leah with condescension dripping in his tone. 'You should leash your pet.'

Brandon gave a low, angry noise and stepped in front of her. 'Don't talk to her like that.'

Pansy let out a small peep and got the hell out of the way. She tugged at the chain holding her tight to the back of the booth. 'Oh, shit. Maurice, back off. This guy's big.'

'MY NAME IS MASTER VENOM!'

Leah put a hand on Brandon's arm to hold him off. She gave Maurice a long hard stare. 'I don't need to leash him to get him to do what I want.' Her tone made it clear what she thought of anyone who had to rely on chains to get obedience.

Master Venom sputtered. A couple of people in the crowd cheered and clapped. Pansy yanked the chain and ducked behind the curtain at the back of the booth. Venom followed after a second.

'Asshole,' Leah heard someone mutter from the booth next door.

'He really gives us all a bad, bad name,' said a man wearing faded jeans and a plain white T-shirt, his blond hair in a ponytail. He gave Leah and Brandon both a smile. 'Look, if you want something to wear that's a little more mainstream than a spiked collar, I've got some great pieces at my booth. Show discounts, too. I'm over there. C'mon and stop over.'

The crowd dispersed. Venom and Pansy didn't return. Leah reached for Brandon's hand.

'You know I said I'd never put a collar on you.'

'I know. But Leah...if there was something...' He hesitated, looking around, then waved a hand. 'Some people wear bracelets, or collars, or get tattoos. Some people get off on wearing chains. I think it would be kind of cool to have ... something. To wear when we're not together. Then when I looked at it ...'

He gave her the grin she never could resist.

'What?' she prompted, aware they were not alone, they were in the middle of a thousand kinky lifestylers who wouldn't think twice if she ordered him to his knees to eat her cunt right then and there. And that the thought of it made her clit pulse.

'It's like the lists,' he said. 'You know. I'd look at it and think of you.'

'Ah,' Leah said and looked towards the booth the blond guy had pointed to. 'Well, then. Let's go see what there is.'

17

'Don't let this go to your head or anything but, muthafucka, you look hot in that tux.' Kate walked around Dix in a slow circle to take him in fully. 'What? Am I lying? It's OK, I won't hurt you if you answer. I swear,' she said, looking to the sales associate.

Dix simply laughed and let her look. The salesgirl too, why the fuck not?

'All right, please thank Marcus for this. I'm sure it's not easy to find a tux to rent on New Year's Eve.' Kate, all business, handed the clerk a discreet tip while he paid for the tux rental.

'Who is Marcus, darling Kate?' He nuzzled her neck as he followed her from the store, his tux in a bag over his arm.

'My lover.' She tipped her head back to look him in the eye. 'What? Oh was I not supposed to have a lover?' Laughter spilt from her lips and he smiled before tipping down to kiss her quickly. 'Marcus is the guy who hooked us up with the room and the tickets for tonight. I told you, *big* legal trouble.' She shrugged and he shook his head, amused.

'Clearly I made a mistake going into in-house work.'

'We can't all have favours lined up from coast to coast. It's difficult to be so respected.' She winked.

'This needs to go in the room and then I want to watch you try things on.' The first time she'd let him accompany her shopping, he'd worked his way into the dressing room. After a minute and a half, he couldn't keep his hands to himself and she never let him go with her after that. He found the intimacy of the secret world of women to be ridiculously sexy.

'I'll wait down here. If I go up there with you, you'll get fresh and we'll lose hours of time. Not that I'm complaining that you take your time or anything. But tick-tock, others will be last minute shopping too.

This is already gonna cost a pretty penny so I don't want to spend a month's salary on some lime green atrocity. You go on and I'm going to get a coffee. You want one?'

'You sure you don't to come up with me? You know how hot it makes me when you get sassy and all girly at once.'

She grinned, tiptoeing up to kiss him. 'Insatiable. Now move that stellar ass or I will go without you. Maybe I'll pick up one of these leather boys and have them watch me try things on.'

The look in his eyes thrilled her right down to her toes. Possessive, masculine, heated. *Mmmm.*

'You'd break one in less than ten minutes. The sweet thing you wear is a total lie. You're a wolf.' He flashed a grin at her and she couldn't suppress a shiver of delight. 'I'll be back and, yes, I want a mocha.'

Smiling, she stayed where she was to watch him amble to the elevators. Hot damn, she was one lucky woman.

'Is he yours?'

Kate turned to the two women who'd also stopped to watch him. 'Yeah. Lucky me, huh?'

'He's delish. Are you here for the con? He's a Dom, right? You share?'

'Yes, no, not in the sense you mean it, and no. I take it you ladies are here for the con?'

The taller one, a blonde about Kate's age nodded. 'Mara and I got into the lifestyle two years ago. It's hard to find a good guy, you know? They all come with baggage or lies. Mara's seeing a guy now, though, he's nice. I want that too. Thought I'd tag along with them to see if I'd get lucky. *He's* lucky.' Blondie tipped her head towards the elevators where Dix had disappeared.

Kate laughed. 'He is very lucky. But he comes with baggage. About five and half feet of baggage in the form of an ex-wife who plays helpless and uses their kids to try to break us up.'

'Bitch!' Mara said.

'Word.' Kate nodded.

'So you're not letting her, right? Women like that don't deserve tasty bits like him.'

'He could be a total asshole for all you know. I could have been the secretary he was fucking on the side.'

Blondie looked her over and shook her head. 'No you're not. You don't look like the type to take any shit. And you're hot enough, but in charge, you don't need to steal anyone's man.'

Kate shrugged and snorted a laugh. 'Good to know, thanks. And no, as a matter of fact, I'm done letting her get to me. Ladies, enjoy the day. I'm off to procure caffeine for me and my tasty bit. Keep your standards high, the right guy is out there. Even if he comes with baggage.'

Truer words were never spoken, she realised as she walked towards the tiny coffee bar in the lobby. He was, without being overly mushy about it, the best thing in her world. He got her. He respected her. He wanted to be with her and she saw how much he loved her in everything he did. All that made him worth it. Made the work of accommodating his *stuff* into a working relationship worth the struggle and the effort.

The Pickles thing would be a problem, but, while she was being honest and all, she was hotter, smarter and *not* Eve. As a woman, Katherine was far better suited to a man like Charles than Eve was. He needed a woman who would push back, who did for herself, but allowed him to do for her too. The doing was a gift, freely given, not expected or a burden.

It was his connection to Eve through the kids that Kate found so difficult to get over. Having children with someone was a million times more intense than just about anything else you could do with a person. Katherine couldn't compete with what Eve was on that level. She wasn't jealous of Eve romantically or sexually, but it was that level of intimacy and connection Eve would always have with him. For a while when she first got to know his daughters, all she could see was that they were a physical manifestation of Charles Dixon loving another woman enough to create life with her.

Kate wanted to have his children. So much at times it was hard not to blurt it out. It wasn't as simple as just going out and getting pregnant. She was very much aware, though, of the children he already had. And the part of her who wanted that with him also realised those girls needed a while to be used to the idea. And she loved them, not only because they were Dix's kids, but they were both pretty exceptional people. He loved them, and she respected that and held it in a place of deep importance. She had fears that Eve would attempt to turn them against her, knew it would most likely cause tension when they moved in together. As much as she wanted to avoid that, she wanted to be with him, and he continued to feel hurt when she put him off about it. Her priority was him and she had to make a choice and do her very best to do things right.

He didn't love Eve. Hadn't in a very long time. He did love Kate and she knew that quite surely. They would have children someday, there was time for that. There was no reason to feel threatened, and continuing to hold him off about moving in together and marriage only meant that bitchface won and he still felt hurt and rejected.

And as for bitchface, Eve had a reckoning due and Kate had a few ideas on how to make it happen. Kate would not be out-manoeuvred by a cow like Eve Dixon. No way. No how. It was like necessary for freedom, justice and the American way or something not to let that skank beat her.

His hands encircled her from behind, his body fit against hers as his lips found her temple. 'I'm not sure I want to know what you were thinking about just now. That look often spells trouble.'

She shrugged and handed him his coffee. 'Not for you, gorgeous. By the way, two hot women and I objectified you when you went up to the room. They asked if I shared. I had to decline. They thought you were a Dom here for the con.'

He laughed and the way his eyes crinkled at the edges made her all gooey. 'Awesome. Did you make out while you did it? Cause you can totally do it again, or describe it to me in great detail. As for the Dom thing? You like it when I tell you what to do.'

'In bed. We didn't make out, but I can make up some salacious stories for you later on. They were both hot and told me you were a tasty bit. They're very right. Doesn't mean I'm going to share you. With anyone.' She sucked down the rest of her latte and tossed the cup. 'Come on. I have a dress to buy.'

The street was busy, full of revellers not bothering to wait until midnight. He walked close, his arm around her shoulders and she felt good. Comfortable and loved.

'Where are we going?'

'Leah and I hit the mall, I bought stuff, but not the right dress for tonight. I browsed the shops in the hotel, but all these big luxury hotels have boutiques now. I thought I'd check out a few.'

'Wherever you go, darling, I will follow. I need to escort you everywhere it seems, there are a lot of horny men in Las Vegas who like to stare at your tits. Now, I can't blame them, I quite like to stare at them too. You get my point, though.'

'Oh you'll spoil me with such flattery. Plus, you're good for carrying things.' She winked. 'Since my money will now be going into two mortgage payments until I can sell my place in the city, I may as well be frivolous before the year ends.' She walked through the doors of the swank, designer boutique in one of the nearby hotels. 'You could really go broke in Vegas on the clothes. Fuck gambling, look at that dress.'

It was red. Bright, brilliant red and it called to her like a siren. She had to touch it. Had to own it.

The sales clerk happily showed them to a dressing room and Dix eyed her while she shucked her clothes and got ready to get into the dress.

'I like it already,' he murmured when she tossed her bra aside.

She smirked at him over her shoulder as the material made her want to sing a song of thanks. 'Zip me up, please.'

Dix's fingertips brushed against the bare skin at the small of her back as he zipped. What there was of a zipper. The little red piece of heaven was mostly backless and had just a wee bit more fabric in the front. Enough to cover the indecent parts of her breasts and to make her thankful she'd been exercising regularly. The cut would not hide any lumps or bumps.

'Christ almighty, you look . . .' He met her eyes in the mirror of the dressing room and flicked a thumb over her nipple. It sprang to life at his attention.

Eve wouldn't wear this dress, she thought, looking at her reflection and then back to the man behind her. His eyes refocused and then he turned her around. 'Wait a minute. It just hit me that you said you'd move in with me. You'll buy a house with me.'

'Don't muss me. This dress is obscenely expensive.' She smiled and he pulled her close, hauling her up against him and taking her mouth in a kiss so raw she nearly came. His mouth was inescapable, his tongue sliding along hers, his taste bursting through her. His teeth caught her bottom lip, his arms held her tight. She sighed, letting him take whatever he wanted, responding to such raw sexuality she grew drunk with it. When he let her go, she had to hold on because her knees were rubber.

'Wow.' She licked her lips, savouring his taste a few moments more. If he'd have asked her to marry him right then, she'd have agreed.

'Katherine, I love you. Let's get this damned dress paid for so I can get you back to the room and fuck you. Twice.'

She looked at the price tag and steeled herself. 'One, I need shoes and a bag. Two, we have to talk before there's any fucking.'

'One, fine, but I'm going to totally look down your shirt while you try shoes on. Two, you've made me so damned happy I'm paying for the dress and three, all right but if we talk about Eve too much I'm not going to be as interested in sex.'

'Empty threats, Charles, empty threats. We both know you'd be able to fuck after just about anything. You're just that kind of man. And if you think I won't take you up on your paying for this dress, you're wrong.'

'Goddamn, you're something. You bring me to my knees and I can't get enough.' He sank to his knees and looked up her body. *He* was something else. That wicked grin was on his mouth and she gave in, sinking her fingers into his hair, yanking his face forwards.

His hands went to the back of the dress, unzipping it so it fell from her body. She stepped from it and laid it aside. 'Shall I lick your pussy right here and now?'

Her breath caught. His hands caressed up the back of her calves as he breathed against the front panel of her panties just before pressing his tongue through the silky material, right against her clit.

'Eat me,' she whispered, a shiver breaking over her as he slid the panties down her legs.

'Lean your back against the wall behind you.' He said it without peeling his eyes from her cunt as he spread her open. The look on his face made her muscles clench – wonderment and hunger. It always made her feel like a queen.

And there she stood, watching in the mirrors, one foot up on the bench in the dressing room, back against the cool wall, Dix's face between her thighs. From all sides they were reflected, the look on her face as she took herself in, the colour of her skin as a flush built, the way he bent over her cunt like in benediction. So beautiful, so decadent and luscious.

'Mmm, oh, God, yes that feels so good,' she moaned as she watched the pink of his tongue against the pink of her cunt. Watched the flick and caress as he devoured her. The clerk was just on the other side of the door, the store was full of people and she was just inches away from coming all over Dix's face.

Dix took the taste of her into himself, knew she was getting off on not only his mouth there on her, but on the nearness of the people right on the other side of the door. Her thighs trembled and when he looked up the line of her body, it was to watch her tug and roll her nipples as she looked down at him.

Her tongue darted out, sliding over her bottom lip and he groaned against her. Her eyes first widened and then went sleepy, half-lidded and sexy. A knock sounded on the door.

'Everything all right in there? Can I get you a different size?'

'Fine, thanks,' Kate managed to say before Dix sucked her clit into his mouth the way he knew drove her crazy. Instead of stopping him, she let go of one nipple and grabbed him by the hair, hauling him closer. 'Nearly done.'

Even with a man's mouth on her cunt in a public dressing room she had a sense of humour.

He finished her with three fingers pressed deep, stroking her sweet spot, sucking her clit in and out until she came with a growl of his name.

He stood as she slumped onto the seat. 'I'll go pay for this while you get dressed, shall I?'

Licking his lips, he grabbed the dress and headed out, wearing a smile.

True to his promise, he did look down her shirt as she tried shoes on, but she barely noticed anything but the hard-on pressing against the front of his pants.

'Keep looking at it like that and I'm going to pull it out and shove it into your mouth right here and now,' he said as he took the packages from her to carry.

'We move in together within the next few months. Once we find a house we like with enough room for all our combined baggage,' she began as they walked back to the hotel. 'I'll put my condo on the market when we get back.'

'Good thing I'm used to the way you just wander around between topics,' he muttered. 'Fine. Agreed. I'd like you to stay over at my old house when I have the girls with me. I know it'll be a bigger hassle work wise for you, but aside from wanting you with me, it sends a very clear signal to Eve. You and I are together no matter where we are. And to the girls that you're behind me being where they need me most when they need it. I know you don't want to be an underline, but this is much more than that. This is the truth staring her in the face without letting her look away.'

'Agreed. Although it'd be nice if I could just slap the shit out of her. I change my mind about the "no Eve calling our house" rule. I only want her contacting you that way. She's like one of those yappy dogs who needs a very hard lesson. The lesson is this.' Kate stopped and took his face in her hands. People walked around them but she heard and felt nothing but him. 'You're mine. She is nothing but the mother of your kids and that I respect. Otherwise, she better deal with the fact that *I* am your woman because I'm not giving her any way around that. I won't interfere in your parenting of your kids, but for all other contact, she has to come through me. We'll nip this little comprehension problem of hers right in the bud. Later, I don't care, but for the next little while, Eve will know who is in charge. And it's a woman who can open her own jars.'

He leant down just a bit, brushing his lips against hers. 'And you'll still marry me next year sometime?'

Kate laughed and jumped back, tugging him towards the hotel. 'God, you're like a dog with a bone.'

'Here's what I know, I'd be marrying you in five minutes if you'd go for it, so yes, I'm not going to give up.'

'All right. October. I want a small intimate ceremony. Less than twenty people. Your daughters will be part of it. Then that night we get straight on a plane somewhere lovely. I don't need pomp and circumstance. I want to make it legal, involve our closest loved ones and then party. This doesn't mean you don't have to provide me with a ring. That needs to happen soon. Let me advise you away from that monstrosity Pickles has. I like big, but I like tasteful too. Then again, I wouldn't wear my engagement ring nearly a decade after I got dumped. But we've established I'm an order of magnitude above Pickles.' She looked down at the ring he'd just given her for Christmas. 'This is beautiful, you can keep going in this direction.'

He snorted a laugh. 'I'd tell you to just pick something out and tell me what you want but I know that would be a violation of the code or whatever. I think I can manage something appropriately fabulous. October it is. I'll talk to my travel agent when we get back to have him start looking into honeymoon ideas.'

'If we hurry I think we can catch that elevator before the doors close,' she said, pulling him along.

18

A simple band of gold. Nothing etched on it or inside it. No words. This wasn't for anyone else, it was for them, and neither Brandon nor Leah needed a reminder of what the ring meant.

He'd never worn rings, not even for a high-school class or a sports team. He'd pierced his ears in college and worn silver hoops in both of them for a short time, but now he wasn't even sure he could force an earring through the old holes. Brandon stood in front of the mirror naked, the hand with the ring on it on his belly. Staring.

Leah, wearing only a pair of filmy black panties and a matching bra, came into the bathroom as she slid on a pair of dangling earrings she'd bought from the same guy who'd made the ring. She paused. Her gaze met his in the mirror.

'You're not dressed,' she said.

His cock stirred at the cool command in her voice and the no-nonsense look she gave him. Angry Leah was formidable to see, but she hardly ever got mad at him. Her discipline always came from a different place for Brandon.

'We're going to be late. You know I hate being late.'

He didn't point out that by the sounds coming faintly through the walls, Kate and Dix weren't exactly rushing to get downstairs, either. Or that it was still early evening, hours away from midnight. Or that they were in Vegas, where you couldn't be late for anything, because nothing ever ended.

'You should get dressed,' Leah continued, circling behind him while he stayed still. 'Brandon.'

He swallowed, his prick thickening further. He'd come from the shower, hair dripping, intending to dry off at once and get dressed for the party. The unfamiliar glint of gold on his finger – the right hand, not the left, had captured his attention. Frozen him.

'What are you looking at?' Leah stopped just behind him, looking around him at his reflection.

He felt the slow tickle of her fingertip on his back, low, just above the crack of his ass. 'This ring.'

She smiled. Her finger whispered along the fine hairs at the base of his spine. Then a little lower. Brandon's dick rose another half an inch and his balls tightened.

'You like it.'

He nodded.

'I like it, too.' Leah's hand cupped his ass for a moment, then squeezed. 'Go over there and put your hands on the counter.'

He flicked her a glance, surprised, but there was no pretending she wasn't serious. He did as she said. The ring clicked on the marble, and Brandon swallowed hard at the sound. He kept his gaze on her in the mirror.

She was so fucking beautiful it broke him apart. All the time, but now, with her hair pulled up to show her neck, the earrings brushing her skin with every step, she took his breath away. Leah's hand lay light on the small of his back as he bent forwards enough to keep his hands flat on the counter.

'Spread your legs. Feet apart. Let me see that pretty cock.'

He blinked and bit back a smile, but did as she said.

'Do you think that's funny?' Leah pinched his hip, not hard enough to hurt.

His cock, fully hard now, throbbed. 'No.'

She reached between his legs from behind to cup his balls. 'I can see it in the mirror, Brandon. How hard you are.'

Her voice had gone husky and when she licked her lips, his breath caught. A small shudder traced its way down his spine as Leah weighed his balls, then ran her thumb back and forth, stroking. She watched in the mirror, expression contemplative.

'I've been thinking what that domina said, downstairs. About the cock harness.'

His entire body jerked and he made to stand, to turn and face her, but Leah's grip tightened on his nuts. Brandon didn't move. His fingers clutched on slick marble. His heart raced.

'Shh,' she murmured. Her thumb stroked, stroked. She shifted her hand so her thumb pressed against his asshole.

'Fuck,' he blurted, voice hoarse and raw, and bent his head so his hair fell over his eyes and he wouldn't have to see her face.

He'd come in another few seconds if he saw the look in her eyes, he knew it. With her thumb pressing him so gently back there he almost couldn't feel the pressure, without even touching his cock at all. She owned him.

'That ring,' Leah said in a low, hot voice, 'was a very, very good idea.'

He nodded, waiting. When her other hand came around to grip his cock, he groaned. She stroked him slowly from root to tip, her other hand keeping up the same gentle pressure. He fucked into her hand and she stopped moving it.

'No,' she said.

He stopped.

She stood so close her breath gusted against his shoulder and the heat of her body warmed his naked skin. 'There is so much, Brandon. So many things . . . there is so much we haven't done.'

Leah's voice quavered, and Brandon turned to take her in his arms. He tucked her close, her head just beneath his chin. She hugged him.

He loved her for being uncertain. For worrying. 'We'll figure it out. It's OK.'

She sighed against him, then tipped her face to look up. Doubt crossed her face, replaced in the next moment by a sly grin. She reached between them and rubbed his cock slowly over her bare belly. But when he bent to kiss her, she turned her head.

'No.'

His mouth stopped a breath away from her cheek. 'You sure?'

Her body moved as her hand also moved his dick against her. 'I'm sure.'

Frustrated, he closed his eyes but didn't kiss her. He kept still, even though he wanted to push against her. Inside her.

Leah laughed, low and throaty, and stepped back. 'Get dressed.'

He opened his eyes and looked at his cock before he looked at her. 'Now?'

'Yes, now. I hear Kate in the living room, and I'm hungry, Brandon.'

He groaned and swept the hair off his forehead. His balls ached a little. So did his prick. 'Can I have a minute or two?'

'No,' Leah said sternly. She tossed him the pair of briefs on the counter. 'Put these on.'

He did. The front bulged and the fabric rubbed him without mercy. Heat flooded up from his chest to his face. 'Leah . . .'

Again, she laughed, teasing. 'I want you hard, or half-hard, until I'm ready to do something with that gorgeous prick.'

He sighed and adjusted himself. 'Yes, ma'am.'

Her eyes gleamed. 'Don't get saucy with me, Béarnaise.'

He laughed and she stood on her tiptoes to brush a too-brief kiss over his mouth. When he reached for her, she stepped away, shaking a finger. Brandon dropped his hands, giving in to her.

'Be good,' she admonished, 'and I will let you lick me, later.'

'I could lick you now . . .'

'No,' she said serenely, and paraded out of the bathroom, calling over her shoulder, 'get dressed! Now!'

He snuck a quick rub through the briefs, but Leah ducked back through the door and caught him at it.

'Cock harness,' she warned.

Everything inside him pulsed.

'Ah,' she breathed, watching him. 'I think we might have to stop back at the vendor exhibition tonight, after all.'

Leah had never been enamoured of Las Vegas, but she had to admit this trip had been a fabulous idea. Impulsively, she reached to squeeze Kate in a sideways hug. 'Thank you.'

Kate, wearing a gorgeous, short red dress laughed and hugged Leah, too. 'For what?'

'All of it.' Leah waved a hand at the ballroom. 'The trip. The party. The suite.'

Kate smirked. 'It has been pretty damn great, huh?'

'Yes.' Leah sighed, searching the crowd for Brandon who'd gone off with Dix to find drinks. 'I'm going to marry him, Kate.'

Kate raised a brow. 'Duh.'

Leah laughed and smoothed the skirt of the simple black dress she'd picked out earlier. Thigh high, strapless, spangled with the subtle gleam of iridescent black beads, the gown had looked like nothing on the hanger but fit her perfectly and made her feel like a goddess the way a good dress should. She shifted, feeling the whisper of her lace stocking tops against each other.

'What about you?' she asked pointedly. 'Have you and Dix figured out the housing situation?'

Kate nodded to the beat of the band on the room's far end. 'I'm moving in with him, wedding bells to follow in October. Something simple. Not like your White Wedding extravaganza.'

'Hmmm, I'm not sure I can get away with wearing white,' Leah said dryly, 'although I'm going to toss out a guess that it will end up being quite a show.'

'You'll be OK with that?' Kate asked.

Leah nodded. 'Brandon will do whatever I want, I know that. But ... I know he'll want the whole thing. The church, the dress, the roast beef reception. Well,' she amended, thinking, 'maybe something classier than that. But yes, I think it will be traditional.'

'Good,' Kate said firmly. 'I'll practise my Chicken Dance. But I'm not doing the Macarena, so don't ask.'

Leah laughed. 'Oh, God. No.'

The crowd moved around them, a horde of fancy dresses and tuxes and pretty people drinking from champagne flutes. Yet even in the crowd, Leah had no trouble seeing Brandon and Dix cutting their way back from the bar, drinks in hand.

'We are two very lucky women,' she said.

'Dude, you know it.'

The women shared a high-five that morphed into the secret handshake they'd made up in eighth grade and could still bring out when the occasion called for it. Breaking up into laughter, Leah added a hip shimmy. Kate threw up rock horns with her fingers.

'I see you're behaving yourselves.' Dix pulled Kate into his arms and kissed her soundly. 'My darling Kate, I brought your drink the way you like your man.'

'Fruity with an umbrella?' she asked archly.

'Strong enough to buckle your knees,' he told her.

Brandon handed Leah her glass as he moved behind her to pull her close. 'Margarita with salt.'

She felt the lump of his semi-erection and rubbed her ass against him, just a little, then turned to smile up at him. 'Thank you.'

They moved together for a minute to the beat, but they were in the wrong place for dancing. Too many people with drinks, and a little too far from the band. And Leah's stomach was growling.

'Where's the buffet?' she asked Kate.

'Other room, I think. Hey, hey.' Kate slapped at Dix's roving hand, but not seriously enough to stop him.

'It's your fault for looking so delicious.'

Kate snorted. 'Do you want to eat?'

'I want to eat,' Brandon said matter-of-factly.

Leah linked her arm through his. 'No surprise there.'

They wove through the crowd and through the arched doorway to the smaller ballroom, where a buffet of truly spectacular proportions had been arranged, along with a number of tables and booths close to both the food and the music. Ice sculptures, lights, platters and trays of food and drink, all laid out in true Vegas style. Brandon let out a low whistle.

'Everything looks so good.' Leah studied the long tables set up with steam trays. 'C'mon, let's eat. I want you to keep your strength up. For later.'

She wiggled her eyebrows at him, and Brandon laughed. He got in line behind her. They both took plates, still hot from the dishwasher, and moved along the line. Leah made careful choices . . . things that could be eaten with her fingers, small portions. Brandon, on the other hand, loaded up with whatever he pleased.

Kate and Dix had filled their plates as well. Now the four of them stood around, hands full of food, while people all around them did the same thing. All the small tables on this side of the velvet rope had been taken.

'Screw this,' Dix said. 'Let's get one of those booths. I'm not standing around nibbling and getting stuff spilt on me.'

'That one's open.' Brandon pointed with his chin. 'We'll have to get bottle service.'

'Worth every fucking penny,' Dix said. 'Ladies, after you.'

'I could get used to this,' Leah said from inside the booth as the waiter brought them a bottle of champagne, the music started, and everyone around them who didn't have a VIP table had to juggle plates and glasses.

Brandon dug into his pile of food but shot her a grin and nudged her knee with his under the table. 'Too bad there aren't any bagels.'

Leah reached to squeeze his knee and watched his grin get a little strained, though the humour stayed in his deep-brown eyes. 'That is truly tragic.'

The jazz trio playing in this ballroom was great, but not quite loud enough to cover up the occasional throb of music from the two connecting ballrooms. Even so, the booth shielded them enough to allow them conversation without having to shout, the food was great and the champagne flowed. It wasn't long before Kate and Leah were giggling over their own conversations while the men discussed stuff that had measurements and scores and point spreads and God knew what else.

Kate shifted in her seat to the upbeat tempo. 'Charles, I want to dance.'

'And I, darling Kate, want to see you shake that sweet –'

Kate stopped him with a kiss. 'C'mon, before I give in to another plate of pasta or a piece of cheesecake.'

She turned to Leah. 'Are you coming?'

Leah looked at Brandon, who was still eating. 'Umm . . . in a little while.'

Brandon laughed but didn't put down his fork. 'I'll be done soon.'

Dix shook his head. 'Christ, kid.'

Kate took him by the hand and pulled him from the booth, calling over her shoulder at Leah, 'We'll be in the electronica ballroom, OK? Text me if you can't find me.'

'Have fun.' Leah watched them go, then leant to drag a finger through the raspberry sauce on Brandon's plate of chocolate cake. She touched the tip of her tongue to it, then offered it to him. 'Yum.'

He took her fingertip in his mouth and sucked gently in a way that sent tendrils of pleasure unfurling all through her. 'Mmmmm.'

Leah's hand slipped under the table and cupped the bulge at his crotch. 'Mmmm.'

Brandon pushed his plate away and kissed her. 'I'm done.'

'Ah ah,' Leah said. 'I'd hate for you to miss out on something good. You should finish.'

His breathing quickened as his tongue swept hers and he pulled back just enough to murmur, 'This is better.'

Leah sat back against the booth's high leather seat. She stroked him idly as they kissed, interrupted only by the waiter asking if they wanted another bottle. Since the one they had was only half gone, she shook her head.

Brandon filled her glass, then his. 'Good stuff.'

She rubbed his cock again. 'This is better.'

His tongue wet his mouth. He was hard under her fingers, and she took mercy on him. It had to be uncomfortable. But when she tried to withdraw her hand, he made a noise of protest.

'I can't get you off right here,' Leah said into his ear as she added a nibble that made him shiver. 'It would make a mess and would be uncomfortable for you. Really. It's for your own good.'

He groaned. 'Leah . . .'

'On the other hand,' she told him, 'you can certainly use your hand on me.'

Brandon laughed and as the jazz trio struck up another song, a singer joined them. Her slow, sultry crooning was the perfect background for him sliding his fingers up her thigh and past the lacy stocking tops, to stroke her clit through her panties.

'Like this?'

She nodded and settled back against him, facing the stage so she could watch the show. Most of the other people were still too busy eating and drinking to pay attention to the singer, who looked every inch the part of a 1930s blues singer, right down to the flower in her hair. Leah didn't know the words to the woman's song, but the music flowed over her, sweet and slow and sensual, a total ear-fuck.

Brandon's hand moved slowly, too. Fingertip barely circling.

Anyone walking by would see a couple intent on the performance, not a man with his hand between a woman's legs. Making her come. Not that she was close, anyway. Not yet.

Brandon knew how to ease her into it, keep her humming. He paused every few strokes. His breath heated the back of her neck and his lips traced her ear. Her nipples stood out, sharp, hard points, inside her gown. Leah arched slightly, pressing herself back against his cock.

'You're so fucking sexy,' he murmured in her ear as his fingers moved again. He shifted to dip inside her panties and find her slick arousal. Her cunt clenched and Leah bit back a moan. 'I want to put my fingers in your pussy and feel how hot you are.'

God, she loved it when he talked dirty. It made her mindless. Made her want to writhe, to sink down on his prick and ride him. Instead she kept still, opening her legs to let him get inside her as far as he could the way they sat.

Brandon took her clit between his thumb and finger and rolled it gently, then tugged. Just once, then again. Stopped. Her muscles quivered and her hips tilted, just a little, pressing herself towards his hand. A couple, drinks in hand, stood just a foot or so away from the table to watch the show. Leah could hear every word of their conversation and knew without a doubt they'd be able to hear her if she cried out.

'So fucking beautiful.' Brandon tugged her clit again and waves of desire broke over her. 'I can feel you getting so tight, every muscle. I want to make you feel so good you come all over my hand.'

Leah's hips rocked as she clenched internal muscles but barely moved anything else. Her fingers bore down on his arm, squeezing. Brandon chuckled into her ear, the heat of his breath sending a chill through her. She felt feverish, more than a little tipsy, drunk not on champagne but on his love. On this pleasure, gained from his hand, his fingers, from the sigh of his breath on her skin.

Brandon tugged her clit, then stroked. She was so wet his fingers slid over her without skidding or catching. He pinched her clit again between his thumb and finger and held it without moving.

Her heart beat heavily in her ears, in her throat, and in her clit.

The pounding of her blood felt as though it pushed her against his fingers. Her inner thighs trembled. She tasted sweat on her upper lip. His pinch loosened and the sudden lack of pressure nearly sent her over, but then he took her clit again and she bucked.

The man next to their table looked over brow furrowed. Leah froze, eyes on the singer who was now moving her hips in sensual circles Brandon echoed with his fingers. Leah held her breath until spots danced in front of her eyes, then let it out.

'Do you want to come?' he asked her, voice low so only she could hear.

Leah didn't trust her voice to answer. Nor could she nod, tense and stiff as she was with waiting for her body to take over and send her soaring. Brandon's laugh tripped up and down her body. He worked her clit a little bit harder until she gripped his arm so tightly she was sure she'd bruise him even through the thickness of his tux jacket.

'Should I make you come?'

Waiting for her to give him permission. How he was holding her off, Leah couldn't tell. Everything in her strained towards release. She didn't think she could have stopped herself, but something held her back. Kept her from tipping. Each infinitesimal stroke pushed her closer and closer, but she wasn't coming. Not yet.

She didn't tell him she wanted to come, though all she could think about was sinking onto his thick, hard cock and riding him until they both exploded. She couldn't make out the singer's words any longer – could hear the woman's voice but simply could not decipher the words. Everything had narrowed to the hand between her legs. Leah relaxed, she had to. Had to breathe in, deep. Had to let her body's tension ease a little, else this tension start to hurt.

Brandon's fingers moved expertly on her, and every time she skated to the edge, he eased off. Leah let her head fall back, onto his shoulder. He kissed her cheek. She shifted on the seat and went with the overwhelming pleasure.

'Now,' she said. 'Oh, God, Brandon. Now.'

Or maybe she didn't speak. Maybe he just knew. But at that moment his pace quickened, just enough. His fingers tweaked and stroked and eased her into orgasm. Her body shook with it, though she did her best to keep still. He cupped her cunt, the heel of his palm pressing her clit.

'Fuck, yes,' he said into her ear. 'I can feel you coming . . .'

The tremors subsided, but she wasn't finished. Hell, no. Leah shifted to look at him and caught her breath.

'I want to fuck you,' she said.

'Now?'

'Now.'

He looked around at the table, and the crowd. 'Leah . . .'

She gripped his hand, already sliding out of the booth, going God knew where. 'We'll find a place.'

19

Dix couldn't tear his eyes from her ass. More specifically, the way the hem of that short red dress fluttered up, showing the tantalising strip of skin on her upper thighs, just below the curves of her ass cheeks.

Kate was so unbelievably sexy. He loved it when she dressed up like this. Her hair was down and styled to look like she'd tumbled from bed. Big curls tousled around her face accented her eyes and that mouth.

The dress fit her like a second skin except for that little flounce at the hem which allowed for the fabulous show of leg. Shoes, delicate and very high, wrapped around her feet, giving her about three inches of height and the toes matched the same red as the dress, her fingernails and the slash of luscious colour on her lips.

The song told him to shake his tambourine and get a whistle but he only wanted to blow one thing and it wasn't a whistle. He licked suddenly dry lips as she lost herself in the music, her hips switching back and forth, those juicy tits bouncing just enough to make him harder than he'd been for at least an hour.

The room was packed, even so, he didn't complain when she moved closer, her ass now sliding from side to side over the aforementioned very hard cock. He saw lights behind eyes he had to close for a moment because the sensation was so fucking good.

Her arms went up around his neck, arching her back. The R&B shifted into a harder hard-driving techno song, one he recognised from the *Blade* movie. In unison, the room began to pump with the bass line, surging back and forth, up and down like the tide. The lights flashed and her scent filled his nose.

His hands had come to rest on her waist but he slid them up a bit, his thumbs resting just at the bottom curve of her breasts. Higher, just a bit, and he flicked his thumbs up over her nipples. They sprang to life and his cock answered their siren call. Ridiculous how in tune he was with this woman.

The sexual tension coiled between them, he could taste her want on his tongue, smell it, feel it on her skin as she rubbed herself over him like a cat. Sex personified, but graceful too. Each time she flipped her head and her hair moved, his body answered, cells wanting to surge forwards, wanting to claim her in the most primal way.

The room was a bacchanal, dancing, singing, drinking, the sticky-sweet scent of marijuana curling around them every few minutes. People made out every few feet, hands roamed over bodies on the dance floor as it swallowed them to the thump of the techno bass beat.

His teeth found the back of her neck, biting down just enough to let her know he was there, just enough to let her know he was imagining what the clasp of her pussy would feel like around him as he fucked her.

'You're so ridiculously sexy. You know I can see into the bodice of that dress every few movements right? I can see the curve of your tits and I want to put my mouth on them. I want to put my cock between them. I want to play with your nipples until you scream at me to make you come,' he whispered.

He knew she heard him when she shivered but just moments later, she spun quickly and pushed him back. He let her lead them into a corner of the room, shadowed by the lights, the railing and the walls. With the heels, she was his height and his hands automatically moved to cup her ass as she snuggled into his body.

'Christ, you feel good,' she murmured, nuzzling his neck.

'The feeling, darling Katherine, is entirely mutual. In case you missed my cock prodding into your belly and all.' To underline that, he rolled his hips, grinding into her, very much liking the intake of breath that made her delectable mouth shape into an O of surprised pleasure.

And then she spun again, her body maintaining some sort of contact with his as she danced, writhing against him with sensual abandon. Her hair covered her face as the flash, flash, flash of the lights provided a show against her body in the otherwise dark of the corner.

A server passed nearby and she grabbed two glasses of champagne from the tray and handed one to Dix. The server's eyes roamed over Kate's body but who was Dix kidding, he couldn't blame the guy for looking.

'Are you getting a wee bit tipsy?' he asked, smirking after she drained her glass and then picked up another from the tray.

'I'm far away from work, from home, from anyone who knows me. Why not get a wee bit tipsy? Do you promise to take advantage of me if I am?' A sexy, teasing smile marked her mouth and he leant in close to brush his own across it.

'I love this no-smear lipstick. As for taking advantage?' He pressed his lips to her ear. 'If we weren't here, I'd shove you face down on that table over there and fuck you from behind.'

She spun again, sliding down his body and then tucked something into his pocket. Turned out to be a very tiny pair of panties. Good sweet Lord.

The look she sent him over her shoulder made him swallow, hard.

'You're a very naughty girl. It's one of your best qualities.' His hand rested in his pocket, holding the small scrap of material.

'Fuck me.'

He blinked. 'What?'

She backed up and slid her ass over his cock again. 'You heard me,' she said, craning her neck to see him. 'Take your cock out and put it in my cunt. In more common parlance, fuck me. You have my panties, there's nothing in your way.'

He banded her waist with his forearm and hauled her close, leaning to speak in her ear. 'You want me to fuck you, here? Really?' As if every day wasn't already a holiday with her? Score.

'I want you to fuck me. Here. Now.'

He wasn't about to argue about getting caught. It was Las Vegas after all and it happened to be one of her turn-ons. God knew he could pound nails with his cock he was so hard. And it made him hot to see her so hot.

The crowd pressed in around them, everyone focused on the music, on the party, on themselves. Inside her, the need for him ached, crawled along her belly, itched over her skin. The idea that someone would know what they were doing excited her wildly.

He kept her against his body and she trembled when she felt his hand working at the zipper of that very natty tuxedo he wore.

His fingers brushed her thighs as he moved the dress up a bit, the heat of his cock against her brought a shiver, even in the heat of the crowded club.

She focused on a group just below where they danced on the main dance floor. Two men and a woman undulated, eyes closed, hands all over each other.

And Dix's cock pressed against her entrance, his hiss vibrated through his bones into her and she heard his murmur, *hot*.

Slowly, the beat of the song thumping, his cock slid deeper. His fingers dug into the muscle of her hips. It was so good she shuddered, so good she had to grab the railing nearby to keep standing.

So much information, so much stimulus coming into her system she would drown if she continued to fight it so she let go, let herself get off on the idea of being caught, of being watched, let herself love the feel of the width of him pressing into her cunt and then pulling out.

She fell into a dreamy place as he fucked her, pleasure ebbing and flowing around her as the crowd danced. Sex hung in the air, possibility spicing it. Las Vegas on New Year's Eve at half an hour to midnight and the people around them were revving higher and higher as they counted the minutes.

'You can't come this way,' he said, leaning to speak in her ear. 'So do it yourself, darling Kate. Touch that clit and make yourself come.'

He continued to stroke into her at an almost casual pace until she lost her resolve to keep her hands from between her legs. One of the men below dancing with the woman looked up and she slid a hand down her thigh and then under the hem of her dress.

Each flash of the strobe was the only real light in the space. But it must have been enough because dancing guy turned fully to watch. She nearly came the first touch of her fingertip to her clit.

'Whoa there, I'm not going to last long as it is.'

She laughed and tipped her head back. 'A guy down there is watching. Watching me finger my clit.'

He thrust a bit harder. 'Good. Let him look and know he'll never have anything as sweet and hot as you. Makes you hot, doesn't it? Knowing he's watching you be a very–' he thrust again for emphasis '–very bad girl. Or I should say, a very *good* one.'

She toyed with herself, lazily sliding her middle finger along her labia, dipping inside to flick at her clit and back out again. She teased them both, knowing no matter how turned on he was, Dix wouldn't come before she did. He was a gentleman that way.

'Kate, don't make me stick my hand under there and bring you off myself. I'm dying here, which doesn't look nearly as handsome in this tux as a man who just lucked out with the woman of the century and fucked her in the middle of a room with three hundred other people in it.'

Catching her bottom lip between her teeth, she found her clit again and kept the pressure, kept at it until wave after wave of pleasure hit her, her cunt contracting around Dix's cock, his cock lodging hard and deep and unloading as he came too.

When her vision cleared, the guy on the dance floor sent a bow and then turned his attention back to his friends.

Dix reeled as he poured into her. He came so hard his teeth tingled and his scalp hurt. He thanked his mother for teaching him to always carry a handkerchief and discreetly handed it to Kate as he tucked himself back in.

She turned and looked up into his face. 'I love that you want me to be happy.'

'Come on, let's both be happy out where the food was. It's too loud in here and I want to be with you, to talk to you without shouting.'

She swayed ahead of him as the crowd parted. He kept a hand at the small of her back, feeling like a fucking king.

Once they were away from the din, she hugged him again, raining kisses over his face.

'If I'd known fucking you in public would make you this affectionate and grateful, I'd have boned you months ago when we went out to get pizza.'

Her mouth, that luscious mouth, curved up into a smile. 'Anything but be serious, Charles? I thought you wanted to be serious,' she teased.

'I am serious, darling Kate. Serious as a heart attack. Now, I need a cigar and I want to sit, drink some good Scotch and look at you before we hook up again with Bingo and his missus.'

'He's probably still eating.'

'I doubt it. I'm wagering they found a dark corner to engage in sexual relations in as well.'

He guided her to a table near the large wrap-around balcony lining the entire length of the ballroom. A warm breeze floated in as she settled in next to him and put her head on his shoulder.

'Happy New Year, Charles Dixon,' she said softly.

He loved her most when she was like this. The Kate she rarely showed anyone else. Soft and sweet, vulnerable and wholly feminine. This was his woman stripped to the core and it was more titillating than if she'd been wearing lingerie.

'Happy New Year to you too, Katherine. You know, you were all of my resolutions last year.'

'I was?'

'I wanted to pursue something more with you than a long-distance relationship. I wanted to see you regularly. I wanted for us to be openly together. Looks like all those things happened. This time next year you'll be my wife. I'm a lucky man.'

'You totally are.' She winked. 'Sweet, handsome, lucky, smart, sexy, awesome in bed, funny even. Oh you have a good job and two really great kids. One major drawback, but I'm over it. OK, I lie, I'm not over it, but I can afford to be magnanimous because your cock is in my cunt at night. Not hers.'

He wrinkled his nose. 'Thank you for everything but that image of my ex.'

She grabbed two glasses of champagne and handed one to him. 'To us. To a year filled with all the things we need and want most.'

He clinked his glass against hers and sipped. He couldn't agree more.

'Let's see if we can find Bingo and Leah. I feel like we should all be together when we hit midnight. Oh, but wait.' He handed her the fabric bundle he'd been carrying in his pocket. 'That dress is short enough that any man in here can get a glimpse of that succulent pussy if you cross your legs or raise your arms over your head.'

She rolled her eyes but got them back on, even as a couple sitting nearby watched her do it with surprised gazes.

Kate, his love, just winked at them and stood. 'Shall we go look then?' She pulled out her phone and texted. Moments later she received a text back. 'They're in the eighties room. They'll meet us near the bar. Come on, it's ten minutes to twelve.'

'Um yeah, totally engaged in sexual relations,' she said quietly to Dix, who chuckled.

Leah had the FFG, freshly fucked glow, and Brandon looked like the boy from Iowa who just got his crank yanked in the middle of Las Vegas on New Year's Eve. The world was a beautiful place.

'Nice FFG,' Leah said first and Kate laughed.

'You too. Floozy.'

'You know it.'

'Damn, I was gonna say cradle robber and I shot my wad on floozies.'

Leah tipped her glass, touching it to Kate's. 'Next time. For now, Happy New Year.'

'It totally is. Congratulations, you know. You two are good together. He loves you. Not who he can make you into, not who you should be according to a book or magazine. He loves you for who you are. That's pretty awesome.'

Leah smiled and Kate saw love written all over her friend's face. 'It is. For both of us. All those lemons and in the span of less than a year, we find the right stuff.'

'If you're going to make out with her, can we watch?' Dix asked.

Brandon nodded enthusiastically. Kate and Leah just looked at each other and continued talking.

The room got very noisy and then hushed as the clock hit the thirty-second mark. Kate turned to Dix and gulped the last of her champagne before reaching up to wrap her arms around his neck.

By the time the room had counted back to one, his lips were on hers, his tongue sliding in like it was meant to. Her own caressing it, welcoming it as his heart beat against where she pressed herself to him. Her heart in time with his.

'Happy New Year, darling Kate. Now let's go back to the room. I want to fuck you, bathe you, order room service, blow you and sleep until noon.'

'We have a flight out at ten. So none of that sleeping until noon business. But I can sleep on the plane. I'm not giving up all the other stuff you just mentioned.'

'You're like my Santa list all rolled into one person. You know that?' He briefly looked up towards Brandon and Leah. 'We're out of here. Heading back to the room. We'll try not to be so loud people call the cops. See you two in a few hours.'

She waved over her shoulder as he pulled her from the room, even as she laughed and tried not to trip over her shoes.

20

New Year's Eve in Vegas. There was nothing like it. Well, maybe a Roman orgy might've been something like it. There was more action going on in this room than there'd been downstairs at the fetish con.

Brandon's mouth tasted sweet on Leah's as balloons fell from the ceiling and the clock struck midnight. Somewhere not far from them, Kate and Dix were kissing too, but for now Leah concentrated on Brandon's hands on her waist and the slide of his tongue on hers. They kissed until it was twelve-oh-one.

'Happy New Year,' Brandon said.

'Same to you.' She stood on her tiptoes to kiss him lightly, once more.

Though the party wasn't over – hell, in Vegas was it ever over? – Kate and Dix were heading back up to the room. Since Brandon and Leah had already spent the past couple hours in the suite taking advantage of the privacy, Leah felt morally obligated to give her friend the same amount of time. They'd all managed to change their flights so they could leave together, and she knew getting to the airport tomorrow by 10 a.m. would be pure unadulterated hell, but she wasn't tired.

'You want to dance some more?' Brandon gestured at the couples bumping and grinding on the dance floor. 'Grab something to eat?'

Leah shook her head. 'Let's go for a walk.'

He cast a dubious look at her shoes. 'Uh huh.'

Leah laughed. 'When I can't stand it any longer, you can carry me on your back.'

Brandon raised one lovely dark eyebrow. 'Uh huh.'

She stood on tiptoes again to brush her mouth on his. 'You'll be my pony.'

He laughed at that, though the cutest faint blush appeared at the base of his throat. 'Whatever you want.'

She linked her fingers through his. 'C'mon, baby. Maybe we'll even hit Nathan's for a hot dog. Or ride the roller coaster.'

Now both brows went up. 'It's after midnight!'

'And we're in Las Vegas,' she pointed out. 'Let your hair down.'

Brandon bent to curl his arm around her waist, lifting and twirling her while she laughed. She didn't care if people were watching, or that the room spun as she got dizzy. It was the perfect excuse to cling to her big, strong man so she didn't stumble.

Hand-in-hand, they wove their way through the crowd, which seemed no smaller than it had at any point during the night, and into the hotel lobby. Here there were more fetish con people. Maybe they'd had their own party.

The chilly air after the heat inside was nice for about five minutes, but then Brandon shrugged out of his tux jacket and slung it over her shoulders. She hadn't even asked. Leah looked up at him.

'How'd you know I was cold?'

'Um, aside from the fact your teeth were chattering?'

They paused in front of the huge M & M store. Leah slipped her arms into the sleeves. 'So it was obvious.'

He shrugged. 'Well, it's cold out here. Your arms are bare. I figured you'd be cold. You're always cold at home, anyway. It's why you always wear a sweater.'

'I love that you know that about me.'

He smiled. 'I should, don't you think?'

They walked a little further, slowly. Brandon's hand anchored in his pocket to make his arm a loop just right for her to hold. 'I'm not sure if it's a matter of should.'

He looked down at her and steered her gently around a scatter of broken glass. 'I think it is. If you love someone you should know the important stuff about them. Not just things like their favourite colour but you know. Stuff that's really necessary for getting along with each other.'

God, he was smart. Not just book-smart, though she knew he was that, too. Brandon was insightful. Intelligent in the way that mattered. And she was an idiot for ever thinking they weren't meant to be together.

'If you're going to live with someone, it's especially important,' she said wryly.

Benches in Vegas were hardly ever empty, but this one was, and Leah grabbed it to give her poor feet a rest. They had a fabulous view of the Bellagio fountain show from here, one of the many Vegas spectaculars she hadn't yet seen. Maybe they'd be lucky and it would go off while they were here.

Brandon laughed and sat next to her. 'Well, duh.'

She gave him a look. 'Did you just "duh" me?'

'Absolutely.'

She watched him stretch out those long legs and put his hands behind his head. A man fully pleased with himself. She leant closer to say in a low voice, 'Pretty cocky, aren't you?'

'Absolutely,' Brandon said again.

'Shameless.'

'That too.'

Leah snuggled against him and watched people pass by, most of them drunk. They were going to be hurting in the morning. God. The morning. She looked up at the sky that was probably still dark, but it was too hard to tell with all the Vegas lights.

'I don't want to go home,' Leah said suddenly.

Brandon slid an arm around her shoulders. 'No? How come? I mean, aside from the obvious.'

She sighed and put her head on his shoulder. 'Back to work, for one thing.'

'Yeah.' He sighed, too. 'I'm sure I'll have a buttload of crap to deal with. If I'm lucky nobody will have quit while I'm gone. If I'm luckier, I won't have to fire anyone when I get back.'

She laughed. 'Same here.'

Brandon kissed the top of her head. 'I thought you liked your job.'

'I do. It's work I don't like.'

They both laughed at that. A very drunk woman wearing a cone-shaped party hat, her dress halfway up her thighs and her date stumbling behind, whirled around at their laughter. She waved a noisemaker at them.

'Happy Fucking Nude Year!'

Leah covered her mouth to hide a guffaw at that – usually drunk people didn't amuse her but this woman was clearly beyond shit-faced. The woman's date, his tux shirt open, tie gone, zipper undone, did a little dance. Brandon snorted.

'Did you hear me, honey?' The woman stumbled forwards and Brandon caught her neatly before she could end up on his lap. 'I said, Happy Nude Year!'

'I heard you.' Brandon, pinned on one side by Leah and by the woman in front of him, tried to get his new friend to stand up straight, but she was too unbalanced. 'Careful, now.'

The woman peered at Leah. 'Zis your boyfriend?'

'Yes,' said Leah.

'I bet he's got a nice big dick,' the woman said and put her hand right on it.

Brandon jumped, laughing, and grabbed at her wrist while Leah got ready to give the woman a big old shove. Drunk or not, you don't grab the dick of another woman's man. Before Leah could do anything, though, the woman managed to back off. She straightened her dress and jerked her thumb over her shoulder at her date, who was staring at them all blankly.

'Thass my husband. He's hung like a bear.'

'Rawr,' said the man.

'Like a bear, huh?' Brandon shook his head. 'Never heard that one.'

'Means he's got fuzzy balls and a furry ass!' The woman broke into gales of hysterical laughter. 'C'mon, hairy ass. Less go fuck and stuff.'

'I'll be surprised if they can find their way back to their hotel,' Leah said, watching them. 'I can't believe she touched your crotch.'

'She was right though. I do have a nice big –'

'Hush,' Leah said and stopped him with a kiss. 'Don't be naughty.'

'I thought you liked it when I was.'

'Pffft.' She waved a hand and stood. 'Come on. Let's walk. We only have a few more hours here and we might as well make the most of them.'

He stood up and up and up, stretching. 'What time's our flight?'

'Ten. So really, there's almost no point in going to sleep.' Leah grinned at him and swatted his very fine ass. 'And since we already made looooooove . . .'

Brandon grabbed her up and pinned her against him, earning a 'woop-woop!' from some passing drunken frat boys. 'That doesn't mean we couldn't do it again.'

She reached between them to squeeze his very fine package – but gently. No point in bruising the merchandise. Only in Vegas would she stand on a sidewalk and fondle him. 'Rawr.'

'My ass,' Brandon said with dignity, 'is not furry.'

'Thank God for that.'

He frowned. 'What, you wouldn't love me if I had a hairy ass?'

'Well, now, see, that's the problem with hair in places you don't expect it,' Leah said as they walked along the rows of shops and hotels. 'By the time you discover it, it's usually too late to be worried about it.'

'Uh huh. So does that mean if I start getting hair in my ears and stuff you'll disown me?'

She paused to give him a look of faint alarm. 'Are you expecting to grow hair out of your ears?'

'My grandpa does. Tons of it. All over the place. His eyebrows too.' Brandon made a scared face and gave an exaggerated shudder 'He's like a sasquatch, that guy.'

'Oh, my.'

He rolled his eyes towards her. 'Yeah.'

Leah hugged his arm closer to her side so she could press against him. 'I think I can handle that.'

He shot her a grin. 'You sure?'

'I'm sure.'

He nodded. 'OK, then.'

'What about me?'

'Do you expect to start growing hair out of your ears?'

She shook her head. 'No. But what about when I start to get hair on my mole?'

Brandon snorted. 'What mole?'

'The one I'm sure will grow on my chin eventually.' Leah raised an eyebrow. 'Will you still love me when I grow a mole with a hair on it?'

'Of course,' he scoffed.

'But will you still want to make love to me?'

He stopped, not caring they caused a minor traffic jam in the stream of people parting around them to get by. 'Leah, I will want to make love to you no matter how many moles you get with hairs on them.'

They'd been being silly, but now tears nudged the backs of her eyes and thickened her throat. 'That is the most beautiful thing anyone's ever said to me.'

'Well,' Brandon said. 'I mean it.'

And even in Las Vegas where so much was made of illusion, Leah had no doubts that this was all truth.

The last time Brandon pulled an all-nighter he'd been in college, pepped up on No-Doz and three pots of coffee, trying like crazy to cram for a Sociology final he needed to pass with an A in order to keep his scholarship. He'd fallen asleep halfway through taking the test, woken ten minutes before the hour was up, and managed to squeak by on the skin of his teeth. Tonight was nothing like that – they stopped to grab steaming cups of coffee from a vendor but not because he was in any danger of falling asleep. Being with Leah was enough to keep him energised.

She was tired, he could see that. Her hair had fallen out of the pretty hairdo she'd put it in for the party, but he liked it that way, tumbled over her shoulders. Her make-up had smudged, too, giving her smoky eyes and fucking incredible pouty lips he couldn't stop wanting to taste.

They had done everything they possibly could in the few hours they had left. Stopped for hot dogs at Coney Island, rode the roller coaster, visited the Eiffel Tower and viewed most of the free shows. Now the sky was finally turning light, though the thousands of lights still gleamed as bright as they had all night.

Vegas in the morning looked hung-over. There were still people on the streets and casino lobbies, a number of them dressed in formal wear. They were the ones who looked like they might pass out at any moment. There were other folks dressed in regular clothes, up early for the buffets or an early shot at the tables and slots. Tourists pulling suitcases towards taxis. Some gave Vegas a last, longing look while others tried slipping away leaving behind a few hundred bucks and probably some dignity, too.

'I'm hungry.' Leah took a deep breath. They were leaning on the railing in front of the Bellagio, having made a full circuit of the Strip. 'Can you believe that?'

He put a hand on his belly. 'Sure.'

She nudged his side. 'You're always hungry.'

'Well, yeah. But it's been at least an hour since we last ate.'

She laughed and tipped her face up to the brightening sky. 'Gawwwwwd, Brandon. Will you still love me when I'm so fat you have to roll me from room to room?'

They'd played this game all night. Will you still love me when...? It was sort of silly, seeing who could top the other, but he liked it. It meant she was considering the rest of their lives together, and, though she hadn't come right out and said, yes, she'd marry him, he was more certain than ever that's where all this was leading.

'Of course. Will you still love me when I lose my hair?'

'I thought you were going to grow hair.'

'In my ears,' he said. 'I'll probably go bald on top.'

She pretended to consider it. 'OK. So long as the hair in your ears is long enough to do a comb-over.'

He cringed even as he laughed. She was rarely this silly. 'Dude. Gross.'

She slapped his arm. 'Do not call me dude!'

'You and Kate call each other dude all the time!'

'Kate,' Leah said archly, 'is my bestie. And a woman. Women can call each other dude. You do not call me dude. I have a vagina, not a penis.'

He slid his hand over her ass for a squeeze. 'Mmmm... vagina.'

She shifted until she was between him and the railing, her ass nice, round and shoved up tight against his crotch. Leah leant against him. 'Yes. I will still love you when you're bald.'

'Good.'

They swayed a little. Exhaustion should've weighted his eyes, but he'd gone past the point of being tired into being hyper-awake. Everything seemed too bright, too colourful.

'It's kinda like being high,' he said out loud.

'What is?'

'Being this tired.'

She twisted to look up at him. 'Sorry we stayed awake?'

'Nope.' Brandon watched people going in and out of the hotel. People just starting their days, heading to work.

'What do you know of being high, anyway?' she said sternly.

He grinned. 'Garsh, ma'am, not a thing.'

'Uh huh.' She pushed her butt back against his crotch again. 'What would your mother say?'

'My mom and dad were kids in the sixties,' Brandon said. 'I'm pretty sure they know about pot.'

'I can't picture that,' she told him.

Brandon laughed. 'Leah, you know ... my parents aren't as squeaky clean as you think.'

She was silent for a moment. 'Your parents are wonderful.'

He hugged her. 'And I told you, they love you.'

'Yeah.' Her shoulders lifted and fell in a sigh.

'Leah ...'

'Yeah, baby.' She yawned.

'We could do it here, if you want.'

She looked at him again with a naughty grin. 'Right here? On the sidewalk? I'm not sure we could get away with it.'

He turned her in his arms to face him. 'No. Not that. I mean ... we could get married here.'

One of the things she'd never said but that he knew was that Leah didn't want a lot of pomp and circumstance. It wasn't that she didn't like being the centre of attention – she loved that, actually, when it was the right sort of attention, and from him. And he knew it wasn't that she had any qualms about planning an event like a wedding, because that too wasn't anything that intimidated her. He simply knew her well enough to know she didn't necessarily want something traditional like a ceremony where they'd have to get up in front of people and exchange vows. And he knew it was because no matter what she ever said, part of her would always wonder if people were questioning their relationship.

'In Las Vegas?' Her brow furrowed.

'Yeah. People do it all the time.' He actually had no idea how much preparation went into getting married in one of those chapels, or even if they had enough time. But if Britney Spears could do it, he was pretty sure they could.

'Oh, Brandon.' She put her forehead against his chest.

'What? No?' Shit, had he screwed it all up?

Leah looked up at him, her eyes dancing with laughter but her mouth holding back on the smile. 'I love you so much.'

He let out a breath. 'OK, good.'

'But I don't want to marry you in Las Vegas.'

'OK.' This was a better answer than saying she didn't want to get married at all.

Leah shook her head. 'No. We'll have to have a wedding. Reception. The whole thing. Kate in a bridesmaid's dress, oooh, she'll kill me.'

He didn't want to admit until she'd said it how much he'd wanted the whole shebang himself. 'Really?'

She nodded, solemn. 'Yes. Really. I'm sure your mom will want a big, splashy wedding.'

'It's not about what my mom wants.'

'I know that. But ... it's what you want, isn't it?' She studied him seriously. 'I know it's what would make you happy.'

His hands settled on her hips. 'Yeah. I'd like a wedding.' He paused, thinking. 'Does that make me a pussy?'

She laughed. 'No. I don't think so. It makes you very sweet.'

He groaned. 'Oh, God, that's worse than being a pussy.'

She poked his chest. 'No. It is not. I love that you're so traditional. I love that you want to get up there in front of everyone we know and wear a monkeysuit and dance the Chicken Dance and toss the garter and all that. I love that about you. Well, that and your huge, gigantic, immense ...'

He was already grinning before she finished.

'Ego,' Leah said with another poke.

He caught her hand before she could poke him a third time. 'Ouch.'

Her other hand snuck between them to give him a quick fondle. 'And this, of course.'

He looked around, hoping they were alone enough for her to keep stroking him, but of course now that the sun was up even more people were bustling about, and they were still on a public sidewalk. Leah held back a yawn that triggered one of his. She laughed.

'Let's have something to eat and head back to the suit to shower and pack up. We have to return your tux, too.'

Brandon sighed. 'Back to reality.'

She flashed him one of those looks he loved so well. 'If you're lucky, maybe we'll have time for you to go down on me in the shower.'

His prick stirred at that. 'I hope so.'

Leah winced. 'But I do think I'm going to have to take you up on that offer of being carried. My feet are killing me.'

He turned around and hunkered down so she could climb up on his back, which she did even as she burst into laughter. He stood, shifting her weight. 'Ready?'

It was proof of where they were that they barely got a second glance as he started towards their hotel.

'Don't drop me,' she warned.

'Have I ever?'

'There was that one time . . .'

'Hey,' he protested. 'That wasn't my fault. You wiggled too much.'

She dug her chin into his shoulder. 'Yeehaw, pony-boy.'

'It's too bad about the wedding thing,' he tossed back at her. 'I can't think of a better souvenir from Vegas than that.'

'Oh,' Leah said. 'I think I can.'

'Are you sure about this?' Brandon looked warily at the design laid out on the paper in front of them.

Leah nodded. 'Yes. You?'

He grinned. 'If it's what you want.'

The tattoo artist had drawn up matching art for both of them. Something small, not too flashy. Something meaningful for both of them, and something unique.

'I gotta tell ya,' the guy said. 'I've had a lot of requests for ink, but I've never had anyone ask for a picture of a belt before.'

'Good,' Leah said.

She was getting hers low on her hip, where it would only show when she was naked. But Brandon was getting his around his bicep where anyone could see it any time he took off his shirt. Not that just anyone would be able to tell what it was, since the design was clever enough to hide the buckle and make the whole thing look like a simple band of colour.

'You both ready?'

'This is so romantic,' Brandon said dryly. 'Getting this done at the same time. How come she gets the cute girl?'

'Because that cute girl's my old lady,' said the tattoo guy with a grin, 'and I don't think you want her getting all flustered and messing up your ink, do you?'

Leah laughed. 'We certainly don't.'

It hurt worse than she'd expected, even though the design was simple and the entire process for both of them took less than an hour. They had just enough time to get back to the hotel and get ready to go. Riding up in the elevator, she couldn't help grinning at the sight of them in the mirror.

'We definitely look like we've been out all night.'

Brandon looked, too. 'You look hot. All messed up and rumpled.'

'Slutty,' Leah said.

'I wasn't going to say so, but . . . yeah.'

She arched a brow. 'Is that a fantasy of yours, Brandon?'

His grin gave her an answer. Leah contemplated the reflection again as the elevator doors opened on their floor. 'Hmm. Maybe we'll fuck first, before the shower.'

Then she stepped out with a grin, not looking back as he stumbled out behind her, and she led the way back to the suite.

21

'You're totally rocking the best-friend thing with this party.' Kate waggled her brows at Leah, who sat across from her sipping a margarita as the assembled women chatted and laughed.

Leah raised one shoulder casually. 'Least I could do for you. You'll be all Mrs Dixon and stuff. Plus I'm next and I didn't want you thinking I'd be satisfied with punch spiked with soda and games involving potential baby names and stuff.'

'Did you see my planner? You're totally ruining the surprise like the selfish bitch you are. And I'll have you know Bingo's mom says her punch is better because it has orange sherbet and pineapples in it. Just for that, you only get pineapples. That'll teach you. I won't even let you have the cool *I'm Getting Married*! tiara she sent me the link for.'

Leah snorted a laugh. 'I may have in-laws who own a BeDazzler but you have a crazy ex-wife. That's worse. My mother-in-law lives a few states away.'

Kate gulped the last of her drink and hooted when the next stripper came out onto the stage. 'You wound me, Leah. You really do. Now shut up while this boy earns his college tuition.'

The bendy, pretty hot, moderately legal male stripped and undulated as he danced, grinning the whole time.

'I've gone to several strip clubs with Dix. Male strippers are just way more fun.'

'You two are total deviants. This one,' Leah said, craning her neck sideways as she watched the show, 'seems to enjoy his work.'

'Always a plus. Being a deviant too. Charles is quite good at it. Of course, I have shoes in my closet older than he is. Not Charles, this happy little stripper.'

'Good thing you don't need to wear him on your feet then.' Leah smirked. 'Or do you?'

'If it amused me to, I totally would. And he'd love it. I'd leave his arms free so he could do his homework and stuff.'

Another snort from Leah, but that died in the din of hoots and squeals as college student stripper guy writhed on the stage and dropped to the ground, heading straight for their table and Kate as the bride to be.

'If anyone gets goo on me, I'm gonna put orange sherbet in your punch. I'm just sayin',' she hissed to Leah.

'Hi there, you must be Katherine. I'm Travis.' Cute stripper was even cuter close up.

He didn't shake her hand, but he did get his very flat abdomen in her sight. Nice. 'Hi there, Travis. Aren't you pretty?'

He rolled his hips, the line of his cock pretty close to her face. But he was careful not to get any of whatever he had greased all over his muscles onto her. Such lovely manners.

Kate yelled over the music. 'Grab a seat. I'm getting married, flatter me and chat with us.'

He laughed in that self-confident way any attractive twenty-three-year-old male has. But he plopped down in a chair at the end of the table. Leah shoved another margarita at her and moved closer.

Few people loved strippers more than Leah, so Kate sat back and watched as Leah turned on the charm. Travis responded right away, like they all did, and Kate wished she had some popcorn to eat as she took them in.

'What's your story, Travis? What I really want to know is, can you move your body like a cyclone?' Leah asked with a smile.

'I totally can. Wanna see?'

'Dear, sweet Travis, with your washboard abs, of course we want to see. That's why we're here.' Kate winked at him.

'Good point, Katherine.' Leah's voice was dry and the other women with them all leant in and eyed him. 'We'd all love to see.'

Sweet baby Travis had not lied. No, he leant back and rolled himself, rippling his abs and his nice, albeit hairless, thighs. Then he did some move where he whipped his body around, artfully sending his hair around his face all coy like.

When he finished, the entire table clapped and cooed over him. Leah grinned over at Kate, who laughed out loud.

Baby Travis became their own personal stripper for the rest of the evening, flirting with everyone, giving a few up close and personal dances, flattering, making sure drinks were ordered and sucking up all the attention and tips.

There weren't too many other ways Kate wanted to celebrate her upcoming wedding than to hang out with Leah and pretty boys as they drank margaritas.

Kate wagged her finger at him as they prepared to leave. 'Good evening, sweet baby Travis. Don't let me hear you've blown off school for another quarter. Just go back, even if it's part time.'

He grinned, very fetching and sort of naughty if she went for men young enough to not understand a single cultural reference she made.

'I know, I know. You two should come back in again so you'll know for sure. I'll be your arm candy any old time you need it.' He kissed her cheek. 'Congratulations again on the upcoming wedding. Make sure he behaves.'

Kate laughed. 'Ha. He's not one for behaving. It's part of his charm really. Don't tell him I said that, he gets away with enough as it is.'

Travis laughed as he kissed Leah's cheek and she told him something that made him blush.

'Dude, you can make a stripper blush,' Kate told her as they got into the limo outside.

Leah buffed her fingernails on her blouse front. 'I still got it.'

'You sure do.' Kate hugged her briefly. 'Thanks again. For tonight and for being my maid of honour and stuff.'

'Enough thanks to get some sherbet in my punch?'

'Pfft, we'll see if you deserve it by then.'

They got into the limo, laughing.

'One thing, on the wedding day, you have to be on Pickles watch.'

Leah looked up from her iPhone where she'd most likely been texting Brandon something dirty, and raised an eyebrow. 'Am I gonna have to bring brass knuckles?'

'If you do, I'll give you twenty dollars to use them on her. After I do of course.' She shook her head as they glided back towards Kate and Dix's house. 'She's just being her usual self, which seems to be a one-woman wrecking crew on her family. It upsets Dix and that upsets me.'

Kate stewed over that statement she made in the limo for a week until the latest incident came up. As Kate had guessed, making Eve go through her to get to Dix had frustrated her ability to yank him around. This pleased Kate mightily. Until Eve simply began to use the girls to do her bidding instead.

'Hi, Kate,' Kendall greeted her when she came through the front door. The girls lived with them in the new house on weekends and, true to Kate's promise to Dix, they all lived in his old house every other Wednesday and Thursday so the girls could stay there and go to school. It hadn't been perfect, but it was how things worked best and it was Kendall's last year of high school anyway.

'Hey there. Hope you guys are up for Chinese for dinner. Your dad just called to say he's bringing some home.' Kate looked up and smiled. 'Yes, you can invite Jimmy.'

Kendall grinned at the mention of her boyfriend. Jimmy and Dix had come to an uneasy truce. Kate liked the boy, but Kendall wasn't her daughter so it was easier for her than Dix. It had been pretty wonderful when Dix had listened to her and took her advice about the Jimmy situation and invited him around. Kendall would have boyfriends and Dix had to accept it. Keeping his daughter close gave him a far better chance of keeping a good relationship with her.

'I'll call him in a minute.' Kendall sat on the couch next to Kate, tucking a foot beneath her and snagging a sip from Kate's diet soda.

Kate rolled her eyes. 'Get your own, girl. You're way younger than me and your joints are in shape enough to take the rest of you into the kitchen to land your very own diet soda. By the way, where's Adrienne?'

'Doesn't taste as good if it's not yours.' Kendall snorted and then a serious look replaced the levity. 'Kate, listen I have to tell you something before Dad gets here.'

'That sounds like I'm going to hate it.' Kate turned to face her fully. 'Go on.'

'You are going to hate it. I'm sorry. Adrienne isn't coming this weekend. She doesn't want to be in the wedding.'

Kate knew Dix's younger daughter didn't like her. It hurt more than she wanted it to, even if she understood it. But this, this was on a whole different level. This would really hurt Dix.

'She what? Why? What's going on? I take it that since you've told me this before he got home she hasn't told your father about it.'

'She hasn't talked to Dad. I'm trying to talk her out of it. But ...'

But Eve. Eve, *that fucking bitch*, was written all over this.

'Your mother,' Kate said flatly.

'I'm sorry. I know it's not fair.' Kendall wrung her hands.

Kate shook her head with a sigh. She squeezed Kendall's hand. 'No, I'm sorry. I know you're caught in the middle and it's not right. I told your father we should wait until you and your sister graduated to get married, but he wanted to go ahead now.' Such a stupid and carefully intimate dance they did around the whole Eve issue. Kendall was a smart girl, but it wasn't fair for Kate to address the situation, no matter how protective she was of Dix.

Kendall made a face. 'Of course you should go ahead now. My dad loves you. You love him enough to love us too, and to take a lot of crap from my mother. I see it, you know. It's embarrassing and I wish she would stop. I've told her to stop. She's a good mother, she is. But this isn't right. How she's acting isn't right. It's just this blind spot she has about him and I don't know why. He was never going back to her. Even when I was just a kid and he left, I knew that.'

Kate smiled, but she wasn't going to address any of those comments about Eve. 'I do love your father. Very much. Enough that it hurts to see him hurting – and this will hurt him. But this is not your fault and, whether I like the decision or not, your sister has every right not to participate in the wedding if that's her choice. If you want, I can clear out for a while when your dad gets here. Or you know what? Why are you stuck with telling him? Who's idea was that?'

'What's up?' Dix called out when he came into the house through the garage.

Kendall squeezed her hand. 'Will you stay when I tell him? I don't want him to hear it from my mom.'

Kate nodded. Not that he would hear it from Eve as long as Kate had anything to say about it. 'We're in the living room,' she called out and his thumping steps neared until he came into view.

'Lookie here, two of my favourite women on the entire planet.' He swooped down and hugged Kendall and then Kate. 'Hope you're hungry. I got extra *kung pao*.'

'Sit down a sec.'

'Uh oh.' He sat on the low table and Kate swallowed back her annoyance that he didn't use the chair or couch. 'You didn't run off to some state where you could get married underage or anything, right?' He turned his gaze on Kendall who exhaled and rolled her eyes.

'Ew. Dad, I don't want to be married. I'm only seventeen.'

'Thank God for that. Go ahead, I've got some good Scotch for afterwards, this has bad news written all over it. You're not pregnant?'

'Again, Dad, ew. I know what birth control is.'

Kate put a hand on Kendall's leg and one on Dix's. 'Let's stop that now, your father is going to have a stroke if we keep talking about your sex life. Or lack thereof.'

Dix shot her a look, both grateful and annoyed.

'Dad, Adrienne doesn't want to be in the wedding. And she's not coming over here this weekend either.'

Kate's heart nearly broke at the look on his face. Rage flushed through her system. This had that bitch of an ex-wife written all over it.

'Why are you telling me, sweetie? This isn't fair for you.'

'I didn't want Mom telling you.'

He bit his bottom lip and Kate barely wrestled back a comment about that. This blended family stuff was complicated and tiring at times.

Dix heaved a sigh and stood. 'You two eat, I'm going over to deal with your sister. She's at your mother's?'

'Wait. Can I speak to you a moment before you go?' She stood and then looked back to Kendall. 'Honey, call Jimmy.'

Kendall hugged her dad and moved quickly from the room.

'I'm sorry about this. But it's her choice, Dix. Let her make it. As for Eve? I'll be back.' She grabbed her purse and her keys.

'This is mine to handle.'

'Bullshit it is. It's mine because she broke the rules about dealing with you through me. This is not about you, it's about me. It's high time this shit ends. Now, eat with your daughter. Eve and I need to talk.'

He sighed. 'I used to think I had the perfect divorce, friendly and good for our kids. But . . . I think I actually hate her. I never would have thought she'd have been capable of this.'

'But since I came into the picture, not so much. Listen, I could just walk away right now if that's what you want.'

'Don't be stupid. That would be her winning and what would it solve? I love you and I'd hunt you down anyway.'

'Good.' She kissed him and headed for the door. 'Don't worry, I won't do anything in front of Adrienne. You should probably call her later to reassure her that you still love her and you're not mad.'

'I *am* mad, Kate. This is not how she was raised.'

Kate laughed. 'Dix, they've got your will. You can't get pissed that she's a teenage girl who hates her dad's girlfriend. It's like one of the five stages of teenage girldom.'

'Don't get arrested.'

'I'll try not to.'

Kate pulled in the driveway at Eve's house, blocking Eve's potential retreat.

Eve had a sparkle in her eye when she opened the door. So satisfied with herself. Bitch. It made Kate want to hit her square in the face and she had to console herself with the idea that she might have to later.

'Is Adrienne here?' Kate didn't waste time on pleasantries.

'No. And you're not going to yell at her.'

She shoved past Eve and into the house. 'Please. As if I came here for that. Shut the door, Eve. You and I have some talking to do.'

'I have nothing to say to you. Adrienne has made her choice. You drove her to it.'

'Like I fucking care if you have something to say to me. As it happens, I've got a few things to say to *you*. Adrienne has a right not to participate in our wedding. I respect that and so does Charles. No, the issue here is that it's *not* what Adrienne wants. It's her selfish, crazy mother who is wrecking her child's relationship with her father because she's petty. Bravo on the parenting job. I think you should send this little gem of a story to one of those women's magazines. You know, "I Was a Selfish Cow Who Turned My Children Against Their Father Because I Couldn't Get Laid". Or something like that.' Kate threw herself onto a nearby couch.

'Get out. I only want to deal with Charles.'

'Yeah, about that. Tsk tsk, you know the rules. Charles is off limits to you. Oh, and do kindly fuck off with your demands. Sit your ass down, bitch, you and I are having a Come to Jesus and you're getting saved.'

'Who do you think you are?' Eve moved from foot to foot like the nervous little bunny she actually was. Right about that moment, Kate felt like a wolf.

'I'm what you might call self-actualised. Imagine that. A whole nation of women who aren't all whiny and dependent on men, especially those who *dumped* us, for our survival. We can open our own jars of pickles and everything. You see, I'm not here to use a pillowcase filled with bars of soap to beat some sense into you. Even though it's mighty tempting. I'm here because I pity you and I figure, if another woman pitied me because I was a hag and a loser and couldn't let go of a man who clearly didn't love me, I'd want to know so I could stop being pitiable.

'You're alienating your kids in this odd crusade of yours. Sure Adrienne is backing out of the wedding and that pleases you to bring chaos into our lives. But you're destroying her relationship with her dad. Why would you want that? It only hurts *her*. In the end, you're going to drive one daughter away from you and the other away from her father and you still won't have Dix. He's mine now. That's not going to change and you know that. You don't have to like me. I sure as hell don't like your worthless ass. But if you have any dignity at all, any true maternal love for your daughters, you'll swallow your self-pity and stop involving them in things that don't have a thing to do with them.'

Kate stood and looked around. God the place gave her the willies.

'You don't know anything about it.'

'I know all I need to know. You're a mother, why don't you act like one? All you're doing is hurting your kids. It's not going to change anything with Dix except to drive him even further away. This isn't a contest. They're your children. They love you and their father both. But *he* doesn't love you, nothing you do will make that happen. Ten years from now, he still won't love you. Even if I walked out on him now, he still isn't coming back to you. So what I'm saying is, all you're doing is being a shitty mother and driving a wedge between your kids and their dad. Eventually between them and you because they can't trust you to put them first. And you'll have nothing then. Let go and move on. Be happy, Eve. Open your own fucking pickle jars and find a man who wants you as much as you want him.'

Kate stood and brushed down the front of her pants before looking at Eve again. 'Don't hurt him again. I love Charles very much and you're hurting him with this petty shit. You're making him feel this way towards his child. It's you, not her. Have some dignity. Stand on your own two feet and stop acting like a fourteen-year-old girl. Next time I will bring that pillowcase, you get me?'

She sailed out the front door with a wave as Eve stood, openmouthed, watching her leave.

Arrested by the sight of his wife standing, steam rising from her body as she reached out to grab the champagne, Dix simply stood and looked at her. Her body was long and lithe, the water sliding down her skin, hair slicked back to enhance the beauty of her features. She took his breath, stole any other thoughts but the ones he had of her.

She saw him and smiled, that smile he knew was only his. That side of her he knew she rarely revealed to others.

The smile drew him in, brought him into motion as he climbed back into the hot tub with her, putting the tray of food down and taking the glass she handed him.

He clinked it to hers. 'Happy wedding day, ma'am.'

She laughed, settling back into his arm, resting her head there as she looked up to the stars. 'Happy wedding day, sir. This place is awesome. I vote we always stay in hotels with hot tubs and private patios.'

Their honeymoon would be spent at a beautiful luxury resort, in their own private villa complete with steps straight down a cliff to the ocean and the aforementioned hot tub right outside a bedroom the size of a small city/state. He planned to take her in every room, on the floor, against the walls, in the huge shower and tub, on the bed, wherever struck his fancy.

'If it means you'll always be naked, I'm totally up for it.'

'What I like about you, Charles, is how very easy and simple you are. If there are exposed boobies, you're happy.'

He laughed. 'Especially if they're *your* boobies. Not that I'd write off any old breast sighting. But yours are my favourites. By far.'

They looked pretty damned good there in the water. Good enough to touch, he thought as he moved a hand to idly brush the back of his knuckles across her left nipple.

It sprang to life, which pleased him inordinately, pleased him to know he evoked such a response from her.

She arched her back, floating a bit and he licked a line up her neck to her ear, tasting salt and that essential whatever that made him crazy to always have more.

'Thank you for the wedding present,' he murmured before nibbling her ear. When he'd seen both his daughters walk into the small restaurant where they'd had the wedding and the reception afterwards, he'd known it had been Kate's doing. Had known whatever the hell she'd said to Eve had struck home because Eve had been more reserved of late and Adrienne had taken to spending at least one night a week at their house.

'I know you don't wear much jewellery but you really do need a watch. Not that I'm commenting on your propensity towards being late. Wait, yes I am.' She chuckled softly.

'Not the watch, although that *was* quite nice and I already promised to make an effort not to be late all the time. It's just that you're so tempting and right as we get ready to leave you get all sexy and then I have to fuck you. You can't blame me. I'm a man in the prime of his life. I gotta get all the fucking in I can. You heard your mother on that score. It's only a matter of time before I'm taking the little blue pill and peeing on myself.'

Delightfully, she began to giggle, all her best parts jiggling as she did. She pressed her face to his neck and embraced him.

'I know I shouldn't laugh. God knows I had enough of her before you came along. But you make such great fodder to toss her way when she starts sniffing around for things to hate about my life. You're so great at handling her. Do you forgive me?'

'Ha. She tried to make a grab at my cock today. Did you see that? I needed a drink or three after that moment.'

Kate sat back, eyes wide as she tried not to smile. 'She did not! Like sexually?' She wrinkled her nose and his cock deflated a little even just remembering it.

'She did. She was regaling your sister with tales of how old men like me can't get it up. Your sister dutifully refrained from rolling her eyes, but reassured your mother I was keeping you happy so she should just stay out of it. That's when your mother lunged towards my junk to emphasise erectile dysfunction. It was not my favourite moment.'

'Did she grab anything? I'm betting you were still young enough to be spry and evade her grabbing hands. If she did get a handful of what you're packing she wouldn't be bugging me about marrying old men with flaccid peens and pee problems. Maybe you should let her cop a feel to end the argument once and for all.'

'No! I jumped back. I'm glad to see you so amused by my misfortune.'

'Whatthefuckever. Eve, Charles Dixon, her name is Eve and she's a giant, hairy, pus-filled carbuncle. With wrinkles because of all her looking down on things. She's so judgy she's made herself even older looking. My mom could have popped out a nipple and it wouldn't have been approaching the street of insanity your ex-wife lives on.'

He groaned. 'Back to my original point. Thank you for the watch, it's great. No, what I meant was thank you for getting Adrienne to attend the wedding. I'd made my peace with her not being there, but it sure would have hurt.'

'Oh. Well. It's all up to Adrienne. She still hates me so don't get excited. But she loves you. You're her father and I just assured her she's allowed to hate me and still love you. I don't think she really understood how much it would have hurt you for her not to come to the wedding.'

He brought her to face him, straddling his lap. 'Thank you.'

'I love you. It made you happy.' She shrugged. 'You do things for people you love.'

'You love my daughter even though she's being an ungrateful brat?' His words were teasing, but there was no denying the truth of what he'd said.

'I do. I'm not their mother, they have one already. But I'm their father's wife, they're part of you, I love them for that if nothing else. Now, this is my honeymoon and I say we give up talking about any other women but Angelina Jolie for the duration. We haven't had sex in hours. Are you neglecting me already?'

He stood, bringing her with him.

'You're right. I've been remiss.' He sat her on the edge of the tub and stood back, just looking at her. The air was cool, but the heat of the hot tub would keep them comfortable.

She was his happy ending. His slice of something far more than he'd ever expected to possess, to love, to wake up to and he'd lured her into his life and never planned to let go. She hadn't had to stay in his life. Hadn't had to open her life and her condo in the city to him, didn't have to move in and accept his proposal. He'd come with more than his share of baggage and yet, she chose him. Chose to stay, chose to love him baggage and all and all throughout, she'd kept her head, remained a strong and independent woman with her own mind. It was so sexy it made him crazy. He hadn't been something she needed to do, hadn't been a reluctant burden she'd taken on. Katherine had chosen him and had become part of him in ways he couldn't even quantify.

Few people had such gifts.

'Nothing but you.'

Kate opened her eyes and looked into his. Took in the features of this man who'd come into her life like a seductive whisper and had managed to burrow under her skin and hadn't let go. Noble, more noble than he'd ever let on, but he was a good man. An honest man who loved his children and now her. Mischievous, silly, intelligent, funny and gorgeous. Not a bad way to spend the rest of her life.

His mouth found that spot just below her ear that brought her entire body to life, her hormones surged.

'Outside, beneath the full moon, the rush of the ocean in the background and my naked, willing wife at my beck and call. Sometimes a man has to just flat out admit when he's got it good.' He quirked a grin at her and she leant in to kiss him at the corner of his mouth.

'You're such a surprise to me sometimes.'

He paused before kissing her again. 'Good. It's good to keep the mystery alive. When you're a hundred I'm still going to fuck you. Just a warning. I should have said so before the wedding, in the interests of full disclosure and all.'

She wrapped her legs around his waist to haul him closer. 'I'll hold you to that.'

His mouth on hers teased at first. Featherlight touches of his tongue against her lips as she opened to him.

Urgency rode her. She wanted more of him, didn't want the teasing or the seduction. Only wanted the hard and fast possession of cock in cunt.

'In, in, in, in. Now.' She urged him closer, her nails digging into his shoulders, widening her thighs to rub her pussy against his cock.

'Impatient. I want to eat you.' He spoke, lips against hers, she took in the breath, the need and it sent a shiver through her.

'No. No. Fuck me. Please, please, please. I want you in me.'

He groaned, the sound raw against her mouth, filling her with it. Stepping closer, he slid his fingertips through her, teasing for a brief moment around her gate and then moving to her clit, a quick side to side and then his cock was there, pressing inside, the pleasure so good it forced a loud moaning *please* from her lips.

There was nothing but the naked sky overhead, the way the sweat on her back dried against the blanket of cold evening air. His body forced the cold back, his skin radiating heat as much as the water did.

Once he'd seated himself fully, her cunt wrapping around him, her calves holding him tight, he took a deep breath and raked his gaze over her face, over her features for the briefest of moments before settling back on her eyes. And then he began to fuck her.

No nuance. No seduction. No finesse. Just barely leashed sexuality, a man who owned his pleasure and loved to give it to her. He thrust hard and fast, his hands to either side of her hips, braced to keep the rhythm steady and intense, slamming into her body, but holding just this side of pain. Pleasure so intense it crawled over her nerve endings, built until she wasn't sure she could stand it. But she hovered, just shy of coming.

He groaned again when she brought her fingers to her mouth and then down between them. It didn't take much at all, just a soft touch, two strokes of her middle finger against her clit and she fell off the edge then.

Her body seized around his cock as she writhed, knowing he was close, wanting him to let go and follow her. The sound he made, when he did climax, tore at her, sent little echoes of pleasure through her system that this man felt that way to be in her.

'Holy shit.'

She managed a weak laugh as she wrapped herself in a towel and they headed back inside.

He grabbed her hand and brought her into a hug. 'I want that, every day for the rest of my life.'

'You got it.'

They ended up on the bed, their legs entangled. 'You know that first time?'

She rolled and leant up on her elbow. 'First time?'

'The first time we were together.'

'How can I forget a knock on my hotel-room door while I'm attending a seminar and, when I open, it's you? That's pretty unforgettable.'

'I knew you'd be there. I wanted to meet you in person. I wanted to fuck you. It was all I'd been thinking about for months. I signed up for the conference because you were there. I wanted you from the first time I heard your voice on the telephone.

'And there you were, all sort of breathless when you saw me. Stayed so very professional and cool while we were in public and then I showed up at your door and you pulled me inside and fell to your knees. You sucked my cock as I stood there, filled with wonder at the reality of you.'

Kate was quite certain no one in the universe saw her the way he did. It filled her with wonder, to be loved the way he loved her.

'So you set out to seduce me?' She grinned.

'Yes. I went there with the express purpose of getting you alone and naked. I had no idea then, what it would do to me. How you'd change everything in my life. I just wanted you to know that even from the start, I've wanted you and I've done what I needed to to keep you.'

'That's so flattering.' She kissed him quickly. 'When I saw it was you, I did a little jump, just a little one so you couldn't feel it on the other side of the door.' She laughed at the memory. 'I hoped to God you were there to fuck me. I figured if you weren't, once your cock was in my hand, you would.'

He shook his head while he laughed. 'You're very devious. Thank God.'

'I didn't expect you.' She licked her lips. 'I didn't expect you or anyone like you. You were just suddenly there and I realised how much I never wanted that to change. I didn't even have the time to fight wanting to be with you.'

'I love you too.' He kissed her and pulled her atop him again. Even as she protested that she couldn't possibly have sex again, he proceeded to show her just how very wrong she was.

22

The list came in, one item at a time, via text message.

Drop off dry-cleaning.

Pick up eggs, bread and milk.

Mail birthday package to your mother.

And the last one, his favourite, the one that made him grin, then shift in his office chair to ease the sudden pressure:

Think about eating my pussy until I can't even speak.

God, he loved that woman. Brandon shut down his computer and gathered up the armful of dry-cleaning he'd earlier hung on the back of his door. He'd already taken care of the birthday package and he'd stop at the store on the way home for the few groceries. He'd probably pick up some takeout Chinese, too, so neither of them would have to cook dinner or wash dishes.

Who wanted to waste time in the kitchen when he could be spending the night with his face between her thighs?

Just before he flipped off the light and shut his office door, his phone rang. It was the trill of an inner-site call, which meant it was probably someone with a fire to put out. But damn it, it was already past five, he'd taken care of everything that needed to be done, and he was tired. Yet with a sigh, Brandon answered anyway.

'Hi, Brandon. This is Ed Daniels.'

Ed Daniels from Corporate, Brandon's boss. Hell, Brandon's boss's boss. 'Hi, Mr Daniels. What can I do for you?'

'I'm sorry to catch you so late.'

'Not a problem,' Brandon said, just barely gritting his teeth. He doubted Ed gave a rat's ass how late he was keeping him. Ed probably had nice, boring wife who wasn't waiting with a blindfold and a belt.

'I'm sure you've heard about the recent restructuring in our national hospitality division.'

'Yes, sir, I have.' Brandon sat heavily, chest going tight. He was about to get laid off, just months before his wedding.

'I'm not sure if you've heard about Chaz leaving us?'

Chaz Solone, one of the three heads of the Tri-County division. Brandon's boss. 'No, actually, I haven't.'

'Well, he is.' Ed offered no explanation. 'We'd like to offer you the position.'

Brandon blinked and sat up straight. 'What?'

'We want you to take over for Chaz. You'd be overseeing all the units in his division. There's a lot of travel involved but the pay and benefits more than make up for it, I think. Are you interested?'

'Yes, of course.' Brandon cleared his throat. 'Absolutely.'

'Good.' Ed sounded firm. 'Chaz himself recommended you, and we just don't have time to go hunting around for someone to step in. You'd start at the end of the month, give you time to find and hire a replacement and get started on your own training. We'd aim to have you in place a month after that.'

'That's some timeline.'

Ed laughed. 'I'll have my secretary send you all the important documents on Monday. You can look them over, make sure you're still interested, and get back to me. How's that sound?'

'Sounds good.' Brandon sat back in the chair, his eyes closed, until Ed said goodbye and hung up. Then he replaced the phone in its cradle and gave a slow, one-two fist pump in the air.

Yes!

A new job would mean a lot of things could change. For one thing, he could pay off his college debts sooner. For another, this more important, Leah could stop feeling like she was 'keeping' him. And Brandon had to admit that more money and a fancier title wouldn't exactly make him feel too shabby, either.

He dropped off the dry-cleaning as ordered, and, while the woman behind the counter had no idea why he was grinning like an idiot, she laughed along with him as she filled out the pickup tag. Then he went to Wegman's, where he loaded the cart not only with the items on the list but a bouquet of fresh red roses, an extra loaf of fresh French bread, a hunk of wasabi cheese, some grapes, and a package of Leah's favourite mint-chocolate cookies. Then he hit the prepared-food area and grabbed a couple containers of everything else she liked, too. She'd scold him a little for going overboard, but so he'd eat it for breakfast. And lunch.

After he was finished eating her, Brandon couldn't help thinking with yet another grin as he flung the bags into the back of his car. His prick was already trying to stand at attention. He could already taste her, smell her, hear the sound of her breathing change as she got closer.

He couldn't wait.

'Hey, asshole.'

It took him a second or two to realise the voice was directed at him, but when he turned to face it, Brandon recognised the man right away. 'Hey, Dickweed! What's up!'

Darren Weedman, also known as Dickweed, grinned and pumped Brandon's hand. 'Haven't seen you in for-fucking-ever man. What've you been up to?'

Brandon ran down the short list, including work and ending with '. . . getting married in a few months.'

'No shit. You? Really?' Darren clapped Brandon's shoulder. 'Good for you. I got married last year. Worst fucking thing I ever did.'

Brandon raised a brow. 'Yeah?'

Darren's grin didn't falter. 'Nah, I'm shitting you. Hey, let me take you out for a beer. Celebrate.'

'Nah. I should really get home.'

'C'mon, dude. It's been –'

'Forever, right.' There'd been weekends spent with Darren and other of their friends that Brandon was half-glad he couldn't completely remember, but he was a good guy for all that. And he hadn't seen him in a long time. 'Sure. Why not? One beer.'

'Great. I'll text some of the other guys, see if they want to hang. You still see Chris and Jerry?'

'Oh, yeah, saw Jerry last week.' While Darren tapped out messages to other people, Brandon pulled out his phone to send Leah a text. He already knew she'd been planning on getting her nails and hair done after work today, so an hour or so shouldn't be a problem.

Ten minutes later they were at some dive bar with sports on the big screen and hot wings on the table. Beers all around, lots of congratulations and a bit of good-natured ribbing. Some of the guys already knew about the engagement, of course, since Brandon still shot hoops with them or had them over to watch a game. But the more Darren drank, the more Brandon remembered why it had been so long since he'd hung around the guy.

'Seriously, my old ball and chain . . .' Darren shook his head. 'Fucking on my ass, dude. All the fucking time. About everything. What about your old lady? She try to tell you what to fucking do every single second?'

Brandon's phone hummed from his pocket with a reminder of Leah's earlier text messages. 'Yeah. Pretty much.'

'Dude,' said Darren.

'Dickweed,' Brandon answered.

And though most of the guys razzed him when he got up after a single beer and a dozen wings, Brandon only grinned and refused to let them rile him. He was going home to get laid. The rest of them were probably going to spend the night with Mary Palm and her five sisters.

'Later, guys.'

He headed out into the dark parking lot, his collar turned up against the cold that at least had kept the groceries in his trunk fresh. He came up alongside a guy leaning against the brick wall in front of where Brandon had parked. Guy was peeing, the splash of urine loud in the night air.

Gross.

'Hey . . .' The man turned, his eyes going wide as he tucked his dick back in his pants.

It was Mike, Leah's ex. Brandon had thought they were done with that douche, who'd finally stopped calling her about a month after Leah and Brandon got together. Now here he was, a pimple that needed squeezing.

'Dude,' Brandon said. 'Go away.'

Mike sneered. 'Saw your engagement announcement in the paper.'

'You're not invited.'

Mike put a hand over his heart. 'Oh, I'm hurt.'

Brandon shook his head. He didn't have time for this jerk. He had a hopefully horny fiancée waiting for him at home. Thinking about it again – the fact she had, indeed, agreed to marry him, that Leah would be his wife in just a few short months – Brandon let out a soft chuckle.

'You laughing at me, you prick?'

Shit. The guy just wouldn't let it rest. Brandon turned again. 'No, man. Look, I know you were carrying a torch and all that and, believe me, I get it. If I'd been stupid enough to let Leah get away from me, I'd be pretty pissed off at myself, too. But you have to back off.'

'Let her get away?' Mike coughed. 'Right. Like I wasn't finished with that bitch?'

Brandon had opened the driver's door but now paused, a hand on it. His shoulders straightened. His teeth gritted. He let go of the door and turned around, and Mike, that stupid fuck, didn't even have the sense to back up.

'Don't call her that,' Brandon said evenly, but through a clenched jaw. 'I've had enough of you and your shit. Get the hell away from me.'

'Or else what?' Mike's eyes shifted from side to side, and he bounced a little. 'What's the big boy gonna do? Whatcha gonna do . . . boy?'

The emphasis he put on the last word forced a hiss of breath from Brandon's lips. He didn't give a damn what Mike thought of him, his age, his relationship with Leah, none of that. All he wanted was the guy to get out of the way so Brandon could get in his car and get home to her. But Mike had never proven himself to be particularly smart when it came to knowing when to give it up. Leah didn't talk about him much. Brandon got the idea she was ashamed at having dated him at all, much less lived with him, and, if there was only one thing in the world Brandon thought Leah should fault herself for, it was that. But hell, it wasn't like he'd never made any dating mistakes. Crissy came to mind every so often, and he always winced at the memory.

Now, though, Brandon stared hard at the other man. 'Back off.'

'Ooh. Is that a threat? Are you threatening me?'

Brandon shook his head. 'No. I'm ... advising you.'

Mike's lip curled back from his teeth. In his seven-hundred dollar suit, his hair carefully combed back from his face, he looked every inch the successful business man – except for the crazy in his gaze. He tugged at the knot of the tie at his throat, then shook his head to toss back a stray hair that had come loose from the gel.

'Fuck you,' Mike said.

Brandon put his keys in his pocket and closed the door to his car. 'Seriously. Back. Off.'

Mike drew in a long, snorting gasp and spit a huge, disgusting loogy onto Brandon's left shoe. 'Or what?'

Shit. Leah had bought him these shoes, and they were nice. Brandon frowned.

'Why are you doing this? Seriously. Do you want to get your ass handed to you? I mean ... really? Haven't we, like, had this same conversation a few times already? I'm pretty sure it ended bad for you before.'

'She won't marry you,' Mike said. 'You know that, right? Leah won't ever get married. It's not in her to do it.'

The slow simmer of anger roiled to a boil at Mike's words. That the prick thought he'd been close enough with her to think he knew what the fuck he was talking about made Brandon want to strangle him. That he might be right made him want to kick the bastard in the teeth.

But, even though Brandon knew he could reach out a fist and grab the guy by the throat and shake the breath out of him, he didn't do it. Instead he pulled a handful of tissues from his pocket and bent to wipe off the already congealing spittle from his shoe. Then he stood, the crumpled, snot-smeared tissues in one hand, and tucked the mess into Mike's breast pocket.

'She'll marry me.'

Mike punched him in the face. Brandon saw it coming but didn't have time to turn before Mike's fist connected squarely with his cheek. Bright stars of pain flared, blinding him, and Brandon stepped back with a muttered curse. Mike didn't wait for him to recover.

He punched Brandon again, this time opening his nose so blood spurted freely.

'Son of a bitch!' Brandon clapped a hand to his face, blood dripping between his fingers. He'd also bitten his tongue, and tasted blood in his mouth.

Mike, the stupid punk, didn't have the sense to run away. In fact, he stood, stunned, like he couldn't believe he'd actually just punched Brandon.

Twice.

Motherfucker.

Brandon grabbed the front of Mike's shirt with the hand not holding his nose. His fingers curled tight in the expensive fabric. He yanked the other guy towards him, up on his toes, to bring him eye to eye. He took his hand from his nose, which was still bleeding.

'I would like to punch your fucking ticket for you, you know that? I would really like to fucking kick your fucking ass,' Brandon said in a tight, furious voice. He paused to turn and spit blood onto the pavement. Mike let out a small whimper. 'The fuck are you thinking? Punching me in my fucking face? The fuck, man?'

Brandon was pretty sure he'd never said the word fuck so many times in a row, but there was nothing better to say than that. His nose was on fire, his eyes watering, and the d-bag in his fist just batted at him with ineffectual fists and couldn't seem to find anything to say.

Brandon jerked him closer. 'I should call the fucking cops on you!'

'No, no,' Mike said in a strangled voice. 'I'm already on probation for a DUI . . .'

'What?' Disgusted, Brandon shook the other man until Mike's face turned bright red. 'You are a fucking moron! Come up here, punch me in the face, and you're on probation? The fuck's the matter with you! No matter Leah dumped your ass, man, you're a fucking waste of fresh air.'

Brandon dropped him. Mike stumbled back, a foot going wrong, and went down into a puddle of oily water. His elbow clipped the car next to him and he let out a howl of pain. Brandon, watching, found another handful of tissues in his coat pocket and held them to his nose, which throbbed and ached.

'I seriously want to fucking kick you in the face,' he said.

'Why don't you?' Mike cried, struggling to get up. He leant on the car, cradling his elbow. His face was still red.

'Because I think you want me to,' Brandon said. 'Maybe it would make you feel better to have me be this giant dick that knocked the shit out of you, so you can feel better about all of it. I don't know. I don't care. I'm not going to punch you. You're not worth the bruised knuckles.'

Mike ran a shaky hand over his hair, smoothing it back into place. 'She's got you that whipped, huh?'

Tired of all of this, his earlier joy thoroughly shit on now, Brandon sighed. 'Yes. She does. And I love it.'

Mike just stared. Brandon swiped a hand over his face again, wincing at the throb in his nose. At least his hand came away without any fresh blood.

'Get the hell out of my way,' he said to Mike. 'Or I'll run you over.'

This got Mike hopping, finally, and Brandon got in the car and drove home.

It wasn't like Brandon to be late, but it was an hour past the time Leah had been expecting him from the last text he'd sent. She'd been looking forward to coming home to a clean house, dinner ready, her errands finished and his eager hands and mouth waiting to please her.

She was entirely too used to the royal treatment. Now, waiting for him, Leah realised she was taking Brandon for granted. She didn't like to admit this, but it was the truth.

When she heard the key in the back door lock she whirled from the sink where she'd been running water into the teakettle. 'Brandon?'

The door creaked open and he appeared in the doorway, his shoulders hunched. At first she thought he'd worn some crazy tie-dye shirt to work today, which made no sense, but once he came into the light she could see the blotches of brown and red were of blood drying on the material.

'What . . . are you all right?' She rushed to him, but he held her off when she'd have hugged him.

'Don't get any on you.'

Leah tipped her head to look up at him. 'Your nose . . . and you have a black eye, and a cut on your cheek. Were you in an accident?'

'If you count your ex-boyfriend's fist hitting my face as an accident, yes.'

Leah hissed in a breath. 'What?'

'He was at the bar when I came out,' Brandon said, then cleared his throat as though it hurt. 'What an asshole.'

'Oh . . . baby, I'm so sorry. Come here.' Leah took his hand and led him to the kitchen chair, where he sat.

Seated, his face reached her chest, and Leah could look down at him. She put her finger under his chin and tipped his head back, then slowly, gently, side to side to view the damage. Her heart hurt at the swelling and darkening bruises.

'I can't believe he hit you.' She went to the freezer and pulled out an icepack, wrapped it in a towel and pressed it to his face. 'Tip your head back.'

Brandon did. 'Forget it. He's not worth even talking about.'

She cupped his face in her hands. 'He hurt you.'

Brandon smiled with a wince. 'Not so much.'

'Did you . . . hit him back?' She wasn't sure what she wanted him to say.

'I wanted to.'

Leah went to the sink and wet a cloth, brought it back to wipe off the streaks of flaking blood from his cheeks. 'But did you?'

'No. I told you. Not worth it.'

Something in his voice made her look deep into his eyes. Most of the time she could read him like a book. Better than, because a book had words and sentences, punctuation that had to be deciphered, and knowing who Brandon was and what he meant came wholly from her love for him.

'What did he say to you?'

'Nothing.' He put a hand over hers to stop her from wiping his face.

'Brandon,' Leah said softly. 'What's the matter?'

He stood, pushing her away a little, to go to the sink where he cupped a handful of water and rinsed his mouth. He put both hands on the sink, his broad shoulders hunched, his head low. Leah had never seen him even close to broken before.

'Brandon.' She knew the tone of her voice would turn him, but she didn't want him to bend to her just now. So when he gave her his profile, Leah went to him and pressed her face to his back, her arms around him, locked tight at his belt buckle.

'He said you would never marry me.'

'Oh, honey.' She sighed against him and felt the rise and fall of his body as he did the same.

Leah stepped back and hooked a finger in his belt. She tugged as she stepped back again, and Brandon turned. He was a big man, and he took care of her, did everything she ever asked, and Leah had come to expect he always would.

But had she not been as forthright in proving the same to him?

'I'll get the groceries.' Brandon's fingers went to hers on his belt, gently prying her free.

Leah didn't let him go. 'No. We can get them later. It's OK.'

'But dinner –'

'I had some toast. I'm fine.'

'Baby,' Brandon said, voice still hoarse. 'If I don't take the stuff out –'

'No,' Leah said again, more firmly this time. 'You're coming upstairs with me. Now.'

He sighed, broad shoulders lifting once more, and Leah softened her tone. 'Please.'

Finally he looked at her, those big dark eyes more distant than she'd ever seen them. Then he let her take him by the hand and lead him upstairs. They didn't speak, and that was fine.

In the bedroom, she stripped off his coat, loosened his tie, opened the buttons on his shirt. She'd been afraid to see more bruises, but Mike had apparently focused his attentions on Brandon's beautiful face. She kissed him over his heart.

Leah tugged open his belt and heard the sweet intake of his breath, but she didn't loosen it from the loops. She undid his zipper and pushed his trousers down and off. Then his briefs until he stood naked in front of her.

It wasn't often that she knelt at his feet this way, but Leah didn't mind. It was her turn to take care of him, now. She slid her hands up his calves, his thighs, around to cup his ass. She nuzzled at the coarse dark hairs of his legs.

His cock was already getting hard. When Leah licked his balls, his hand found the top of her head, his fingers twisting in her hair. They twitched, pulling, but Leah didn't move. She used the flat of her tongue, then the point to stroke and tease at the soft flesh.

He breathed her name. She took him in her mouth, and he groaned. When she drew him in deeper, the head of his prick nudging at the back of her mouth, his fingers twisted harder, and Leah's own groan eased out over her mouthful of cock.

She sucked him, stroked him, until the sound of his breathing changed and his knees shook a little, and then she pushed him back towards the bed and pushed a pillow beneath his head. She stripped for him, not too slowly.

Naked, she climbed onto the bed and straddled him. At another time she might have shifted upwards to cover his face with her cunt, ridden his tongue until she burst into ecstasy. But not tonight. Now Leah bent over him, her mouth skimming his body in all the places she knew would please him the best.

Only once did he try to stop her, to urge her up over his mouth, but she shook her head and Brandon fell back on the pillows and let her have her way with him. Leah took her time, relishing every second of it.

She was so wet and ready for him by the time she slid up his body and pushed his delicious, thick cock inside her, there was no resistance. Only pleasure. Only exquisite delight.

It took more than this to make her come, but Leah didn't ask Brandon to touch her. She touched herself, instead, intent on making sure he gave himself up to pleasure without having to worry about hers. Watching him, his eyes closed, brow furrowed, his gorgeous mouth thinned with his concentration, Leah found she barely needed a fingertip on her clit to push herself towards orgasm. All she needed was to watch him heading for his own.

They came within seconds of each other. It took her by surprise, the force of it. She always came with Brandon, often more than once, but this time the first surge of sensation was so fierce, so full, all she could do was ride it. Ride him. Grip his cock with her cunt, his body with her thighs. All she could do was let her head loll back and cry out his name.

In the minutes after, when she'd sunk onto the pillows beside him, both breathing hard, Leah turned to rest her head on Brandon's shoulder. She put her palm on his chest, feeling his heartbeat slow. He turned to kiss the top of her head.

'I love you, Brandon.'

'I love you too.'

Leah tipped her face to look at him. 'And I intend to marry you. I said I would.'

He said nothing. Leah sat up to look down at him. She kissed his mouth.

'Are you worried?'

He swallowed and shifted in the sheets. 'No.'

If he'd ever lied to her, Leah didn't know about it. She wasn't offended, now. If Brandon had doubts, she couldn't blame him, what with running away to Vegas and all that – she'd told him over and over since then that she was more than ready to marry him. But maybe she hadn't done enough.

'Look at me,' she said.

He did.

'I love you, and I want to spend the rest of my life with you. I want to be Mrs Brandon Long.'

His mouth tipped at the corners. 'I thought you didn't want to change your name.'

'Would it make you happy if I did?'

He got up on one elbow to look at her. 'Only if you wanted to.'

She smiled and kissed him. 'I want to marry you, Brandon. With the cake, the dress, the Chicken Dance at the reception. Everything.'

'The Chicken Dance? Are you sure?'

The Chicken Dance was probably the last thing in the world she wanted to do at her wedding reception, but Leah nodded anyway.

'All of it. I promise you. And I'm so, so sorry if anything I've ever done or said made you think otherwise.'

He stroked a hand over her hair. 'You didn't.'

Leah raised a brow. 'Are you sure?'

He laughed, low. 'I want you to be sure, that's all. I want to know that when you get up there with me that it's with . . .'

'No reservations,' Leah said with a laugh, thinking of the trip to Las Vegas and everything that had happened since then. 'I promise you, it's true.'

'We don't have to have the Chicken Dance,' Brandon said.

'Oh, thank God.'

They laughed together and snuggled close. Brandon fell asleep first, and Leah looked at him for a while. She'd have to make sure not to take him for granted again. Not ever.

Visit the Black Lace website at
www.blacklace.co.uk

LOOK OUT FOR THE ALL-NEW BLACK LACE BOOKS – AVAILABLE NOW!

All books priced £7.99 in the UK. Please note publication dates apply to the UK only. For other territories please contact your retailer.

Also to be published in September 2009

MISBEHAVIOUR
Various
ISBN 978 0352 34518 9

Fun, irreverent and deliciously decadent, this arousing anthology of erotica is a showcase of the diversity of modern women's erotic fantasies. Lively and entertaining, seductive and daring, *Misbehaviour* combines humour and attitude with wildly imaginative writing on the theme of women behaving badly.

TAKING LIBERTIES
Susie Raymond
ISBN 978 0352 34530 1

When attractive, thirty-something Beth Bradley takes a job as PA to Simon Henderson, a highly successful financier, she is well aware of his philandering reputation and determined to turn the tables on his fortune. Her initial attempt backfires, and she begins to look for a more subtle and erotic form of retribution. However, Beth keeps getting sidetracked by her libido, and finds herself caught up in the dilemma of craving sex with the dominant men she wants to teach a lesson.

To be published in October 2009

THE THINGS THAT MAKE ME GIVE IN
Charlotte Stein
ISBN 978 0352 34542 4

Girls who go after what they want no matter what the cost, boys who like to flash their dark sides, voyeurism for beginners and cheating lovers . . . Charlotte Stein takes you on a journey through all the facets of female desire in this contemporary collection of explicit and ever intriguing short stories. Be seduced by obsessions that go one step too far and dark desires that remove all inhibitions. Each story takes you on a journey into all the things that make a girl give in.

THE GALLERY
Fredrica Alleyn
ISBN 978 0352 34533 2

Police office Cressida Farleigh is called in to investigate a mysterious art fraud at a gallery specialising in modern erotic works. The gallery's owner is under suspicion, but is also a charming and powerfully attractive man who throws the young woman's powers of detection into confusion. Her long time detective boyfriend is soon getting jealous, but Cressida is also in the process of seducing a young artist of erotic images. As she finds herself drawn into a mesh of power games and personal discovery, the crimes continue and her chances of cracking the case become ever more complex.

ALL THE TRIMMINGS
Tesni Morgan
ISBN 978 0352 34532 5

Cheryl and Laura decide to pool their substantial divorce settlements and buy a hotel. When the women find out that each secretly harbours a desire to run an upmarket bordello, they seize the opportunity to turn St Jude's into a bawdy funhouse for both sexes, where fantasies – from the mild to the increasingly perverse – are indulged. But when attractive , sinister John Dempsey comes on the scene, Cheryl is smitten, but Laura less so, convinced he's out to con them, or report them to the authorities or both. Which of the women is right? And will their friendship – and their business – survive?

To be published in November 2009

THE AFFAIR
Various
ISBN 978 0352 34517 2

Indulgent and sensual, outrageous and taboo, but always highly erotic, this new
collection of Black Lace stories takes the illicit and daring rendezvous with a lover
(or lovers) as its theme. Popular Black Lace authors and new voices contribute a
broad and thrilling range of women's sexual fantasy.

FIRE AND ICE
Laura Hamilton
ISBN 978 0352 34534 9

At work Nina is known as the Ice Queen, as her frosty demeanour makes her
colleagues think she's equally cold in bed. But what they don't know is that she
spends her free time acting out sleazy scenarios with her boyfriend, Andrew, in
which she's a prostitute and he's a punter. But when Andrew starts inviting his
less-than-respectable friends to join in their games, things begin to get strange
and Nina finds herself being drawn deeper into London's seedy underworld, where
everything is for sale and nothing is what it seems.

SHADOWPLAY
Portia Da Costa
ISBN 978 0352 34535 6

When wayward, sophisticated Christabel is forced to take an extended country holiday she foresees only long days of bucolic boredom and sexual ennui. But she has reckoned without the hidden agenda of Nicholas, her deviously sensual husband, and the presence of unexpected stimuli within the grounds of a brooding old mansion house. Soon, she is drawn into a web of transgressive eroticism, where power and pleasure shift and change like the shadows playing across Collingwood's secretive walls. Drenched in this unusual and kinky atmosphere, Christabel learns lessons the jaded city could never teach her.

ALSO LOOK OUT FOR

THE BLACK LACE BOOK OF WOMEN'S SEXUAL FANTASIES
Kerri Sharp
ISBN 978 0 352 33793 1

The Black Lace Book of Women's Sexual Fantasies reveals the most private thoughts
of hundreds of women. Here are sexual fantasies which on first sight appear
shocking or bizarre – such as the bank clerk who wants to be a vampire and the
nanny with a passion for Darth Vader. Kerri Sharp investigates the recurrent themes
in female fantasies and the cultural influences that have determined them: from
fairy stories to cult TV; from fetish fashion to historical novels. Sharp argues that
sexual archetypes – such as the 'dark man of the psyche' – play an important role
in arousal, allowing us to find gratification safely through personal narratives of
adventure and sexual abandon.

THE NEW BLACK LACE BOOK OF WOMEN'S SEXUAL FANTASIES
Edited and compiled by Mitzi Szereto
ISBN 978 0 352 34172 3

The second anthology of detailed sexual fantasies contributed by women from
all over the world. The book is a result of a year's research by an expert on erotic
writing and gives a fascinating insight into the rich diversity of the female sexual
imagination

Black Lace Booklist

Information is correct at time of printing. To avoid disappointment, check availability before ordering. Go to www.blacklace.co.uk
All books are priced £7.99 unless another price is given.

BLACK LACE BOOKS WITH A CONTEMPORARY SETTING

- [ ] THE TOP OF HER GAME Emma Holly — ISBN 978 0 352 34116 7
- [ ] UP TO NO GOOD Karen Smith — ISBN 978 0 352 34528 8
- [ ] VELVET GLOVE Emma Holly — ISBN 978 0 352 34115 0
- [ ] WILD BY NATURE Monica Belle — ISBN 978 0 352 33915 7 — £6.99
- [ ] WILD CARD Madeline Moore — ISBN 978 0 352 34038 2
- [ ] WING OF MADNESS Mae Nixon — ISBN 978 0 352 34099 3

BLACK LACE BOOKS WITH AN HISTORICAL SETTING

- [ ] NICOLE'S REVENGE Lisette Allen — ISBN 978 0 352 32984 4
- [ ] THE SENSES BEJEWELLED Cleo Cordell — ISBN 978 0 352 32904 2 — £6.99
- [ ] THE SOCIETY OF SIN Sian Lacey Taylder — ISBN 978 0 352 34080 1
- [ ] TEMPLAR PRIZE Deanna Ashford — ISBN 978 0 352 34137 2
- [ ] UNDRESSING THE DEVIL Angel Strand — ISBN 978 0 352 33938 6
- [ ] A GENTLEMAN'S WAGER Madelynne Ellis — ISBN 978 0 352 34173 0
- [ ] THE BARBARIAN GEISHA Charlotte Royal — ISBN 978 0 352 33267 7
- [ ] BARBARIAN PRIZE Deanna Ashford — ISBN 978 0 352 34017 7
- [ ] THE CAPTIVATION Natasha Rostova — ISBN 978 0 352 33234 9
- [ ] DARKER THAN LOVE Kristina Lloyd — ISBN 978 0 352 33279 0
- [ ] DARK ENCHANTMENT Janine Ashbless — ISBN 978 0 352 34513 4
- [ ] WILD KINGDOM Deanna Ashford — ISBN 978 0 352 33549 4
- [ ] DIVINE TORMENT Janine Ashbless — ISBN 978 0 352 33719 1
- [ ] FRENCH MANNERS Olivia Christie — ISBN 978 0 352 33214 1

BLACK LACE BOOKS WITH A PARANORMAL THEME

- [ ] BRIGHT FIRE Maya Hess — ISBN 978 0 352 34104 4
- [ ] BURNING BRIGHT Janine Ashbless — ISBN 978 0 352 34085 6
- [ ] CRUEL ENCHANTMENT Janine Ashbless — ISBN 978 0 352 33483 1
- [ ] DARK ENCHANTMENT Janine Ashbless — ISBN 978 0 352 34513 4
- [ ] ENCHANTED Various — ISBN 978 0 352 34195 2
- [ ] FLOOD Anna Clare — ISBN 978 0 352 34094 8
- [ ] GOTHIC BLUE Portia Da Costa — ISBN 978 0 352 33075 8
- [ ] GOTHIC HEAT Portia Da Costa — ISBN 978 0 352 34170 9
- [ ] THE PASSION OF ISIS Madelynne Ellis — ISBN 978 0 352 33993 4
- [ ] PHANTASMAGORIA Madelynne Ellis — ISBN 978 0 352 34168 6
- [ ] THE PRIDE Edie Bingham — ISBN 978 0 352 33997 3
- [ ] THE SILVER CAGE Mathilde Madden — ISBN 978 0 352 34164 8
- [ ] THE SILVER COLLAR Mathilde Madden — ISBN 978 0 352 34141 9

❑ THE SILVER CROWN Mathilde Madden   ISBN 978 0 352 34157 0
❑ SOUTHERN SPIRITS Edie Bingham   ISBN 978 0 352 34180 8
❑ THE TEN VISIONS Olivia Knight   ISBN 978 0 352 34119 8
❑ WILD KINGDOM Deanna Ashford   ISBN 978 0 352 34152 5
❑ WILDWOOD Janine Ashbless   ISBN 978 0 352 34194 5

BLACK LACE ANTHOLOGIES
❑ BLACK LACE QUICKIES 1 Various   ISBN 978 0 352 34126 6   £2.99
❑ BLACK LACE QUICKIES 2 Various   ISBN 978 0 352 34127 3   £2.99
❑ BLACK LACE QUICKIES 3 Various   ISBN 978 0 352 34128 0   £2.99
❑ BLACK LACE QUICKIES 4 Various   ISBN 978 0 352 34129 7   £2.99
❑ BLACK LACE QUICKIES 5 Various   ISBN 978 0 352 34130 3   £2.99
❑ BLACK LACE QUICKIES 6 Various   ISBN 978 0 352 34133 4   £2.99
❑ BLACK LACE QUICKIES 7 Various   ISBN 978 0 352 34146 4   £2.99
❑ BLACK LACE QUICKIES 8 Various   ISBN 978 0 352 34147 1   £2.99
❑ BLACK LACE QUICKIES 9 Various   ISBN 978 0 352 34155 6   £2.99
❑ BLACK LACE QUICKIES 10 Various   ISBN 978 0 352 34156 3   £2.99
❑ MORE WICKED WORDS Various   ISBN 978 0 352 33487 9   £6.99
❑ WICKED WORDS 3 Various   ISBN 978 0 352 33522 7   £6.99
❑ WICKED WORDS 4 Various   ISBN 978 0 352 33603 3   £6.99
❑ WICKED WORDS 5 Various   ISBN 978 0 352 33642 2   £6.99
❑ WICKED WORDS 6 Various   ISBN 978 0 352 33690 3   £6.99
❑ WICKED WORDS 7 Various   ISBN 978 0 352 33743 6   £6.99
❑ WICKED WORDS 8 Various   ISBN 978 0 352 33787 0   £6.99
❑ WICKED WORDS 9 Various   ISBN 978 0 352 33860 0
❑ WICKED WORDS 10 Various   ISBN 978 0 352 33893 8
❑ THE BEST OF BLACK LACE 2 Various   ISBN 978 0 352 33718 4
❑ WICKED WORDS: SEX IN THE OFFICE Various   ISBN 978 0 352 33944 7
❑ WICKED WORDS: SEX AT THE SPORTS CLUB Various   ISBN 978 0 352 33991 1
❑ WICKED WORDS: SEX ON HOLIDAY Various   ISBN 978 0 352 33961 4
❑ WICKED WORDS: SEX IN UNIFORM Various   ISBN 978 0 352 34002 3
❑ WICKED WORDS: SEX IN THE KITCHEN Various   ISBN 978 0 352 34018 4
❑ WICKED WORDS: SEX ON THE MOVE Various   ISBN 978 0 352 34034 4
❑ WICKED WORDS: SEX AND MUSIC Various   ISBN 978 0 352 34061 0
❑ WICKED WORDS: SEX AND SHOPPING Various   ISBN 978 0 352 34076 4
❑ SEX IN PUBLIC Various   ISBN 978 0 352 34089 4
❑ SEX WITH STRANGERS Various   ISBN 978 0 352 34105 1

To find out the latest information about Black Lace titles, check out the website: www.blacklace.co.uk or send for a booklist with complete synopses by writing to:

Black Lace Booklist, Virgin Books Ltd
Random House
20 Vauxhall Bridge Road
London SW1V 2SA

Please include an SAE of decent size. Please note only British stamps are valid.

Our privacy policy
We will not disclose information you supply us to any other parties. We will not disclose any information which identifies you personally to any person without your express consent.

From time to time we may send out information about Black Lace books and special offers. Please tick here if you do not wish to receive Black Lace information. ❏

Please send me the books I have ticked above.

Name ....

Address ....

....

....

....

Post Code ....

Send to: Virgin Books Cash Sales, Black Lace,
Random House, 20 Vauxhall Bridge Road, London SW1V 2SA.

US customers: for prices and details of how to order
books for delivery by mail, call 888-330-8477.

Please enclose a cheque or postal order, made payable
to Virgin Books Ltd, to the value of the books you have
ordered plus postage and packing costs as follows:

UK and BFPO – £1.00 for the first book, 50p for each
subsequent book.

Overseas (including Republic of Ireland) – £2.00 for
the first book, £1.00 for each subsequent book.

If you would prefer to pay by VISA, ACCESS/MASTERCARD,
DINERS CLUB, AMEX or MAESTRO, please write your card
number and expiry date here: ....

....

Signature ....

Please allow up to 28 days for delivery.